STICKS
AND
STONES

STICKS
AND
STONES

PATRICIA THROCKMORTON

A NOVEL
OF
LIFE'S TRIALS

TATE PUBLISHING
AND ENTERPRISES, LLC

Published by Tate Publishing & Enterprises, LLC
127 E. Trade Center Terrace | Mustang, Oklahoma 73064 USA
1.888.361.9473 | www.tatepublishing.com

Tate Publishing is committed to excellence in the publishing industry. The company reflects the philosophy established by the founders, based on Psalm 68:11,
"The Lord gave the word and great was the company of those who published it."

Book design copyright © 2014 by Tate Publishing, LLC. All rights reserved.
Cover design by Joseph Emnace
Interior design by Jimmy Sevilleno

Published in the United States of America

ISBN: 978-1-63063-367-7
1. Fiction / General
2. Fiction / Historical
14.02.25

DEDICATION

FIRST OF ALL, I must thank my dear husband Keith for the many hours he gave me the solitude to think and write. Then my children Andrea Register-Sanz and her spouse, Jesus, and Parrish Register and his spouse, Jennifer, for hurling me forward in this endeavor.

Acknowledgments

To Kent Henson, dear friend and editor extraordinaire, thank you. Thank you, Diane Huff, long-time family friend, for your thorough scrutiny. Judy Burch, thank you for your valuable input regarding reader appeal.

FOREWORD

A PRODUCT OF THE pride and prejudices grown in the 1950s Deep South, Patricia donned an enduring shell of tenacity and grace. A developing, embryonic shell layered and calloused with personal loss and interpersonal gains, refortified and hardened against a bittersweet endearment of a loving home sheltering a broken stick family. A shell so frequently stoned by unspoken words and unshared sacred secrets that it must intrinsically crumble if it be rent.

Otherwise, the lines etched through laughter as well as those creased by sorrow are all for naught and the broken heart emerging healed is nil. It is her ever present *life-grown* love that now releases my daddy's sister, finally coming of age. May God bless and keep this survivor as her heart continues spilling ink across the pages of life.

—Deborah Watson Merritt

Preface

ROM AN EARLY age, I was fascinated with legends, myths, and fables told to me by my mother at fireside. She was a superb storyteller and could keep one spellbound for hours. Back in the day, that was all we had for entertainment—no electricity for a radio and well before the invention of the television set. As I birthed children of my own, I carried on my mother's tradition. Throughout the years, each has pleaded for me to put some of these stories on paper so they would have them to pass down to children of generations to come.

This is a work of fiction. Any resemblance to actual events, locales, or persons, living or dead, is entirely coincidental. Enjoy…

ᵠNTRODUCTION

SOME INDIVIDUALS EQUATE life's events to that of climbing mountains and being in valleys. In the valleys, where I have spent an inordinate amount of time, it seems, I have learned much. I have learned unconditional love, unconditional respect to use things and love people and not to use people and love things. I have learned how to survive anger, fear, heartbreak, and broken spirits. Sometimes I am on top of the mountain and so appreciate the reprieve, yet I know it is in the valleys that life's lessons are truly learned. I believe God prepares me for the next mountain with the one I am climbing at the moment. I have experienced some rather catastrophic events in my lifetime, but at no time has my faith faltered.

In the mid-1980s, when my marriage was failing after twenty-five years, I begged God to *make it right*…to bring about changes…changes in me and the father of my children so that we could remain a family unit. Changes occurred. However, they were not what I had prayed for, and the unity came to an end. How could I possibly survive such emotional distress? How could I continue onward?

Years ago, my mother became severely ill for no apparent reason. I stayed by her bedside in the hospital for the last two weeks of her life. Constantly I was in prayer, asking God to make her comfortable and to give her life for just a while longer. My request was partially answered. In late winter of that year, He made her more comfortable and took her home in her sleep. I had lost my best friend. For the first time in my life, I had no one to communicate with or turn to that I could trust with my deepest secrets…what would I do now?

A few years later, my eldest sister Lucy, suffered a long, painful death from the throes of chronic lung disease. I prayed all day each day for God to aid and comfort her in her suffering. The days dragged slowly by as she struggled for every breath, drifting in and out of consciousness. Not once did I leave her side and would even nap in the hospital bed with her, talking to her about happy times, never knowing if she was aware or could comprehend. After ten days of this suffering, God took her home, in her sleep, as well. If only I had been a better sister, if only I had spent just a little more time with her. How could I possibly live with the guilt associated with this?

Words cannot describe the years of suffering that I saw my eldest daughter, Megan, endure. Such a young, beautiful woman she was never to have the option of truly experiencing life… At the age of thirty-two, her life was essentially over. The uncontrollable pain she suffered…the faith she exhibited. What agony the whole family experienced. I prayed to God always to take the cancer from her; if anyone must have it, let it be me. I begged for this for six years, but that was not to be the outcome. Again, God took her home as she slept. How could I possibly make it through one moment without this child of mine?

I prayed to God for months, asking that my daughter Angela and her husband, Ricky, be able to have a child. In secrecy, I chose names: Dylan or Sawyer if it's a boy and, without a doubt, Megan if it's a girl. That pregnancy, through means of *in vitro*, failed. The sorrow was too vast to discuss. Only they knew the depths of the emptiness *they* shared.

How heartbreakingly painful it was to observe Aaron, my youngest and only son as he cried out, "If there is a God, then why did he let Megan suffer as she did for so many years?" Never has there been, to my knowledge, a sister and a brother so devotedly and lovingly attached one to the other. The death of his sister scarred Aaron more than most realize.

Death can be such a grim reaper. It struck again. My eldest brother, was diagnosed with bone cancer in the summer of his eightieth year. He survived only a few months and passed away quietly in his sleep. Then, just before Christmas of that same year, my niece lost her husband to kidney failure. Although he was surrounded by an intimate loving family until the end, he suffered immensely and they with him.

Each step I take, climbing the mountains, presents with a larger obstacle, and I wonder whether I can take another. But God gives me strength and comfort even when I do not realize it. He makes it possible for me to face each day, each new experience with fortitude I do not realize I have. He makes it possible for me to look forward, after a while, and establish a new direction to follow that will bring happiness in its own way. I realize that I cannot, in this lifetime, get beyond the suffering and sorrows of losing my dear loved ones…but I know that there are mountains still there, waiting to be climbed.

For all eternity, God has a plan, one that is microscopically revealed. He gives us free will and allows us to make choices. He tries to steer us, gently. That is how He has worked in my life. Each valley, every mountain, every step of my life, I believe, has led me toward Mark. I've known Mark since early childhood and have held a certain fondness for him. It was not until the autumn years of our lives that we became one when we joined in holy matrimony. God is good!

—Kathleen

PROLOGUE

MY STORY BEGAN in 1942...the year in which I was conceived. However, I am not sure I should start there. From the very beginning, my life was filled with turmoil and disorder, confusion and chaos. It was difficult to know when truth and fantasy traded places. And who knows which is which? My parents were married by a Justice of the Peace in 1925. My father was thirty-six years old that September and my mother turned nineteen in August. I was fifth in a group of six children born into this family. I remember my mother remarking on several occasions that my baby sister and I were sent to her at a late age so that she would not be alone and isolated in her later years; this prophecy became a reality.

CHAPTER ONE

TWO HOUSES ON MY MAP

I COULDN'T BELIEVE I did that! I looked at the map of the area I had just drawn. It was a map of the neighborhood in which I lived in my early childhood years. Sure enough, there, in bold, number 2 lead pencil, were etched two houses, much larger than all the other tiny little squares on the map. They stood out like colossal structures; these were the homes of my cousin Bertha and my friend Sarah.

I always felt not quite as good as they or the other children I played with. I guess I blamed these feelings on lack of material things. Much later, in my middle years, I would recognize the true reasons neighbors whispered behind my back and peers shunned my presence.

Like opening the lock on a dam, the memories began to flow. How interesting to look at the map and see the disproportionate size of these two houses that I subconsciously drew. I was amazed at how they compared to all the others in this, the area of my origin. It rekindled the feelings I had through childhood, adolescence, and even into adulthood: the feelings of being poor, of not being on the same social standing as my peers, the embarrassment I would feel wearing homemade and hand-me-down clothes.

Somewhere, I read that an exercise such as drawing a physical map of where one had lived would open floodgates of memories. What an understatement! Am I brave enough to write the truth as I remember it? Am I brave enough even to recall the memories of my childhood years? Do you suppose anyone would believe them anyway? Perhaps I will proceed, knowing I can never tell it all...

MY FAMILY

The Great Depression, affecting every country, began in 1929 with the economy at its lowest in recorded history. Industry and construction came to a halt, rural areas suffered as crop prices plummeted. Only until World War II did the economy see improvement.

As documented by written words and pictures, in the early morning hours of Sunday, December 7, 1941, the surprise military attack by the Japanese Navy on the US Naval Base at Pearl Harbor in the Hawaiian Islands catapulted us into World War II. Volunteers flooded local draft board offices and the economy shifted to war production. In May of 1942, the US Office of Price Administration (OPA) froze prices on everyday goods; war rationed books and tokens were issued. Thus the stage is set for the unfolding story of the Barnabas and Savannah Willoughby family.

Initially, four children were born into this family with Louise being the first. Over the next twelve years, three more children were to follow: a son, Lawrence; another daughter, Hazel; then Nicholas, the last.

Eight years after Nick's birth, my mother found herself pregnant again at thirty-seven. Nine months later, the *ugly child*, a girl named Judith Kathleen was born. This birth was followed two years later with another daughter. Her name is recorded in the family Bible as Pamelia Marie, but I think she changed the spelling of her first name along the way. She was to be the last child born into this family. Judith Kathleen became Kat because her baby sister could never pronounce Kathleen, and Pamelia became Pam.

Rarely was anyone recognized by their given name. Many ended up with quite extraordinary nicknames, such as Pogo, Ned, Bootsie, and Nod. Mostly, though, this story is about Kat…

Louise, nicknamed Lucy, the eldest, a tiny baby girl, weighing less than one pound at birth, was delivered near Mama's twentieth birthday. At the time, Daddy was about thirty-seven years old. I have been told she was swaddled in her first baby's blanket, which was Daddy's pocket-handkerchief; her first cradle a cotton batting–lined shoebox. She was placed on the fluffy cotton, and they waited for her to die…

But she didn't, not then anyway.

She always seemed sickly, Lucy did. Born prematurely, her skin, was transparent, with a map of veins distinctly visible lying underneath her translucent skin. The fontanels of her scalp were enormous; her ears were soft and floppy with no cartilage. Her actual gestational age was never determined.

Larry was the second son, named Lawrence Butler after a prominent lawyer there in Bakers County. He was born with a head full of black, coarse hair and dark brown eyes. His skin was light tan, like an almond, his personality sweet like caramel candy. He never cried unless he was hungry. The third child was a daughter they named Hazel. From a very early age, it seemed like Hazel was more than a handful and was the cause of many a worry for Savannah. Mama said she was colicky for nearly two years, crying day and night and spitting up on everything in sight. In 1936 along came their fourth, a son they named Nicholas, the one they called Nicky. He was scrawny and short at birth and had fine blond fuzz for hair.

LUCY, 1942

Schooling was difficult for Lucy, and at roughly thirteen, she just stopped going to school altogether. By age fourteen, she was pregnant and forced to marry Rufus Hardy, a hard drinking, sullen man twice her age. He was cruel and physically abusive to her especially during pregnancy. My brother Nick says he distinctly remembers the bruises on her arms, legs, and face. Lucy's first-born, a son, died of a respiratory infection before he was one. Twin sons delivered the summer following were born much too prematurely from labor induced by a brutal beating from her cruel husband. They survived only days. Their gravesites, in the cemetery behind the Baptist church, were identified with silvery metallic markers that framed a cardboard plaque with their names, dates of birth, and death—children giving birth to children.

In the 1940s infant and toddler death rates were around twenty-five deaths in one thousand births. They were subject to cholera, smallpox, and measles; but then childhood diarrheal diseases were the most terrifying. The infant or child would develop diarrhea, become dehydrated, and die. Such deaths were directly related to poor sanitation conditions. Prenatal care to the residents of Crossroads was as alien to them as Belgium chocolates. Lucy's infants died from ignorance and cruelty.

To escape this abusive marriage, the teenaged Lucy returned to Crossroads to live with her parents and siblings. She brought with her a tiny mason jar filled with artificial flowers salvaged by her from small floral bouquets at each of the graves of her children. Rufus never appeared in her life again.

WHEN IT ALL BEGAN

On reflection, it must be admitted the disposition of Crossroads dwellers was slightly askew. We were at times intellectually blind, morally unacceptable. It is possible I do some injustice to my ancestors albeit you can reach your own conclusions.

I was conceived in August of 1942, the same month of my mother's birthday. There must have been much gossip and many whispers in regard to my mother's behavior. After all, she was a woman before her time; she smoked cigarettes and cigars, wore perfume and short-skirted dresses, and many colored people were her friends, entering her home through the front door! And she had a secret romance with a handsome traveling man just passing through. She must have been around thirty-seven, so she might have been searching for her youth; maybe she was tired of the ill-treatment shown by her husband's family and the snubbing in general. "Barney shouldn't have married someone from the low country in West Virginia," they would say. Maybe she was bored; maybe she was tired of her husband Barnabas, who was seventeen years her senior. Some memories she shared, some went with her to her grave.

LARRY AND HIS WALLET 1944

As is prevalent today, county school buses made their journey picking up children along the way to be delivered to the district schoolhouse, which contained grades one through twelve. The buses were driven by older students who were of high integrity and were licensed to operate a motor vehicle.

In Crossroads, there lived a woman who was certified to teach first grade. Her name was Rumley—Roberta Rumley. Because of some hardship she presented to the school principal, she was granted permission to ride the bus along with the students to and from school each day.

Toward the end of the school year, when Larry was about fourteen, the bus stopped in front of our home at the end of the school day. He jumped off the school bus, nose all snotty, with tears streaming down his cheeks, and ran into the house through the front door.

"Mama, Mama! I tried to keep her from taking it. I held on real tight, but she wouldn't stop pulling. She slapped me and took my billfold and wouldn't let me have it back. She said it wasn't mine that I stole it…that it belonged to someone else," he sobbed erratically to his mama. Lucy told me there were four scarlet red finger prints across his tender little cheek. She said Mama went into a rage!

What a travesty this was and so demoralizing to such a gentle, obedient, and honest adolescent. My mama, Savannah, with her passionate and fiery personality, hired Cousin Freddie to drive her to the school the following day. She went directly to the office of the principal where she found Mr. Todd. Savannah demanded Ms. Rumley be called in and to bring Larry with her; he was to wait in the hallway. She was to be told to bring the billfold along, and this was arranged.

Savannah was waiting by the door when the teacher entered. Roberta Rumley was surprised indeed when Mama slapped her hard across the face, sending her glasses flying across the room.

"Those fingerprints on your face resemble the ones you put on Larry's face on the bus yesterday," she remarked casually. "What needs to happen now is that you return my son's billfold to him and apologize to him for what you did."

Ms. Rumley was speechless. She looked at Mr. Todd then back to Mama then back to Mr. Todd again. "I think an explanation is in order," Mr. Todd said to the two of them. The teacher walked over and picked up her glasses.

Mama remained silent but thought, "Let her talk first. She'll be digging her own grave when she tells what happened."

Roberta Rumley stuttered and stammered but eventually got the story out with a meek. "I didn't think the boy's family had enough money to buy him a billfold."

Mr. Todd gave the teacher a tongue lashing and called Larry in. He pointed at Ms. Rumley, saying, "You know what to do!"

She apologized profusely to Mama and to Larry as she handed his billfold back to him. Needless to say, Mrs. Rumley was stripped of her right to ride the school bus ever again. She had to overcome her "hardship" finding her own transportation to school. Larry's formal schooling ended there.

This led to Larry being hired on at the sawmill there in Crossroads. The manual labor was difficult for one in his early teens. For four long years, he was up at the crack of dawn to catch a ride to the sawmill with other workers; he would retrace those steps again at dusk. Mama packed his lunch in a tin pail like all the other workers. He was, most of the time, bone weary, but he rarely complained and never missed a day of work.

Before modern sawmills, boards were rived and planed or more often sawn by two men with a whipsaw using saddle blocks to keep the log secure and a hole for the pitman who worked below and got the benefit of sawdust in his eyes. Sawing was slow and required strong and steadfast men. The top sawyer also had to be the stronger of the two because the saw was pulled in turn by each man, and the secondary had the advantage of gravity. Larry was the pitman. Early sawmills adapted the whipsaw to mechanical energy as was the case at this particular mill. The back-and-forth motion of the saw blade by a pitman thus introduced a term used in many robotic applications.

Winters were bitterly cold in Crossroads; at the sawmill campsite, a fire burned throughout the day. The crew ate their noon meal by this campfire as a welcomed reprieve from the cold. While standing and backed up to the campfire on such a penetratingly cold day, Larry's pant leg caught fire. He was so badly burned he was unable to return to work that winter. It was months before he could wear his wool socks and work boots.

IN THE SUMMER OF 1945

On May 8 that year, World War II officially ended and the date declared VE Day. This is the same year Pam was ushered into the world. It was also the year the doctor predicted I would die.

I don't remember the actual hand-colored photograph being taken. But I do remember the homemade chicken feed sack dress I was wearing on that occasion. I was two years old. "She has Bright's disease…her kidneys have shut down…certainly no salt, no meat, no bread…limited amount of fluids. She can have mostly egg whites and maybe a little clabber," Dr. Nathanial Morgan, our family doctor, had told my mother a few days earlier. The term Bright's disease, is no longer used, as diseases are now classified by more stringent categories. It was diagnosed in boys more often than girls between the ages of one and a half to two years old and could be acute or chronic. To my misfortune, the latter was to be my fate.

I was in good company: Mikhail Bulgakov, the twentieth-century Russian author of the novel *The Master and Margarita*; Ty Cobb, Hall of Famer baseball player; Emily Dickinson, nineteenth century American poet. Then there was Bram Stoker, most famous for writing *Dracula*, who died from the disease in 1912.

I vaguely remember the retching and the back pain. I distinctly remember how tight and swollen my skin was and how difficult it was to breathe. I can remember, more intensely, how hungry and thirsty I was. I remember sneaking a homemade biscuit from the platter on the side board then hiding in the back of the closet to eat it. I was to be discovered, and the biscuit taken away only to be replaced with whipped egg whites and clabber. To this day, I dislike yogurt and meringue. I remember how ugly I felt. Maybe it was based on my daddy's opinion of me being ugly and rejected by him.

Mama would demand, "You have to pee. You just have to pee." I would squat over the sunbaked sand as instructed. Occasionally, I would deposit a few drops of dark pumpkin-colored urine onto the ground. Eventually, this condition stabilized, life resumed and the eight-by-ten photograph was tucked away. I think folks went back to talking about Adolf Hitler who had committed suicide that spring…

THE BASTARD CHILD

Illegitimate bastard child is what my father called me. "Get away from me! I said get away! God, what an ugly girl you are, and you certainly don't belong to me! Look at *you*, with your *black, curly hair* and your *black eyes. You look just like that railroad man! You'll turn out to be nothin' more than a scalawag, just like him!*" My father growled viciously at me. The pain of that moment was excruciating; surely it will go with me to my grave. I remember the emotional aching of rejection as I sat there looking at him. He, cuddling my baby sister and scorning me, a feeling I would become accustomed to more and more as time went by.

There he sat, the one I called Daddy, by the front door, on the wooden slat floor of the porch with his feet resting on the second step. He was a thickset man and smelled of cheap aftershave and sweat and flimsy cigars. His teeth were yellow, decaying. To hide his thinning hair, I imagine, he always wore a fedora-type hat, the brim slick and oily, and for field work, it was the straw hat, headband slimy, as well.

On his lap sat my baby sister, less than two years old. My father turned back to her and spoke lovingly, murmuring to her, telling her that *she* was such a beautiful child with such a cute smile and such pretty brown hair. What an impression to have as a child. But this cruel, mean-spirited behavior of my father set the stage for the multitudes of emotional pain and fear that came to be the basis of my life during my early years.

LARRY DRAFTED, 1948

Three years passed, and by the time the next mill season rolled around, Larry had been drafted into the army. There was no general military draft in America until the Civil War. The Confederacy passed the first of three conscription acts April 16, 1862, and barely a year following, the Union began enlisting men. Government officials plagued with manpower shortages regarded drafting as the only means of sustaining a powerful military and to encourage voluntary enlistments. But compulsory service embittered the people, who considered it an infringement on individual free will and individual freedom and feared it would gather absolute power in the military. President Franklin Roosevelt signed the Selective Training and Service Act of 1940, which created the nation's first peacetime draft and formally established the Selective Service System as an independent federal agency.

Larry was sent to Fort Campbell, Kentucky. This military base lies on the Kentucky-Tennessee border between the towns of Hopkinsville, Kentucky, and Clarksville, Tennessee, and is about sixty miles northwest of Nashville. It was here that Larry lost some of his shyness and became a more outgoing, carefree young man. He made friends quickly and easily, although he retained a portion of his shyness that only added to the evolution of his charm and air of innocence.

The fort itself was opened in 1942 and was named after William B. Campbell, a Tennessee statesman and brigadier general of the United States Volunteers during the Civil War. Although nearly two-thirds of the 105,000 acres of the place are actually in Tennessee, the post office is located in Kentucky, and the establishment lies within that state. You can only imagine what an eye-opening experience this was for a naive young man who had spent his entire eighteen years in the backwoods of North Carolina. Most likely, Larry would have made his a military career but for the sudden illness of his dad. That resulted in him receiving a hardship discharge that Mama worked diligently to secure. Larry came home to Crossroads to provide for his ageing parents and his two much younger siblings. Daddy's sudden illness miraculously resolved.

HAZEL (1949–1950)

She was born third in line to Barnabas and Savannah. At sixteen, Hazel was living in the town of Elder at a crossroads named Tinkerton with Daddy's sister, Aunt Sarah, and attending the city school. Perhaps Hazel was too good for the farm and county schools. She was a beautiful young lady, with a thick mane of strawberry blond hair and eyes as blue as the Carolina sky in summer. I was only around six years old, but I would sit on the bed with my feet dangling over the side and watch intently as she combed her beautiful hair.

On one particular Saturday night, I was not sent to bed at the usual time but allowed to sit by the pot-bellied wood heater and listen to the adults talk. Their voices were soft and hushed, almost whisper-like and none of the conversations I could understand. I heard the words, but I could not decipher their meaning.

"Mama, why are you crying?" I asked. She removed the hot flatiron from the top of the wood-stoked heater, replacing it with the cold one, appearing not to hear my question. "Where is my sprinkling bottle?" she remarked, obviously ignoring me. A white cotton blouse was retrieved from the stack of clothing that had been sprinkled with water and rolled into a tight ball. As the iron pressed out the wrinkles of the damp cotton, the fragrance of the freshly ironed clothing, pleasant and familiar, filled the air.

Another garment was neatly folded and placed in the suitcase that was resting on a chair by the ironing board.

Summer had come to a close, and Hazel was in preparation to go live with Aunt Sarah for the new school year. At least that is what I thought…

"Why are you putting your clothes in the suitcase with Hazel's? Mama, why are you still crying?" I asked again.

"I'm just tired, and there is a long journey to make tomorrow. Stop asking so many questions. You need to go to bed now and try not to soak it this time."

I was eight years old but still wet the bed on occasion, the purpose for which you will find unraveled in yet another story. Moreover, wetting the bed interrupted that horrible recurring nightmare it seemed I would experience most every night.

Truth is, Hazel was pregnant; the long trip Mama spoke about was to Granville, North Carolina, to a home for unwed mothers. The name of the house was Jocelyn Hammermill Home for Unwed Mothers. Mind you, that wasn't my only encounter with this home, but that is another tale. Hazel birthed a healthy female and then left her behind for adoption. She returned to the town of Elder to live with Aunt Sarah and complete her senior year at Elder High.

NICK (1948)

My brother Nick… He was the fourth in line of six children. Somehow he seemed to come out last, well, except for me maybe. Nick and I held an extraordinary relationship most likely because we both suffered and shared so much pain during our growing-up years. I always admired Nick for his fortitude and resilience. The tenderness in which he dealt with nature was exceptional. I think I was one of the few who understood just how misjudged he actually was. He was a scrawny, wiry child and was constantly in some kind of face-off with the bullies of our surrounding communities. They teased and taunted him, foolishly believing they could intimidate him because of his small statue. However, my recollection is that Nicky never lost a battle. Well, except with Mama…

Seems Nick got the most whippings of anyone I knew. Mama was merciless with him, short on insight. Nick took whippings for his three older siblings more times than I want to remember. With every lash of the switch on his tan, young body, I cried and silently begged God to make her stop. She didn't. Did she secretly enjoy this despotism, the exercise of sovereign power in such a cruel and oppressive manner?

Nicky worked the fields together with the rest of the family. In summer, when night fell, he was the one who stoked the brick wood-burning furnace to keep the coals at the right temperature to cure the golden leaf. The tobacco barn was built with skinned logs and the cracks were chinked with muddy clay. This made them mostly air-tight.

The barn had four rooms, each room had five tiers. The barn itself was about sixteen-by-sixteen-by-sixteen feet. Occasionally, the chinking dried out, fell out and needed replacing. The chore of filling these holes took place in the winter. Buckets of muddy clay would be dug out from the bank of the big ditch that ran behind the barn and then hand-carried to the nearest side. We worked our way around the structure with children chinking between the logs they could reach and the adults climbing wooden homemade ladders to reach those higher up. I remember how cold my hands became, dipping up hands full of the sticky, sour-smelling black earth and packing it into those empty little spaces.

Unless you have had personal exposure to the curing leaf, you cannot know how strong and mellow and sweet the aroma was. Or you could not understand the pride the tobacco farmer had when he removed the bundles of leaves from the tobacco barn and carefully graded out the finest, most perfect leaves for cigars.

The leftovers were processed for making cigarettes, chewing tobacco and snuff.

Daddy would stretch out on the rickety wooden bench, still in his overalls, and pull his sweat-stained straw hat over his face. He slept while Nicky placed fat ears of yellow sweet corn, still encased in silks and shucks in the edge of the burning embers. As the fires burned in the brick wood box in the barn, Nick roasted marshmallows and ate the fleshy, plump roasted ears of corn and dreamed of faraway places.

Occasion would find him wandering into the edge of the woods; bare feet picking up sand from the dew-covered earth, capturing fireflies in a pint-sized glass mason jar. With an icepick from Mama's kitchen, he pierced the lid with minute holes, preventing the fireflies from dying from suffocation. Sometimes, he, too, would nap as his daddy stoked the fires. Nick never forgot to release the fireflies before dawn, so they could sleep through the long day and be ready for capture again when night fell. And another summer and another winter went by.

Chapter Two

Early Years

THERE WERE MANY enjoyable days playing with my baby sister, Pam. With small twigs and tobacco twine, we built houses in the warm, dry sand beneath the Muscadine grape arbor attached to the old smokehouse. The sand was like powder between our bare toes and we would spend hours organizing the little houses into bedrooms, kitchens and living rooms. When we tired of playing house, we would search for doodle bugs in the sand. We were protected from the boiling hot summer sun by the leaves and branches of the grapevines interwoven onto and around the wooden framework above us. Sometimes we made "snuff" by mixing sugar and cinnamon and packed it in our bottom lip, just like Aunt Eliza, Cousin Frankie's mother, did.

Mama made jelly with the grape pulp and pies with the hulls. Daddy and my eldest brother, Larry, prepared wooden barrels of whole squeezed grapes and sugar with a little water, which fermented slowly, turning into tangy, sweet, homemade wine.

I adored Pam, practically worshiped her for the obvious; she loved me unconditionally. She didn't think I was ugly or unattractive; she didn't think I came from an unclean beginning… She loved me as only a child can love. And I loved her back fiercely. There were undercurrents that pervaded our home on a regular basis, but nothing that I was able to explain, not always visible. There seemed to be unknowns waiting to happen. Those feelings left me feeling uneasy, it's difficult to explain.

Pam *was* a beautiful child. *I* could see that. She had pretty soft brown hair with almost ebony eyes, such a lovely round little face. She was quiet, though, and Mama fretted over "why isn't she talking yet? She just never tries to say a word, and she is almost four." I don't think she was mentally slow. In fact, looking back, she was probably the smartest of all. She learned early on that tears would get her almost anything. All Pam had to do was point, indicating what she wanted, and Mama, Daddy, or Larry tripped over each other to get her that particular thing. So it was not necessary for her to speak. I have been told that one of the first words she spoke was Kat in trying to pronounce my name, Kathleen, thus the tagging of that nickname. Only until she was around five years old did she begin to talk, speaking in short sentences of three to five words.

My goodness, yes, she was pouty. That bottom lip could roll out in less than the blink of an eye. She especially formed a sullen face when Larry tried to comb her hair in preparation for attending church. I can see her now. He gently combed her hair, creating the cutest little part down the middle of her scalp and placing each soft fiber of her bangs in a pretty straight row. As he stood there admiring his mastery, what did she do? Both hands shot to the top of her head, and by her own doing, her hair would be tousled again. This process would be repeated over and again until she tired of this adventure. She certainly was a spoiled little thing! But we didn't care; we adored her so.

INDOCTRINATION

Ms. Virgie and Mr. Vinnie Outlaw lived north of the white Baptist church. Ms. Virgie was plump and short. She kept her chopped-off graying hair secured behind her ears with bobby pins causing her chubby cheeks to appear even more so. Mama stood at the bottom step of the front porch as Ms. Virgie looked down at us. Pam clung to Mama's left hand, me to her right.

Ms. Virgie shifted her weight from foot to foot as she stood behind the screened door, blocking our view into the long corridor behind her, the one onto which the interior rooms opened. She wheezed a bit as she spoke, "Vinnie's just finishing his breakfast. I rather you wait out here 'til he goes out to milk the cow."

I was afraid of Mr. Vinnie; he reminded me too much of Daddy. He was tall and thin with thinner hair that he plastered across his scalp with mineral oil and beeswax. His hawk-beaked nose always seemed to be in competition with his pointed chin. Some of his teeth were missing with others decaying, looking like a half-shelled ear of yellow sweet corn.

I heard the back door slam and watched him cut across the back yard toward the cow pen with the empty milk bucket swinging at his side. His strides were long, but he had a funny kind of walk as if his knees were double-jointed. He talked out loud to no one, spreading his hands and arms in grotesque mannerisms for emphasis. Not even one glance did he send in our direction.

This morning, Pam and I had accompanied Mama as she followed the winding dirt road that led past the Baptist church to the where Mr. Vinnie and Ms. Virgie lived. We made this trip three times a week so Mama could help Ms. Virgie care for Mr. Vinnie's bedridden mother. Her name was Mary Martha Outlaw, but folks just called her Ms. Mary.

How I detested climbing those seven steps. With dreaded expectation, I followed Mama through the door and into that dark hallway. I could hear the screech and squeal of Ms. Mary's shrill voice. I wondered about demons and goblins. The hinges creaked as Ms. Virgie pushed open the door to Ms. Mary's bedroom. I was overcome by the stench of rotting flesh, lye soap, and pine oil that permeated the room in thick, heavy currents of air, rising and falling.

As Pam and I played make-believe in a far corner of the room near the heavily draped window, Mama and Ms. Virgie tended to Ms. Mary's needs. They log-rolled her frail, contorted body; joints twisted, distorted, and bent from disease and old age. They cleansed the bedsores, filling the deep pockets with salve. They rubbed petroleum jelly on clean white rags and applied them as dressings. Plastic sheeting was laid down on the putrid lumpy cotton batting mattress; worn sheets were placed over that.

The queasiness did not subside and my uneasiness rankled, unaware that this was my indoctrination to death and dying.

ABOUT POGO

What an obscure and microscopic reality we commanded. Personalities were ambiguous; behaviors not without aberrations- odd and peculiar. Was it possible Crossroads was duplicative of rural farming communities across the south?

According to Mama, Larry's induction into the army caused a noticeable hardship on the family left behind. The hardship discharge explains why he was back at home in his bed asleep when Pogo stopped by on that night in June 1950. Pogo was a cousin to us, and he and Larry were nearly the same age and best of friends throughout childhood and adolescence. Pogo should have been drafted at the same time Larry was; seems he was a dodger of his responsibility to serve our country. The loud exchange of words between Mama and Pogo awoke the entire household. He was drunk as a skunk, reeling in the doorway, demanding Mama to roust Larry out of bed so he might "ride off with me for a while." Pogo was good-looking with a thick shock of curly blond hair, a good-natured and fun-loving guy, yet quite scrappy and reck-less. He just couldn't handle the hooch. He drove a short dog as means of transportation. The cab of the truck was high off the ground; the big flatbed was the body of the truck. If you were standing nearby, you would lose your breath at the overpowering gas fumes. The sound of the engine was deafening.

Hearing all the racket, Larry jumped out of bed and was there at the door, stuffing his shirttail in, buttoning his trousers. He had all intentions of joining Pogo. No matter how hard Larry and Pogo begged, they did not shake Mama's decision. Rather, she told Pogo he should stay the rest of the night at our house, stay off the road, and sober up. He gave it some thought or prob-ably pretended to, then tumbled, stumbled around, and made his way back to his truck. I can still hear the belching and wheezing followed by an incredible bellow of the engine as spark met fuel of that old short dog. Pogo and his short dog roared away, head-ing west, kicking up a plume of dust, on the dirt road toward the white Baptist church.

Mama gave Larry at least fifty reasons it seemed as to why she wouldn't let him to leave with Pogo. It made no difference to Larry; he sulked and pouted. Shortly thereafter, we were all back in bed. I did not fall asleep right away, so it was easy for me to hear the soft tapping on the front door. Fearfully, I peeked around the curtain covering the doorway and could see Cousin Freddie Parks standing on the porch, hat in hand, talking to Daddy. Cousin Freddie was a colored man who lived less than a half mile away, just a stone's throw from the juke joint, known as *Jake's Place* and frequented only by the colored folks. Cousin Freddie explained he would appreciate Daddy accompanying him to the general store located in the center of Crossroads because "he's gone. Mr. Pogo is dead. Someone has to go right away to tell Miz Eliza that her son was just killed in a terrible accident right there in front of Jake's Place."

Thaddeus Brightwell (Pogo) Underwood was twenty-one. He was the first of many sons and grandsons Aunt Eliza, my daddy's mother's sister, would lay to rest.

EUDORA (1948)

Her name was Eudora Johnson, but we called her Aunt Eudie. Her husband was Uncle Charlie Johnson. He was kind, gentle, and soft-spoken. These were the grandparents of the little Johnson boy who lost his life to blasting caps that fateful Sunday morning. Aunt Eudie managed to keep a sizable tin of molasses in her cupboard. She would stir up a mixture of flour, lard, and buttermilk then pour the whole batch into the black iron skillet on the eye of the stove. Our tummies would growl as the fragrance from the flour bread filled the kitchen. Pam and I couldn't wait to swirl her cakes of flour bread in that molasses. She was petite in stature but mighty in character. Her skin was ebony, likened to fine silk and just as soft and delicate.

It must have been around 1948 because I was about five years old. I remember on previous occasions sitting at the plank board kitchen table, eating fried chicken and licking my fingers. I remembered the scent of menthol rub that floated gently about as Aunt Eudie leaned in close to me when she spoke. Her voice was soft. She spoke near-perfect English.

This middle-aged couple owned a Bluetick Coonhound that generally lay on the floor at the side of the kitchen stove. He must have been a splendid specimen in his heyday, treeing raccoons all night and sleeping all day. He would have been speedy and muscular. Even in his old age, he still had those large catlike paws. His mottled black-and-white coat left the impression of navy blue, but his long floppy ears were solid black.

Now he was old—old, irritable, and cantankerous. He was about as deaf as a doorknob and most likely nearly blind. His name was Blue; not terribly original, kind of like naming a black-coated horse Blackie or a chestnut-coated horse Red. Maybe our vocabulary was so small that was the best we could manage. That's hard to believe though as the folks in Crossroads had more vivid imaginations, mostly on the dark side.

We were sitting at the kitchen table that was pulled close up to the cook stove because it was warmer that way—we being Mama, Aunt Eudora, Pam, and me. Uncle Charlie sat nearby in his old platform rocker, puffing on his wooden tobacco pipe, puffing and lighting and rocking, saying not a word.

But getting back to old Blue...we were sitting there at the table, sopping up Blackstrap molasses with Aunt Eudie's flour bread, and I just couldn't get it to run out right. I either had too much molasses and not enough bread or vice versa. Well, too much molasses was the case for me at this point. I slid off the wooden bench and made my way to the stove to get another piece of bread. I could feel the heat from the stove getting warmer as I approached, so I took considerable pains not to burn myself.

We ate a lot of blackstrap molasses in those days. It was believed to be the best medicine you could keep in your cupboard; they said it would cure canker sores, palpitations, and anemia and heart dropsy. Some even said it would turn gray hair back to its original color, but I never saw any evidence of that. Blackstrap molasses was much higher in iron than regular old molasses they said because of it being a product of the third boiling.

I should have taken the same precautions with old Blue that I did in protecting myself from getting burned, but I didn't. I stepped backward away from the stove and right smack dab in the middle of old Blue's belly. He let out an awful yelp-growl then sunk his egg yolk–colored canine teeth deep into my left buttock! Naturally, he finally let go, and I received considerable attention from Aunt Eudora, Uncle Charlie, and Mama, but mostly from Aunt Eudora.

"He was always such a friendly mindful dog and followed Charlie's every command, would recognize my Charlie's voice in a slew of men," Aunt Eudie nervously explained.

She cut a paper-thin slice from the salt-cured pork belly laying on the sideboard, applied it to the now-purple tooth marks, and secured it around my body with a long strip of cloth she tore from the bottom of her petticoat.

"That will draw all the poison out. Leave it there for three days, then you can take it off," she said to Mama.

It must have worked like a charm because in no time, it was all healed up.

Aunt Eudie and Mama were best friends. Each would walk unhurriedly down the little path through the woods to the other's house frequently.

"Ms. Savannah, I brought you some fresh ground cornmeal," she would say as she padded up the front steps in those tiny, black ballerina shoes she always wore.

"Come in, Eudora," my mama would say to her as she guided her through the front door and into the parlor. Mama insisted on all her friends entering by the front door; it was just more respectful that way.

Mama would show up at Aunt Eudora's door. "Eudie, I know you have a plenty of frocks to wear, but I thought this pretty floral cotton chicken feed sack would make a respectable apron for Sundays." Aunt Eudie would *oohhh* and *aahhh* over the fabric because she knew Ms. Savannah had a Sunday apron in that very pattern. They would sit and talk privately, with their heads together, sharing thoughts and feelings while my baby sister and I played with Aunt Eudie's children. Then, at dusk dark back down the little path we would go. One never left the other's home empty-handed.

For prominent events such as church revivals or funerals, we attended each other's church. There was always a reserved front row pew, at Aunt Eudie's church, for Ms. Savannah and her two little girls. When Aunt Eudie and her children attended our church, they sat on the back pew. That is the only time my mama ever sat at the back of the church…when we joined them.

What a sight to behold, these two resolute, headstrong women…one colored and one white…in a time when this was not accepted, quite often not even safe. They went about their lives, scolding each other's children then praising them for good behavior. They worked side by side in the tobacco fields and shared their secrets with each other. Aunt Eudie knew of my mother's deepest secret…

CHAPTER THREE

CROSSROADS: THE COMMUNITY

A S THE OLD saying goes, you can choose your friends, but you can't choose your family. You can't choose the origin of your birth or where your roots are laid down. Such is the case with me. Crossroads is a farming community nestled deep in the county of Bakers, North Carolina, near the Little Scissor River. Keep in mind that what I am about to tell you is strictly hearsay. Knowing the characters inhabiting Crossroads there may not be a lick of truth to any of it at all.

By 1949, Crossroads had turned into a bustling community. The population was 732 and growing. There was a livery stable with a blacksmith shop complete with a farrier, post office, general mercantile store, sawmill, dairy farm, and two Baptist churches, one for the white folks and one for the colored. Crop farming was the backbone of this region where tobacco, corn, peanuts, and cotton were planted and harvested. Strawberries were grown in the nearby town of Rosemont.

Wild huckleberries grew in abundance in the woods that surrounded the community. My mother would watch, in the spring, for honeybees that would feed from the sweet nectar of the flowers in her garden. The more bees, the promise of more honey that could be collected from that old tree she found the previous fall; the tree that felt alive from the vibrations of the colony of bees inside. For some reason, she seemed to be exempt from bee stings. She said her daddy always complimented her on being a worker bee, not a drone, so maybe there was some camaraderie there—who knows.

On a warm dry day in early summer, Mama would assemble all the tools needed to collect the honey—a little serrated knife from the kitchen, a couple of large clay pots, a pair of work gloves, a box of "strike on box" matches—and place them in a basket. From the smokehouse, she would retrieve the bee smoker, stuffing it with damp rags. She would then don an old shirt and pair of trousers that belonged to my daddy and secure her wide-brimmed straw hat to her head with a scarf. Off into the woods she would go.

On her return, with honeypots filled to the brim, Mama would tell my baby sister and me an embellished story about collecting the honey. "I lit the rags on the way so they were putting out some pretty heavy smoke. I was pumping the bellows on the smoker, creeping up on the beehive when suddenly there approached an old brown bear. He was a big one too. Well, I scared him off easy enough, waving my straw hat at him and puffing smoke in his red eyes," she would begin. "Then I lost my footing, nearly falling off that rickety ladder I put there last year, but I held on. I got my knife out and stuck my hand into that hole in the tree and started cutting away at the honeycomb. I almost had the second pot filled when the ladder started shaking, and lo and behold…"—her voice dropped to a whisper—"there on the ground was a humongous black honey badger, making like he was going to climb right up that ladder to get me."

I know we must have had that dropped-jaw, deer-in-headlights look by this time! "I had to think of something, else the badger would surely climb the ladder to steal my honey, so I reached back in the hive and cut off another big chunk of honeycomb dripping with honey and tossed it as far as I could throw it." She leaned forward at her waist and swung her right arm in a wide arc then paused for effect, her eyes twinkling.

"What happened next?" we squealed in unison. "Then what…?"

"Why you children will never believe this. I watched the badger as he scrambled toward the honeycomb. I heard a crashing noise coming through the woods, and mercy me, there was a ruckus to behold: that old bear and the badger fighting over that honeycomb. And that's when I made my getaway." We knew for a fact there were brown bears around Crossroads because we had seen one late one afternoon. We didn't know honey badgers were confined to South America with no chance of one being in Crossroads.

My mother, she must have been the original spin doctor!

Mama would frequently pack a tin pail with tasty bits of leftover food from a previous meal, top it off with a worn table cloth, and exclaim to Pam and me, "It's time for a picnic!" You would think we were embarking on some magnificent extravaganza. And to the two of us, that is exactly what it was in the tiny little world we lived in.

We would strike out with the pail, and it seemed we walked forever, but we were untiring. What's more, Mama told tales along the way to keep us entertained. Upon reaching our destination deep in the back woods on the banks of a little flowing stream, Mama would spread out the tablecloth and place the contents of the pail on top: food for kings! We would stretch out on the wooden planks that bridged the banks of the stream, leaning over and stretching our arms as far as they could reach to scoop up a dipper full of fresh water to drink or to clean our messy hands and faces.

COUSIN FRANKIE AND COUSIN TILLEY

Eldon Franklin Underwood, eldest son of Eliza Ruth and Charles Donald Underwood inherited the mercantile store from his father, who died of consumption they said, at the young age of thirty-nine. I think everyone knew the cause of death was consumption, not the pulmonary kind, but the kind that resulted from consuming too much rot-gut moonshine whiskey. Aunt Eliza was left a widow to nurture six sons and four daughters alone. Eldon Franklin, a.k.a. Cousin Frankie, married Tillie Westerly; and they carried out the ritual of Charles Donald's way of conducting business in the general store. Cousin Frankie and Cousin Tillie both wore gold, wire-rimmed glasses with thick bifocal lenses to improve their limited eyesight. Leaning into and over the balance scale, they would dip their heads down, up, then down and up again, scrutinizing the balancing needle as it teetered precariously to the proper mark on the scale. This was all to convince the customer the "accurate amount" of weight for their purchase.

The old weighing scales sat on the three-inch thick wood-topped counter near the cash register. A customer would enter and say, "Mr. Franklin, I need half a pound of that cheese." Cousin Frankie would tear a piece of thick brown waxed paper from the dispenser and place it on the scale. Then he would remove the round wooden cover from the hoop of cheese that was resting on the cheese cutter. You could hear the *click, click, click* of the wheel bearings as the Lazy Susan turned to position the cheese at just the right angle. Then he would bring the self-attached cleaver down to cut the wedge of cheese. The cheese was placed on the paper for weighing. As the customer watched, the needle in the upright window of the scale moved to four…five…six… ounces. Mr. Franklin eased his thumb up under the paper, pressing the scale down until it reached eight ounces. Thus the customer was cheated out of two ounces of cheese.

It was common knowledge, I have been told, by folks of Crossroads that the head bobbing was intended to be a distraction to the patrons, most just feigned unawareness. But they were savvy; they knew to watch the couple's left thumb creep up to the scale while their heads bobbed to the up position. Patrons were cheated out of ounces of cheese and other commodities as well. Ounces make pounds, and cents make dollars.

Cash money was scarce to most that lived in Crossroads. So most were carried on *The Book* until crops were in and arrangements for payment could be made. Consequently, I have been told, as Cousin Frankie and Cousin Tillie were holders of *The Book*, no objection was made about the standard of weights.

To me, it appears, unfairness and foul play were ever-present to the inhabitants of this small rural community.

STOVE WOOD

When we were young, I was Pam's guardian, shielding her from every conceivable danger. The latter years of the 1940s were tumultuous and disturbing. There were many card-party nights Daddy would host. The men would drink moonshine and play cards and laugh and lose their temper and drink more moonshine. Pam and I would be sent off to bed early in the evening after which the partying would begin.

Sometimes altercations would erupt. I recall the shabby cloth curtain that substituted as a door into the bedroom. On one occasion, I cautiously pulled the curtain aside to peek into the other room. I saw a man, stumbling around, following Mama, groping at her bosom, her buttocks.

I watched as Mama snatched up a stick of stove wood by her right hand and swing it mightily, striking the reveler across his left temple and cheek. It seemed blood was everywhere...on his hands covering the left side of his face, spilling over to his dingy white button-up shirt and the bib of his faded blue overalls. I saw him stumble backward, colliding with the table. I remember Daddy yelling and cursing at Mama as cards, glasses, and jars went crashing, spiraling across the floor. Mama stood there trembling; the piece of bloodstained firewood still clutched in her right hand. I scrambled back to the bed and crawled beneath the covers, shivering in fear at the fray I had just witnessed.

"Kat, what is it," Pam whispered, sobbing into my ear.

"It's just part of the games they play. Don't cry. Let's try to go to sleep," I said to Pam as she clung to me.

Most nights we would lie in bed, trying to stay awake for fear of what might happen in our sleep. Sleep usually won, but I would awaken repeatedly throughout the night, drenched in perspiration because of the heavy homemade quilts I had wrapped around us as protection against the unknown.I remember how we huddled in bed with her sniffling herself to sleep.

Pam cried each time I received yet another whipping from Mama. Nick and I always had to fetch our own "switch," and Pam would follow me into the yard begging, "Kat, please cry. If you will just cry, Mama will stop whipping you. You know that's all she wants you to do." I was too stubborn, though, to take her advice. The whippings grew increasingly fierce.

CHAPTER FOUR

THE FEAR OF GOD

DID YOU EVER meet someone who was so evil you wondered how in the world he got that way? I did, and his name was Ambrose—Ambrose Underwood. Born in the 1880s and died in the 1960s. I was forced to call him Cousin Ambrose owing to the mores of the times. His wife was Cousin Lilly. Although she has no place in this story, I am left wondering if she knew his secrets. He just didn't die soon enough. He should have died before he scarred my life and that of my baby sister forever.

A multitude of events took place in the 1950s. Hazel started nursing school but dropped out, Pogo lost his life carelessly, Nick ran away from home and joined the army, and Hazel married George. Surely, there are other skeletons in my closet that will rattle their bones at me, begging for the door to be flung open, for their tale to be told as this chronicle unfolds.

From about the age of seven to twelve or so, I experienced this dreadful recurring nightmare and awakened drenched with sweat, my heart beating rapidly. In my dream, a band of wild

Indians hid in the woods between my house and the general store at Crossroads. It was the same stretch of road that Mama would send me and Pam to the store to buy her Camel cigarettes and Coca-Colas. You could purchase "Cocola" (as it was pronounced in Crossroads) for five cents, but if you bought a carton of six, you could get them for a quarter.

Anyway, in my dream, the Indians, wearing nothing but war paint, loin cloths, and feathered headdress, would bolt out of the woods with tomahawks raised and arrows primed in their bows chasing Pam and me, yelling and yipping and moving closer and closer, about to catch us and… The warm puddle of pee always woke me; I would have to face Mama in the morning, but morning couldn't come fast enough for me; the bad dreams would be over. The nightmares were intensely vivid; the Indian war cry was piercing, the brilliant colors of war paint and headdress glowing. I prayed for the rapid beat of my heart to slow. I prayed for it to return a more normal rhythm, in the unlit confines of that bedroom. Nausea would overwhelm me again, starting at the pit of my stomach and welling up in my throat; always occurring when I felt something dreadful was about to happen.

The bed-wetting had begun. Poor bladder control left me in many embarrassing situations; I would be so ashamed sitting in my one-piece desk in the first grade, surrounded by a puddle of pee because the teacher refused me an outhouse break, saying, "You will have to wait until recess." I was even more mortified by the appalling events that led to the bedwetting even though I never told…

Pam and I loved to attend Sunday school at the Baptist church that was about a mile and a half from our home. We had no way of transportation, so we were dependent on neighbors to take us places too far a distance to walk. On Sunday mornings, Mama would help us get dressed then send us out to stand on the front porch to wait for Cousin Ambrose to stop, load us up, and drive us to church. Mama would stay behind, begin preparation of Sunday dinner, then attend the worship service that followed Sunday school. What started as such a joyous occasion turned lewd and terrifying for the two of us—a little girl just five years old and another outwardly brave seven-year-old girl.

At times, we didn't wait on the porch; we would sneak off and start walking in the direction of the church, hoping to get there before he drove by. "Get in the car," he would demand the two of us, swinging the passenger door open as his vehicle inched to a stop beside us on that long deserted, sand-rutted road. I remember the wave of nausea rising up in my throat, feel the sweat pepper my body, and can still relive the experience of inhaling the dust as it swirled in and around the vehicle. "I'll get in the back seat first, I will sit forward, and you sit behind me," I whispered to Pam; as always, she did exactly as I asked.

Although the distance was short, the journey seemed as though it lasted an eternity. In horror and fear, I became victim to this so-called prominent citizen and steward of the church as he pulled my panties down, probing and jabbing and pressing his fingers around and about my most intimate areas. I remember his raspy, rapid breathing and the odor of the smelly after-shave he wore. He would grapple past and around me, trying to replicate this horrid act with my sister; however I always blocked him, keeping my body positioned, so this was never allowed to happen.

Cousin Ambrose tugged, pulled at my panties, yanked at my homemade dress in an attempt to make me presentable to the public again. "You better not tell a soul about this because if you do, you will both burn in hell for the bad things you have done and your mother will never love you again," he would say as we slid from his car. I had no reason not to believe this undoubtedly would happen. There is a euphemism widely used in the South: "It will put the fear of God in you." That pretty much described my fear of ever telling… I felt so contaminated, violated, and impure, so riddled with guilt, thinking somehow this was of my own doing. And what if my mother wouldn't love me any longer… That particular feeling was just too overpowering.

This scenario continued Sunday after Sunday until, one day, I had an idea; it came to me that we would lie down in the deep culvert beside the road to hide ourselves from him when we heard his car approaching; accordingly, we did just that. Finally, he pursued us no more. It wasn't until I was twelve or so that I was able to overcome the dreaded bedwetting incidents that were, what I believed, a result of this person's twisted vulgar and lecherous behavior. Certainly, neither Pam nor I ever told anyone of this molestation.

A WORD ABOUT NOD

It was in that same year, 1951, that Marvin Underwood a.k.a. Nod passed away at twelve years old. Nod was born with a condition called water-head baby. He wore diapers, required to be fed pureed food, and couldn't really communicate with anyone except through his pleasant persona. Everyone enjoyed his jovial nature and loved to hear his laughter, only you didn't *hear him*, *you watched him* laugh as his plump body convulsed into motions mimicking laughter. It was a true fact; Nod always had a smile on his face.

Aunt Eliza had a colored lady, a live-in nanny that provided most of the personal care Nod required. Her name was Azaleigh. She was pint-sized and as round as she was tall. She dressed in dark-colored frocks and always wore a clean, white apron. Her hair was hidden from view by the kerchief she kept wound around her head. Sometimes she would let me climb onto her lap where I teeter-totted, playing with Nod. She smelled of snuff and mothballs, but you can certainly feel safe when held in her bosom.

I wondered at the origin of his nickname. Was it derived from the Book of Genesis 4:16 in the Hebrew Bible, "And Cain went out from the presence of the Lord, and dwelt in the land of Nod, on the east of Eden"? Or was it just a pun on that mythical land of sleep, the Land of Nod? It could have been because he *nodded off* more than he was awake.

Nod was a good fit with all the other characters in Crossroads. There was never a thought in my mind to tease or badger him, never an inkling of an idea to play roughhouse with him or pick on him in any way. He was as helpless as a baby throughout his short life. Cute as a bug's ear he was. As a young child, I adored Nod and loved to play with him. The day he died was a sad one indeed; the unsullied baby child was no longer with us. Another of Aunt Eliza's children laid to rest…

It was in this year too that I discovered the Bookmobile, piano lessons, and Trudy, Hazel's second daughter, was born. Lordy did I love the Bookmobile. It followed the same route Thursday of every other week. We would be standing on the front porch, me, Pam, and Mama, looking west up the road for the initial glimpse of the panel truck to arrive. Stepping into the Bookmobile was not unlike entering another world entirely. The interior walls were lined with books, hardbound and paperback; magazines, and newspapers.

We chose our books of interest. Mama picked up a *Life* magazine then put it back, choosing *Look* because it had more about culture and fashion. Then she reached out and took the new novel *Catcher in the Rye* they had displayed. I chose two *Children's Playmate* magazines first, then *The Butterfly*, consciously knowing I would have to keep it hid from Daddy because it was about a Jewish family.

I felt sick to my stomach whenever he started cussing about people he didn't even know. The preacher said God loves everybody and we should too, so why was Daddy so different? Pam chose *Bambi* and a comic book. We left the Bookmobile clutching our choices tightly and ran eagerly back inside the house. There we would sit for hours, pouring over the revelations of the written word.

Although we were poor as dirt, Mama tried to give us some of the finer things in life; for example, she introduced us to piano lessons. Pam was not the least interested in piano, although I was. I will never forget Mrs. Burnett, the piano teacher at school. She dressed in snug-fitting skirts and blouses with a belt cinched tightly at her waist; she smelled of ammonia and kerosene. She wore her long brown hair piled on top of her head, and she never smiled. I was terrified of her! If you missed a note, she would crack your knuckles with a wooden ruler, and I missed a lot of notes... Piano lessons, needless to say, ended after only a few sessions.

Now the ice cream truck was a seasonal event, occurring only in the summer months. The truck was a step-side kind of van with an undercoat of white paint. There were images of ice cream cones and sundaes on the fenders, back, and alongside the drop-down window where orders were placed. There was a rainbow ribbon of colors painted around the bottom. Most memorable, though, was the jingling chimes that started so faintly miles away but grew louder as it approached, which made you think of church bells, beckoning each and all to respond. What a distinctive sound of summer, the jingle of the ice cream truck song!

With great expectancy, we waited on the front porch for the first sound of the music played from the loudspeaker on top of the white van. Mama would never let us remain in the yard or by the road for fear someone would snatch us up and away. We could hear the ice cream truck jingle well before the van rounded the bend at Jake's Place and Cousin Freddie Parker's residence. The coins in the palms of our hands became sweaty from holding them so tightly in our young fists. We eagerly watched as the truck stopped at houses along the way. Then all at once, there it was, stopping right by our mailbox. We jumped off the porch and ran to the ice cream vendor, exchanging metallic smelling coins for cold, deliciously sweet ice cream.

JAKE'S PLACE

Jake's Place, located on the right side of the ninety-degree curve a half mile from our front steps saw a lot of activity. Frequently, drivers would lose control of their vehicles when trying to make that turn just a little too fast. Sometimes the curve just snuck up on the driver.

In summer, some Saturday nights, we would sit on the front porch, listening to the sounds from the jukebox and the laughter that floated on the airwaves. It was just a ramshackle hole-in-the-wall shanty, but on Saturday nights the place came alive. The juke joint was where the colored folks gathered to socialize, and they did just that. The jukebox was turned up real loud, and with the drop of a coin, the music began to play. They danced away the early part of the evening, quenching their thirst on moonshine and beer. Toward midnight, the proprietor would serve up a plate of chicken stew or rice and gravy with greens and hocks, all for a fee. "It's a rowdy place, Jake's is," Mama said.

Daddy would pipe in, "All them low-class niggers know how to do is eat, drink, gamble, and fight!"

His comments, even his presence, always put a damper on my disposition. Mama was clever, though, as she turned the subject to the music. The slow drag dance music was her favorite while Pam leaned toward boogie-woogie. My choice was the live music they would sometimes have, the fiddle and the banjo—that and the blues.

There were nights we could hear gunshots ring out then some screaming and yelling. All at once, the pulsating crowd would flee the building, darting in all directions. One time, I got real brave and crept up the road to Cousin Freddie's yard, dragging Pam with me. We were nervous and silly by the time we found a good vantage point to observe. We could hear the music real good now, and they were playing that slow drag music Mama liked so well. This night, the crowd was so big it spilled over into the yard. We listened as the loud music filled our ears. We watched as the rambunctious crowd became more high-spirited. Our eyes widened, and our mouths fell open as we watched a bare-knuckled fight right before our eyes. We just turned tail and ran back home for fear someone would find us out!

The patrons of Jake's Place may have been a little rowdy, could have been a little disorderly, but they never infringed on the white folks—that would have been against the law. I heard Daddy say more times than one, "They know their place, and by damn it, they well better stay in it if they know what's good for 'em."

When Nick was around sixteen, he would sneak up to the joint and was probably the only white boy they ever invited in. Most likely, Margie had something to do with that, even though the Jim Crow Laws were alive and well in Crossroads, the laws that forced segregation on us all. The coloreds had their schools, churches, and cemeteries…and joints; the whites had theirs.

Nick said they sold moonshine and a few cans of Pabst Blue Ribbon beer. "They offered to give me a shot of that liquor, but I was afraid Mama would find out and tan my hide. It was worth the risk, though, just to be there. Everybody was laughing and joking and dancing. Kat, I wish you could have seen it," Nick remarked wistfully.

Listening to the music and hearing Nick recount his visit at Jake's Place set me dreaming of better times.

NICK'S QUANDARY (1953)

It was early June. This particular morning, Nick was out in the field, with plans to plow tobacco. No matter how hard he tried or how quickly he turned it, the hand crank refused to release the spark that would allow the tractor engine to respond. Every muscle in his body was stretched taut, little rivulets of sweat trickled down his lean torso. The frustration of it all reduced him to tears. With a hopeless sigh, he lowered himself to the warm, soft earth.

A cloud of dry powdery dust, almost vaporlike, rose up around him, settling on his fatigued, damp body.

He was exhausted...tired through overuse of his tense muscles, beating plow-sweeps back into shape, tillage tools used to remove the grass from the tobacco rows...wore down by the constant beating from Mama...tired of being turned away from any prospects of a job in the nearby towns. He had tried to get on with one of the mills, but they were not hiring. Nobody wanted to give a seventeen-year-old boy even the time of day. "What can I do to get away from here and away from her?" He wondered over and over to himself. "I have no money, no way to get anywhere except by hitchhiking or any place to sleep when I have decided to stop. Oh well, I could always..." And suddenly, he had his answer.

Chapter Five

The Great Escape

I T WAS THE end of September on a late Sunday evening when Nick told her. "Mama, I'm leaving tomorrow. I've signed up for the army. I've already talked to the recruiter, and I have to be on the Greyhound bus at eight in the morning. I'll be reporting to Fort Jackson, South Carolina, to get all my army gear."

The house was quiet with only the two of them still awake, she sitting by the oil lamp reading and he fidgeting about. Pam and I were already in bed, and Pam was fast asleep. Daddy was on his cot in the corner of the bedroom, snoring away. But that didn't keep me from hearing their every word. I began to tremble violently, that familiar sense of panic welled up inside. I knew how difficult it must have been for Nicky to say these words out loud to his mama, whom he loved so much despite the particular way in which she dealt with him.

Nick's voice was melancholy. Mama put her book aside. "You are sure this is what you want to do?" she asked with deliberateness, and her stern face softened a bit. "Why, you are still just a boy, only sixteen! They can't take you in the army at that age!"

"I lied about my age, Mama, and I'm not sixteen, I just turned seventeen two weeks ago. The recruiter thinks I am eighteen, and you can't won't stop me from going!" They sat for a long time—a face-off, not exchanging words but each lost in contemplation of days and events past. I began to cry. Already, I was missing him…

Nick was quick and bright and with God's gift of sensibility. He was just poorly directed and ahead of life and times of our little community. The time had come for his bold escape. The year was 1953.

At Ten Years Old

Many things happened that year; it was a year of coming of age for Nick and somewhat of redemption for me. Larry had been called back in the army by the second draft in April; he did so not want to go. Nick volunteering to serve, could not wait to leave, ecstatic to get away from his torturesome mother, and the hard labor of the farm. By the third day of June, Nick had made his getaway.

With Larry and Nick now both gone from the farm, I was next in line to work the fields assisting Daddy with the labor. Daddy would attach the plow sweeps to the cultivator, using U-bolts, tightening the lock nuts at just the correct measured distance apart. The drawbar had to be unlocked and in a free position to assure the lift lever would work properly. At that point, he would turn the hand crank on the old Allis Chalmers farm tractor then step aside so I was able to drop the sweeps into the dark loamy soil below. I would plow one row and then another, stopping occasionally to clear the sweeps of the clumps of fragrant grass all tangled up in the sand spurs they had picked up along the way. Those times were happiest of all. I didn't mind the fine powdery dry earth that rose up around me filling my nostrils.

Nor was I concerned with the potato rows of grime and dirt that grew deeper and deeper on my face and around my neck.

The scorching summer sun that fell across the tobacco field caressed my skin, added warmth to my soul. "See how dirt just sticks to ugly people?" Daddy would taunt me. "If I didn't know better, I would think you were one of them Jews or maybe even a nigger. Your daddy wasn't a nigger, was he?" Then he would sneer at me in self-satisfaction, waiting for a response, one that never came—well, not quite yet anyway.

This was the year I rose up against Daddy, said I wasn't going to take it anymore. As long as I could remember, he was constantly swatting at me, sometimes with his hand, sometimes a stick, sometimes a switch. Always I tried to maintain an arm's length between us; I learned to move quickly avoiding most of the blows.

In years past, we routinely plowed the fields with horses. We still owned two mares; one was coal black with the other the color of roasted chestnuts. These mixed-breed draft horses stood almost sixteen hands tall; to a ten-year-old, they were goliaths. Daddy mocked me for naming them, said they were "nothing but dumb animals and don't deserve no names." I guess I wasn't exactly creative in naming them, which probably added to his ridicule. The black one I named Blackie and the chestnut-colored one I called Red.

It was my job to fill the large washtub with fresh water for the horses. The sun was setting behind the dense forest of trees behind the barn when Daddy brought Blackie out of the stall to drink. She stood there, and filled her belly till I thought it would burst. I kept on pumping, pumping until my arms ached with the effort of pushing down on that iron handle. Water flowed out of the spout in gushes with a *whoosh-whoosh* sound. Daddy put Blackie back in her stall, removing her halter. I always believed Daddy was scared of the horses because he maintained such a tight grasp on the reins with the bit of the bridle cinched tightly in their mouth with one hand, and in the other, he held a long sturdy stock whip.

He then haltered Red and led her to the pump where the tub was waiting, refilled. She would not drink; she just stood there. A cussing man my daddy was; he must have held the record on how many ways he could use the Lord's name in vain. It would make my stomach ache. If he didn't have any fear of the Lord striking him down, I had enough for the both of us. He had an impressive set of lungs too; he would have won any hollering contest.

Well, Red wouldn't drink. Daddy started cussing and hollering, jerking on the reins; Red started shaking her head. Daddy yanked even harder; a little trickle of blood formed in the corner of her mouth, cut by the bit. Daddy started hitting her with the whip, across her beautiful chest, leaving whelps and broken skin in its wake. Red shuffled backward a few paces, Daddy following; a heavy cloud of dust building up all around them. Lash after lash fell across her shoulders, legs, and upper body. It all happened so fast. I screamed at him, screaming to stop; I saw Red as she rose on her hind quarters, front legs high in the air, tucked under, ready to attack the attacker. Her eyes were wild and frenzied. Her handsome coat now covered with white, salty sweat and trickles of blood. Daddy lost his footing, fell backward, losing his grip on the reins. I ran toward them, filled with terror. Daddy twisted away, Red took several steps forward with front end still elevated before she came crashing back to the ground. She snorted, shook her head wildly, then wheeled and galloped back to the safety of the pack house and her stall.

The only thing hurt about Daddy was his pride, to be "outdone by a mangy horse," he said. I made sure, from that day forward, I was the one who took the horses from their stalls, gave them water to drink, fed them hay and fodder, brushed their salt matted hair, plucked the cockle burs and sandspurs from their manes and tails.

The pack house was a fairly new building, more elaborate, more finished than our own home. This two-story barn served many purposes. Prior to the pack house being built, cured tobacco was stored in symmetrical stacks in a front bedroom of our home. With the new building in place, the sticks of tobacco were passed upward through the wide opening on the upper level and packed away in the same fashion. The ground level had a dirt floor with a wide-ranging breezeway down the center. There were two stables on each side toward the back half; two for horses on the left and two for cows on the right. We only had one Holstein milk cow, so the empty stall came in handy to store bales of alfalfa hay and stacks of fodder for winter feeding. Two other cows with their heifers, along with a prized Hereford bull Daddy stood at stud for a fee, were kept out in the pasture. To the left in the front half, hundred-pound bags of guano, nitrogen of soda, other chemical compounds, and chicken feed were stored. These bags were stacked high on top of wooden pallets to protect them from moisture of the damp earthen floor.

We may not have had cash money, but we were never hungry, being fed off the fat of the land—beef, pork, poultry, eggs, and vegetables. We raised Rhode Island red chickens; when they were young pullets some were fried up for Sunday dinner. The older hens were the layers and produced well over 150 extra-large brown eggs each in a single year. When she became too old to lay eggs, the hen was served up as chicken and dumplings. I had to be on the lookout for the two roosters. They didn't like each other much—competition in the henhouse I guess. One in particular didn't like me. I was spurred by that red-headed rooster more than once. The only purchases of staples were for sugar, tea, salt, and coffee. Wheat and corn were ground at the gristmill to produce flour and cornmeal.

Even on the hottest and most humid days, the atmosphere on the ground floor was comfortable. There was no front or back doors to cover this wide breezeway, and this allowed for the gentlest of breezes to find its way in. The nutty sweet fragrance of alfalfa hay would fill your nostrils even as you approached the building. After all the tobacco had gone to market, the upper level became a place to play. Upstairs, on the wide expanse of the wooden floor, a prominent, wide, circular track was entrenched, created by numerous laps from clamp-on roller skates worn by me and Pam and our friends.

It was my chore to collect the eggs from the hen nests built high off the ground on the right front wall. Farm equipment, plows, disc harrows, and cultivators were stored underneath these. So I had to climb up and over this equipment in order to reach the nests. One particular day exactly when as I reached out to collect the eggs, I lost my footing and tumbled down into that jumbled mess of iron.

I heard it and felt it at exactly the same moment, the snap, the grating together as the two bones of my lower right arm cracked. I untangled myself from the heap of iron, staring at the area about three inches above my usual wrist where my arm now bent, flopping down at a peculiar angle. It seemed I was in that plaster cast forever although it was only about six weeks. That injury caused me to learn to do most everything with my left hand. This is how that school year ended.

Just before school started back that fall, Cousin Bertha came one afternoon to play. We were lost in our own little world, playing make-believe, when Bertha's brother, Wallace, showed up on his bike. I always, always, always wanted a bike; however, there never was money to buy one. This day, I begged Wallace. "Let me ride your bike, just one time. I cross my heart and hope to die. I'll ride it around the house just once!" He finally agreed, helped me mount, straddled the center bar, stabilized myself on the seat as I put a death grip on the handle bars, and he gave me a shove to get me rolling.

This was my first experience being on a bicycle, and it was exhilarating! I kept my word, and as I approached my starting point, I suddenly realized I did not know how to stop the thing! The bike was rolling quite slowly now, and I was having trouble maintaining my balance, which led me to reach out with my left hand touching a vehicle in an attempt to stop. I heard it, felt it again, the now familiar snap, crackle, and pop of bones breaking. It just couldn't be true—I had broken my left arm right above my wrist! Consequently, I completed the fourth grade with my right arm in a stinky plaster cast and began the fifth grade with my left arm casted.

WHEN I WAS TWELVE (1954)

It was summer again. The heat was sweltering this July day as tobacco barning season began yet again. There was a little narrow path leading from our backyard around by the big ditch toward the tobacco barns, the same barns where my brother Nick roasted corn and captured fireflies. Daddy was making his way to the house from the barns; I was on my way to the barns from the house when our paths crossed. I heard him coming, cussing, and yelling. I wondered what had set him off this time. It didn't matter.

He was storming down the path, tobacco stick in hand, in a rage, shaking his fist, and then he saw me. He swung that tobacco stick with all his might, directly at my upper body. I had learned to be ever vigilant and to be able to get out of his way, and I easily sidestepped this blow. I could see the dark circles at the armpits of his thin cotton shirt; I could smell the pungent odor of his days-old perspiration. He swung again, but now I had moved up close to him and grabbed the stick in both my hands, wrenching if from him. Stepping away, I crouched ever so slightly, raised the stick over my left shoulder, like a baseball bat. My breath was coming in short choppy wheezes as I allowed the anger to fill me up.

I watched him backing away, away from me, this child whom he had labeled the bastard child. I could perceive the fear in his see-through pale blue eyes, the same eyes he had bequeathed Hazel, passed on through his evil genes. We were at an impasse, a standoff like two animals in battle. I remember the rivulets of sweat that found their way down my back, under my armpits. My whole body screamed at me that this was my turn; I was now in control! Act! Do something…

Daddy turned his back on me and walked back to the barns. We never mentioned this incident to each other, but the rules had now changed…

This was the year the lights came on in Crossroads; when the Rural Electric Association uprighted poles and strung wire across the farmland. The hookup fee was five dollars, and the monthly fee was three dollars. Mama said when the string was pulled on the bare bulb overhead, and the light came on, "Look at these grimy walls! They didn't look that dirty in daylight!" She put us right to work, scrubbing the walls with rags and lye soap. The first thing Daddy bought was an electric water pump to hook up to the deep well: no more pumping water by hand for Red and Blackie. The electric lights sure made it easier to read and study homework after dark. It was also easier to see the Coca-Cola bottle caps on the checker board Mama had fashioned out of an old cardboard box.

That same year, Hurricane Hazel destroyed our outer banks and came inland to wreak more havoc and destruction. It was also the year my sister Lucy and her second husband, Harvey, moved from the tenant house in the country to Hillsboro to live in free housing—free as long as she climbed the fire tower every day and stayed from sunrise to sunset, watching for signs of wood's fires. Lucy said, "Once I climb that flight of stairs, reach the trap door at the top, and enter the little room, I feel overjoyed. There I am isolated, away from it all." She continued, "I feel closer to heaven at this time than at any other. It is when the sun goes down and the blue sky turns purple then black, and the stars begin to appear that the sky is most beautiful."

In this year, another cousin met tragedy and a traveling carnival tent show came to Crossroads in the grassy lot by Underwood's General Store.

CHARLES

He was a tightly knitted mass of sinew and muscle for such a young fellow. I guess it was in his genes because he didn't do any more hard labor than my brother Nick who was about the same age. And Charles was just too plumb pretty to be a boy. He had curly russet-colored hair, dimples, and eyes the color of sea foam. He was a cross between Marlon Brando and James Dean in my book, and I'm sticking to that!

Charles seemed to be fearless; he would meander out into the cow pasture and taunt Poodles, the bull. Poodles's body was a deep reddish brown color. His face, thick deep chest, and under-side were white as was his switch of a tail. The hair around his face was thick and curly similar to that of a poodle, thus the explanation of his name. His horns curved out right around the top of his ears, pointing downward somewhat.

He would take his shirt off; Charles would and wave it at the bull just like one of those Spanish Matadors, flap it in the wind, making it pop and snap just to agitate the bull even more. We all know bulls don't like to be teased like that, but it was just a game for Charles, always a little on the wild side. The bull put his head down, low to the ground and swung it slowly back and forth, snorting and blowing. First, his left hoof then his right would rake backward slinging dirt and grassy particles flying behind him. Left, right, snort, left, right, blow, snort. "Watch out Charles! Here he comes!" Pam and I would scream at him.

Charles had picture-perfect timing, sprinting away from the bull, sliding under the fence gate just barely but always in the nick of time. He would stand, brush the grime from his naked torso with his shirt, slowly put it back on, grin, and wink at us and swagger away. It seems it was more than the bull he was teasing...

The gorilla fight was a highlight of the summer. I am sure there were other facets of entertainment surrounding this occasion, but the main event was the boxing match. Excitement was at such a level it made goose bumps stand up on my skin. Even though it was July and sweltering heat inside that tent, I felt a chill from the beads of perspiration forming on my brow, on my skin.

There was a purse, I don't remember the amount of cash involved, but it seemed like a sizeable amount. It didn't have to be much to seem like a lot to me. The ringmaster led the gorilla into the ring; the spectators moved closer. The ringmaster cracked his whip and barked some words at the gorilla; the gorilla pant-hooted back at him, beating himself on his chest with his gloved hands. This went on for several minutes to prove to those present the handler had perfect control over the beast. Then a carnival worker led Charles in, and the crowd roared in a loud cheer of support.

He sure did look cocky; Charles did, bouncing around on that piece of tan colored tautly stretched canvas. He was wearing nothing but swimming trunks and black PF Flyers, the white laces securing the shoe tops just above his ankles. The bell rang, and the match began. Charles circled the gorilla who circled Charles. A punch here, a punch there, circle, bounce, punch...then the bell rang. The first of three rounds was over. On-lookers indulged in taking care of Charles; others observed the gorilla, watching him pad about! Round 2 went pretty much as the first then the bell rang again. Round 3 was a little different. The gorilla swung at Charles and made a connection with his left jaw; Charles went down. The crowd was in an uproar; the excitement was mounting even more! Regaining his footing, he sparred with the gorilla again when suddenly, out of the blue, the gorilla was down—out like a light! Arms and legs propelled away from his body.

He just lay there sprawled out on that mat, not moving; he hardly breathed all the way through the count of *"ten, you're out"* from the ringmaster. The crowd was jubilant, cheering, shouting; Charles pranced around with his winnings in his hand, like any real boxer would. The ringmaster was flabbergasted; it just wasn't supposed to end this way. How could that young boy... Unobserved by the lookers-on, he motioned to the gorilla and the two of them slinked furtively out of the ring.

I could hear the mumblings in the background from some disgruntled spectators because they had put all their money on the gorilla. The smart ones, though, put their money on Charles! Was the fight rigged? And am I sure if it was a gorilla or was it really a chimpanzee? Or could it have been a man in a monkey suit? Now this is where fact and fantasy collide.

CHAPTER SIX

WARPED AND TWISTED

REALITY REVEALS ITSELF in the emotional and creative context of our minds. Not only do we perceive reality, we sense it. Some personal experiences I have found to be beneficial, others injurious. Unquestionably, there was nothing monotonous in the every day of my childhood.

Pam cried a lot, it seemed to me anyway. There were so many times she would beg me to make it go away that I cannot recall the specifics. I do remember, though, one day in late spring of 1955 in the early afternoon. The sky was just clearing from a heavy downpour of rain from the dark clouds that had been hanging low overhead for most of the day. Although a few light raindrops were still falling, the sun was unquestionably brilliant.

Pam and I were outside, searching for that ever-elusive rainbow when we heard our mama scream, "Kathleen! Kathleen!" I felt panic well within me. Pam started crying.

"What is it?" Her faint little voice trembled as she asked me the question again. "What? What is it?" She cried even harder… I started running toward the sound of Mama's voice.

I was not even a teenager yet, chronologically that is, yet my heart and soul was already weary. I had witnessed and experienced so much fear, so much pain and dealt with so many mean-spirited people. I knew what it was instinctively; I had been through this twice already…I knew what it was. I prayed a child's prayer, "Dear God, don't let him do it. Please, please, please, Lord. Don't let him do it. Let me reach him in time again. Lord, I promise to be good and never ever sin if you will just let me get to him before… oh, God, please…"

I was drenched in sweat, yet I felt so cold I shivered; my body trembled violently as I rushed past Mama, through the kitchen and into Daddy's bedroom. There was no door on the doorjamb, just a curtain to pull to the side. I tried to focus; it seemed like an eternity before my tunnel vision brought his outline into view. At first, all I could bring into focus was the outline of his body against the bright sunlight spilling in from the window. It was as though the entire area was blacked out, and he was radiating light, somehow. The atmosphere was strange and peculiar, yet filled with déjà vu.

He was sitting in a cane-bottomed ladder-back chair. Some years ago, I suppose, he had shortened the legs, so he was seated close to the floor. The thin worn T-shirt sagged at his armpits, and I could smell the stench of sour body odor and cheap cologne. His boxer underwear was ragged and stained.

The butt of the shotgun was wedged securely against the windowsill with both barrels planted firmly in his mouth. I swallowed repeatedly to suppress the nausea that welled up filling my esophagus. He never turned, but I could see him steal a glance toward me as I approached him. The walking stick he held precariously by the slender handle teeter-tottered, trying to latch onto the trigger.

"Daddy, please. Please don't. Please don't," I begged. It is astonishing what the eye sees and the brain computes in milliseconds. I felt I was moving in exaggerated slow motion, and every little squeak in the wooden floor was magnified and prolonged. My ears were roaring, and my words sounded sluggish, hollow, and garbled as though they were spoken by another. I could see him watching me as I moved closer, even closer.

"Daddy, we love you. Please don't…" I said as I reached out with my right hand and took the stick away. The fingers of my left hand closed around the wooden shaft of the shotgun. I backed slowly away. He sat motionless but turned his head slightly and stared blankly in my direction. "It will be okay, Daddy. It's all right. Don't worry, Daddy. I will try to make it better," I stammered as I backed out of the room. I turned my back to him, walked out of the bedroom, clutching the double-barreled shotgun. The curtain fell quietly into place behind me.

As darkness approached that evening, Pam and I secretly stole our way into the woods behind our home. I carried a broad ax along with the double-barreled shotgun. She carried a shovel. I remember her crying and saying how mad Daddy would be and that he would beat me again. I didn't care; nothing could make me as afraid as the thought that he actually would blow his brains out. With the gun stock splintered and the firing chambers damaged by the broad ax, I began to dig.

It had been raining throughout the day, and the mud made a sucking sound with each shovel full of pungent, sour-smelling clump of dirt I removed. Blisters formed on my fingers and palms, they burst only to emerge again. Pam was of no help with the labor; all she could do was cry and snivel. Finally, a long deep trench was dug in that pasty, foul-smelling clay; fitting for a burial place for the gun that belonged to my foul-smelling Daddy. The shotgun was laid to rest. Interestingly, Daddy never asked of the whereabouts of the shotgun. This was the third and final time I would see my daddy in an attempt to take his own life.

THE DIGGING OF MILLER'S POND

There was a day when I could give you the full history of Miller's Pond located just on the county line of Bakers and Dumford, barely past the Bakers' side. It was a man-made pond, a reservoir of sorts, dug deep into the dark dense soil of Dumford with the banks piled high with the innards from the hole. The water seeped in from the natural springs of the nethermost part, becoming darker and murkier as the level rose.

Mr. Miller was a man of wealth and power. He had this artificial lake dug as a reward to him for achieving much in the farming business. This would be a money-making venture for him as well as farming—that is, if he maintained it properly. It would be a nice recreation site for all to come with fishing gear and Jon boats and picnic lunches. He wouldn't have to charge much, he thought, because folks would come from far and wide for the pleasure of boating and fishing.

The site he chose was picture-perfect, surrounded on three sides by tall Carolina Pines. There, just where the hill of the dirt road crested, every passerby would literally catch his breath at the sight of this enormous lake as the road snaked past. Besides, the twenty-five–acre boggy plot was filled with natural springs and not fit for anything more than a pond so why not take advantage of this natural phenomenon?

Mr. Miller was a busy man, so he did not oversee the final digging of this massive hole-in-the-ground so he knew little of what lay underneath this shadowy body of water that grew deeper and deeper and deeper. After all, he had hired professionals out of the city to do the excavating and paid them good money for a turnkey job.

My brother Nick said he was about five years old when the project began so that would have been late 1939 or 1940. This would have been before the war, before the Japanese attacked Pearl Harbor on December 7, 1941, before the United States became fully, militarily involved. So the residents of the County of Bakers and surrounding areas felt far removed from any threat of this kind of danger.

Nick said that the excavating and shaping of the pond provided enormous excitement to the area, bringing onlookers from across the region to watch this massive undertaking. The heavy equipment rumbled, growled, and snorted, bulldozing its way over the land, piling the scraggly shrubs and pine tree logs to one side, then bucket after bucket of heavy black soil was dug out and hauled to other sides of the soon to be pond. The water seemed to rise, he said, quicker than they could dig, so the rush was on to complete the final stages. The contractors were keen in their trade, building a depth control device, an overflow facing the road side of the pond so that when the water level threatened to rise to the top of the berm, it was diverted through this device, snaking under the roadway and into a fairly large creek on the other side. The pond's edge, the berm was tamped neatly down and sloped to perfection but what to do with the nasty eyesore of timbers piled up on the far side?

The natural springs filled the gaping emptiness rapidly; fresh shoots of Bermuda grass and clover quickly covered the barren berm, creating a beautiful clean cushion that wound its way around the perimeter of the pond. Old men would sit on overturned buckets and idle away many an afternoon, fishing for the catfish, bass, and Crappie Mr. Miller had stocked the pond with. Kids played at the water's edge, swimming out, going deeper. Younger men unloaded their Jon boats, and with their paddles, wound their way farther onto the surface of these dark waters.

Nick told of a time when a city slicker came to the pond with his strange-looking fishing boat. "It's a skeeter boat," the man told me as he and his son angled it into the water. "We've just moved to Raleigh from Shreveport, Louisiana. This is my grandson Billy. He paddles me around while I fish for bass."

"It was strange-looking, kinda like a box, but the front was pointed. The bottom was wider than the sides and they slanted in, you know, like they curled in. You could stand on the sides and not even turn the boat over, that's how much they sloped in. That's where they kept their fishing poles. I could've laid down under the side and hid from Mama if I had a need to."

He was the envy of all as he and his son situated themselves along the edge of the pond bank and cast out, spinning their worms slowly back in. Onlookers watched as the old man reeled in bass after bass. Nick told me Billy used a strange-looking paddle, the likes he had never seen before, said he called it a sculling paddle. "The old man and his grandson talked real funny too. I couldn't half understand what they said," Nick recalled.

Over the years, it became quite natural for the teenaged boys of the community to rent one of the little wooden flat-bottomed paddleboats from Mr. Miller's inventory, then take it out to the very center of the lake and use it as a jumping off place to swim in circles and have chicken fights in the water, one trying desperately to sit on the shoulders of another in piggyback fashion, seeing how long the bottom fellow could tread water before slipping beneath the surface. What better way to relax those tired muscles after a long week's work on the farm! So it was on that dreadful day…

INDEPENDENCE DAY

Tobacco barning season would begin in a few days, and there would be little time for horsing around. This was a big weekend in Crossroads with relatives returning to their roots to celebrate with their families left behind on the farms. Barbeques, cookouts, and picnics would happen this long weekend with folks trickling in late Friday night, then Saturday and Sunday. The big celebration would conclude on Monday evening, July 4, with fireworks throughout the neighborhood.

Aunt Eliza's children were no exception; they flocked back to the home place to enjoy and participate in the festivities. Her eldest daughter, Mary, passed away just two years earlier at the age of forty-four, leaving behind a grieving widower and three small children. Gordon, the youngest of the three was present on Sunday to hang out with the other boys around his age. Lester Louis Underwood (brother to Cousin Frankie) and his wife, Eunice, had arrived all the way from Suffolk, Virginia, with their two sons, Elton Lee and Carlisle. Cousin Jettie, fifth in line of Aunt Eliza's children, still lived in Crossroads, and her son, Wilbur, hung out with the other boy cousins at Underwood's General Store located at the center of Crossroads.

❦❦

It was Sunday, July 3. The Baptist church was packed full that morning what with all the aunts, uncles, cousins, nieces, and nephews coming home to Crossroads for the Fourth of July Celebration—such a happy occasion! That afternoon, the boy cousins played tag football in the same field where Charles fought with the gorilla. There were about six in all: Wallace, Wilbur, Henry Alston, Carlisle, Elton Lee, and Charles. Mark, the cousin from Washington, DC, would not arrive until the *day*, July 4, but he was to stay longer as this was the traditional two-week vacation his family spent in the country (his mother, Sudie, was sister to Cousin Tilley, the wife of Cousin Frankie). They always poked a little good-natured fun at him, calling him the City Boy. The girl cousins hung out doing what twelve-year-old girls do, whispering behind their hands, giggling about boys, imagining what a real kiss from a boy would feel like.

Covered with grime from the mixture of sweat and dirt, the boys tired of this roughhousing and decided they would walk

74

the mile and a half to Miller's Pond to swim and play. The dip in the pond might even wash the grunge away accumulated from the long day's activities. Off they went with the blessings of the adults. They whooped and yelled, pushed each other, tripping over each other's feet as they made their journey to Miller's Pond. Not a worry in the world...

History has a way of writing itself, though, and the tranquil weekend turned deadly on this very Sunday afternoon. Leaving a trail of billowing dust particles behind on the dirt road that ran from Crossroads to Miller's Pond, a car came to a skidding sudden stop in front of the house where Cousin Frankie lived and where the activities were centered. Cousin Wallace jumped out of the passenger side door, running helter-skelter up the driveway, losing his balance, bare knees making contact with the graveled path, forcing his way into the group of men standing out near the grove of cedar trees on the perimeter of the property. It was obvious the boy was in shock, crying and shaking uncontrollably as he told the story...

The boys did nothing out of the ordinary. They paddled their rented boat out to about center way the pond, and one by one, over the side they dove, swimming, pushing, shoving, splashing, chicken fighting, showing off to each other, competing with each other to see who could stay under the water the longest. But then, there was a foreboding, an ominous feeling when Elton Lee outstayed all the others. Fear gripped the boys and one by one they dove, swam wider, diving deeper, searching for their cousin in the murky, dark waters of Miller's Pond. None of the boys would be able to recall how long they searched for him before going to shore, begging help from the folks there.

Every adult that could tread water was mobilized in the search for Elton Lee's body that evening, until darkness of night drove them away. With strange and guttural sounds, Cousin Eunice, mother of the drowned boy, wailed and lashed out at the bedraggled group of teenagers. In a menacing surreal voice, she asked each of them, calling them by name, "Why couldn't it be you, Charles? Why couldn't it have been you, Wallace? Why couldn't it have been you, Wilbur? Why couldn't it have been you, Henry Alston?" Then turning to her surviving son, she asked the same question, "And why couldn't it have been you, Carlisle!? God knows my favorite was my dear sweet Elton Lee!"

All festivities were canceled, and the entire community went into mourning. There was nothing to celebrate that night.

The search lasted three days. Professional divers found his body held captive amid the tangle of old tree trunks, roots, and tentacles; the same timber that had been felled on the very day the pond's digging was completed. In the essence of saving time and money, the contractors had simply pushed the whole mess of debris back into the pond, and over the years, the natural movement of the waters swept the trees to the center of the lake, at its deepest point, just where the boy cousins dove deep into the murkiness, the blackness of those waters.

Cousin Eunice never forgave Carlisle for surviving his brother; Carlisle was never able to feel the warmth of his mother's love, and she went to her grave in the same state of depression to which she succumbed after Elton Lee's drowning.

Mrs. George Perkins (1957)

At eighteen, Hazel married George Perkins, the father of the daughter she gave up for adoption. Together they had two more children with only one of the latter being fathered by him. As time advanced, Pam and I took on the role of co-conspirators of sorts, babysitting Hazel's children while she held rendezvous with other men under the guise of "getting my hair done" or "shopping with the girls." She would pay us off, with a fifty-cent piece, to keep our mouth shut.

Hazel and George lived with his parents, Ms. Charlotte and Mr. Walter. It was easy to see that George was his mother's heartbeat doing no wrong in her eyes. Stubbornly Ms. Charlotte denied that George suffered with any issues with alcohol. It was also abundantly obvious that she hated Hazel and thought her not good enough for her son. Their marriage was rocky from the start, too much partying and drinking, too much in-fighting with George's mother and siblings.

The real trouble started in the summer of 1959 when George became deeply depressed. He began consuming large amounts of alcohol from early morning until late at night. This led to fits of crying all the time; he was fraught with anxiety and paranoia. It could not be determined whether his tears were from rage, sadness, or pain—probably a combination of the three. Eventually, this led to a dangerous mental breakdown; dangerous in that he threatened repeatedly to take the lives of, not only his wife, but the children as well. By 1960 or thereabout, he was hospitalized for an extensive period of time at the Asylum for the Insane in our state capital. What led to this was the birth of their last child, well, the birth of Hazel's last child. George discovered the truth of who fathered this child, sending him over the edge. He started drinking even more heavily; his mood was wrathful and despairing. Under great pressure, Hazel "gave" this toddler to Lucy and Harvey. Their next step would be to formally adopt this child, with Hazel giving up all rights. George would have no affiliation with this little one he determined not to be his own.

Maybe it was the electrical shocks he received at the hands of psychiatrists and therapists that mellowed him a bit. Back in the day, these treatments were administered without anesthesia, which carried the potential to produce memory loss, fractured bones, and other side effects. The purpose of the shock therapy (electroconvulsive therapy, ECT) was to trigger a brief seizure, causing changes in the brain chemistry that could reverse symptoms of certain mental illnesses such as schizophrenia and bipolar disorder. It was also favorable in treating the deep depression George succumbed to prior to his commitment to the facility by his wife.

GRIM AND DEADLY SUNDAY

I do know he was dangerously troubled, Earl Willoughby, a cousin of mine. He did put an unnatural fear in me. He had a very small frame, had a nasal twang to his voice and wore thick, rimless glasses. He walked with a limp, slightly dragging one flaccid foot behind him.

As children, we were used as fetchers and gofers by the adults...fetch the hoe, fetch the horse, gofer some cool water... Although he was three years my senior by adolescence, we were basically of the same body built; however, I was the healthier, stronger of the two. Despite the fact, I still was afraid of him. It seemed Earl was always lying in wait, to jump out of the woods surrounding the path I would be following. He would grab me from behind, clutching at my tiny, budding breasts, pulling at my clothes, trying his level best to drag me down! I always managed to get away with nothing occurring more than the groping. I didn't understand what might follow if he overcame me, I just felt instinctively it would be nasty and repulsive.

As time passed and I grew older, even bolder, I believe Earl came to be afraid of me. I have no other explanation of his disgusting behavior coming to a halt. I turned sixteen, seventeen, then eighteen; the year was 1961. I would be graduating from high school at the end of May, and then I would marry my high school sweetheart. I was lost in thoughts of those events as I drove into the churchyard.

The crowd was large—simply too large for a Sunday morning service at the little country church where I attended Sunday school and preaching each Sunday. It was obvious something wasn't quite right this Sunday morning as I maneuvered my vehicle to a parking place alongside the others in the churchyard. No one was inside the church; rather, they were standing in little clusters out near the old logging road to the right at the edge of the church property.

Men stood together, some with their hats in their hands, shifting their weight from the right foot to the left, repeating the process over and over. Others toyed with a mound of dirt, pushing it back and forth with the toes of their freshly polished shoes till the dusty cloud they created settled around the cuffs of their dark gabardine suit pants like ash. Most were silent.

The women huddled in small groups and spoke in whispers, leaning in toward each other, talking behind their hands in tight-lipped fashion. From somewhere in the crowd among the women, a sob could be heard followed by a nervous, high-pitched giggle. Heavy white plumes of frosty breath hung suspended in the air this cold January morning.

It was intriguing to note there were also people of color, our neighbors, included in the group. In our community, in the early sixties, the two races came together only at a time of immense celebration or devastating tragedy.

I watched Daddy, studying him, standing off to one side with his younger brother, Feldon. Daddy was wearing his black Sunday suit and a white shirt with the collar buttoned tightly against his Adam's apple. He was without a necktie. His appearance was stern and cold, austere; his effort with soothing words had little success in comforting his brother. Uncle Feldon's body shook with the sobs he uttered, and tears were trailing down his aged, wrinkled cheeks. He was in constant motion, removing his glasses, wiping fiercely at the heavy plastic-rimmed lenses, replacing them, only to repeat the process again. His head was set in a palsied state.

Near the tree line and just onto the logging road, a car was parked. It was easily recognized as belonging to Earl. Uncle Feldon's son, the same person the neighbors believed to be the fire setter who had nearly burned down, on more than one occasion, all the forest between our home and the crossroads at the general store.

The driver's side window was open an inch, maybe a fraction more. A towel was wedged into the crack in the window. A black rubber hosepipe snaked its way from inside the vehicle down the side panels and to the rear bumper where it entered the exhaust pipe. A rag was stuffed around the connection. The engine was still running.

I heard snatches of hushed conversation as I drew closer. I could hear folks saying

"Well, he was successful this time…"

"He finally did it."

"How could he do this to his family and on Sunday morning?"

"He knew his father would be early to church…"

"Didn't he know his family would discover him?"

Now, it all came together—my uncle's son had committed the ultimate, final act of taking his own life.

Earl had multiple brushes with disaster of one kind or another. This was not his first undertaking at suicide either. It never occurred to me that he really intended to take his own life. I rationalized it as yet another attempt to manipulate his family and the community. I had witnessed this many times before…the staging of a suicide attempt, only to be interrupted in a timely manner by family members. My reflection was that he was not successful at all but failed in his timing for the first time… Earl Willoughby born in 1940 died at his own hands in 1961. He was twenty-one years old.

Chapter Seven

In the Beginning

I MARRIED MY HIGH school sweetheart just two weeks after graduation. I was eighteen, and Douglas was soon to be twenty-two. From the very beginning, I felt this union and the relationship was doomed. The opposition was just too overwhelming with the ratio being 12:1: one being me and twelve being my husband Douglas, his ten siblings and his mother. Early on, his family made it clear they felt I was not suitable for the baby of their family. To my chagrin, I discovered Douglas's family had already chosen a wife for him. It was the sister of a sister-in-law.

I do believe Douglas's father was a good and gentle man. When I came to know him, he was confined to a chair due to crippling rheumatoid arthritis and could only take a step or two with the aid of a walker. He was unable to shave himself, bathe, or perform other activities of daily living because of this. His foods were pureed; his son's shaved him daily, and his wife fed and bathed him.

For the first six months, Douglas and I lived with his parents. I don't know whether I can even explain that scenario. Douglas spent every Saturday night and Sunday at regional drag strips, racing his fast hot rods. Some of those days, I would spend visiting with my parents.

Late one Sunday afternoon, I returned home entering the house by way of the sun porch. I could hear loud conversation coming from a number of people. All at once, I heard my name being repeated over and over from these excited participants sitting around the dining room table. I stopped in my tracks, recognizing to whom the voices belonged, listening to the insults and gossip that was attached to my name.

Slowly, I made my way forward and leaned against the frame of the French doors separating the dining room from the kitchen. The conversation came to an abrupt halt midsentence as my presence was now discovered. What a surprise to them that they had been found out for the nasty people they indisputably were. I was eighteen at the time, suffering from the naiveté of youth while these seasoned older adults defamed my character and my name! But I am not known for burying my head in the sand.

It was like waving a red rag at a bull! All at once, a rage built up within me, and one by one, I called them out. Who did they think they were, slaughtering my character in such a way? I paused, intensely making eye contact with each of them, then turned and walked back to the tiny little bedroom that had been assigned as our living quarters. My breathing was rapid, my heart was racing. How satisfied I was for standing up to those mean, spiteful, cowardly people.

I must have been hit by the stupid stick because they struck again. One Sunday afternoon, I returned to my "home" from visiting with Mama, Daddy, and Pam while Douglas was spending the day and evening drag racing. His dad was just sitting there in his favorite rocking chair.

"She's gone. She has disappeared," he said in a trembling voice, tears streaming down his face. Lucille said she has disappeared. No one will tell me where she is." "What on earth are you talking about!?" I thought as I tried to piece the puzzle together. "She can't have just disappeared!" Douglas, along with his siblings, all expressed surprise as well and questioned where their mother might be.

Day after day, I gave Douglas's dad a bath, got him dressed, cooked and pureed his food, fed him one spoonful at a time. I arranged for Douglas to be free to put him to bed at night and to lift him out of bed the following morning. I agonized over where she might be. I asked if we could notify the sheriff. The response was always an adamant *no*!

Again, my youth and inexperience was obvious as I fretted and cried and worried over the absence of my husband's mother. I was astounded that her children were not exhibiting the anxiety and fear that I had. Some two weeks later, Douglas's mother reappeared in perfect health and with a nonchalant response of "I just needed a break." All eleven of her children, I was soon to discover, were in on the plot for her to take a two-week sabbatical at the home of their sister, Lucille…at my expense. And worst of all, Douglas was a member of this reprehensible plot! Now they had *all* turned out to be the thorn in my flesh.

That was the last straw. From that day forward, I demanded we have a place of our own. Finally, after six months had passed, we moved into a share-cropper's house that was owned by his brother-in-law. I was in heaven! I scrubbed the walls and floors, made curtains from hopsacking trimmed with Wright's Rick Rack. I polished and waxed everything in sight. We had no telephone, indoor toilet, or hot water; but I didn't care. What we had was ours. It is easy to be wise after the event I heard someone say one time.

The Death of My Father (1962)

It was on a Saturday in June that I visited my parents, primarily to spend some time with Mama and Pam. I sat on the front porch and made small talk with Daddy, reminding him at seventy-four, he might be getting too old to clean shrubs and saplings from ditch banks with the bush hook. He disagreed, saying he had spent the morning doing just that. "That's what keeps me young," he said as he chewed on his cigar, shifting it from one corner of his mouth to the other. Our relationship had evolved into one of courtesy even though there was still a level of tension between us. My stay came to an end, and I returned home to my sweet haven. Sometime around midnight, I was awakened by loud banging on the back door. I rushed through the kitchen and flung open the door to find my cousin Wallace standing there.

"You have to come with me," he said with his voice breaking. "Your Mama needs you. Your Daddy is seriously ill, and they have called for a doctor." He added, "And it's high time you get a telephone!"

We sped off into the night, arriving at the home place at the same time the doctor arrived. I watched as that long black Lincoln funeral hearse backed up to the front porch. I listened to Daddy's raspy, gurgling respirations as he lay unresponsive and unconscious on the gurney as his ravaged body was transported into the vehicle.

"No, he cannot be transported to the veterans' hospital. He is too critical to make that long trip, he just could not survive it," the young doctor, still wet behind the ears, said in answer to Mama's question.

My daddy passed away from a massive stroke before ever reaching the hospital. The physical albatross ceased to exist; the burden of the psychological impediments lingered. This turn of events, unforeseen, all of a sudden left Mama and Pam alone.

BREAKING UP

George was released from the asylum, and Hazel reintroduced him to society. On the drive home, they stopped for a visit where

Douglas and I lived. He laid on the sofa in our home, a broken man. He wept with overpowering emotion. He talked about the shock treatments, said they were horrifying. Eventually, he got around to talking about the child, Amy. He told Hazel he forgave her for her infidelities. George was in too weak an emotional state to resist any longer. After a great deal of pressure from Hazel, he agreed to accept the little toddler as his own. So with their hearts breaking, Lucy and Harvey returned the child to Hazel.

What a mockery Hazel's life became. She was a Jekyll-and-Hyde prototype. The relationship between her and her spouse only worsened, with Hazel becoming more and more indiscriminate in her relationships with other men. Eventually, she left George, taking her children with her. Cousin Frankie allowed her to live in an old tenant shanty in Crossroads. It was in great disrepair but it was free; after all, she had no job and no funds. The part about no job was correct. The part about no funds was not as she secretively hoarded hundreds and hundreds of dollars from her estranged significant other in preparation for the day, the exact moment she would be leaving him. But Hazel didn't share the truth of the sizable nest egg with anyone—anyone except me.

I've always heard that paybacks are hell, and I believed it to be true with Hazel. Some weeks after leaving George, Hazel decided it was time for her to return to Perkins Town in the adjoining county of Maysville, mockingly renaming the community where George's family dwelled to retrieve her personal belongings.

Hazel contracted with her first cousin, Edward Underwood, better known in the community as Ned. He was the high sheriff of Bakers County, and she asked him to escort her back to Maysville County. Ned was a daunting figure of a man: six feet five inches tall, weighing nearly three hundred pounds. He was lean, all muscle and grit. Mama said later on that he looked daunting that morning when he stopped in his official patrol car to pick Hazel up. "He was dressed out in full uniform," she said. "So there was nothing to worry about. Hazel was in good hands."

Full uniform for Cousin Ned consisted of dark brown slacks with a razor crease in the pant legs, a tan shirt with the collar and sleeves buttoned down tight, a dark brown clip-on necktie attached neatly just below his Adam's apple. Ned explained to me once, "We don't wear regular dress ties because we don't want to give the perpetrator any advantage if we get in a scuffle, so if someone grabs my tie, it will snap right off."

The high sheriff's silver badge in the shape of a five-point star was pinned to the left, over his heart. Underneath this were numerous smaller police service medals—one for marksmanship, another for meritorious service, one for valor. On the opposite side, a silver police whistle was attached as were medals to signify heroism and lifesaving efforts. At his waist, he wore a .38 Smith & Wesson on his right, a billy stick and handcuffs on his left. His shoes were black patent leather lace-up, blemish-free. He wore his dark-brown felt Stetson hat when conducting business.

To their surprise, there was a whole gathering of folks waiting for them at their arrival: George's three brothers, two brothers-in-law, two sisters, and a couple of strapping young cousins. This group of people turned out to be nothing short of a nest of vipers. Hazel recounted afterward, "We got out of the patrol car. I told them I was there to retrieve my clothes and other personal items and started walking toward the house, when all at once, I was grabbed from behind and thrown to the ground. There were just too many of them, punching and kicking me. Some of the men holding Ned hostage, pinned him to the side of his car." She sobbed. "I just blacked out." Hazel was brutally and mercilessly beaten, kicked, and even rendered unconscious by these frenzied attackers. They had their revenge…

What happened next is unclear. It seems the mob of kinfolk became frightened at the outcome of this attack and dispersed. Ned, having no law-enforcement jurisdiction in this county loaded the unconscious Hazel into his patrol car and sped away to the nearest hospital. Hazel was unrecognizable, face distorted with contusions and edema, clumps of hair missing, ribs broken, internal injuries. I felt so much rage at those heathen people for the damage they had done to my sister. No person deserved such reprehensible treatment. Eventually, she was discharged from the hospital after a lengthy convalescence.

The trial was lengthy, foul, and smutty. Only one prison sentence was passed down; three were placed on probation, and the others acquitted. Even with all this, they accomplished what they set out to do—cause bodily harm and for the community to brand Hazel as a scandalous woman. After a full recovery was accomplished, Hazel decided it was time to really start her life over.

Leaving her children behind with Mama, Hazel moved on to a little town in the western territory to live with Lucy and Harvey where she secured a job with a real estate agent. It was about a year after that she had rented an apartment and moved her children there with her. Mama was distraught as she had developed a strong bond, such an emotional connectedness with Hazel's children…but mostly Amy, the illegitimate one. Amy…the straw that broke the camel's back, the one the marital breakup was about in the first place. Oh, how Mama adored that lass Amy, lavishing her with more love and attention than could be imagined.

The Klan

I always believed the Ku Klux Klan was alive and well in Crossroads. I could hear whispers, watched men talk with their mouths covered, blocking your vision for fear you could read their lips. When Daddy was alive I could see the pamphlets he read even though he kept them tucked inside the Sunday Grit as he feigned reading about President Eisenhower suffering a heart attack. They were there at his fingertips, right beside the family Bible, the red-lettered King James Version.

Klan members were a threat to Negros, Indians, and even whites if they supported the rights of those suppressed. I remember Daddy threatening Mama, "You keep on mingling with the likes of them people and the Klan may come pay you a visit!"

The threat didn't sway Mama, though; at least she didn't show any fear. When I asked her what Daddy meant by that, she half-smiled and said, "It's nothing but malarkey. They're not going to mess with me."

The National Association for the Advancement of Colored People (NAACP) had little power. *Everything was segregated*—schools, churches, doctor's offices, restaurants, water fountains, transit buses, and trains. Coloreds sat at the back of the bus, but riding the Shoofly steam locomotive was different. The Negros sat in the forward car, the one closest to the noisy engine. The soot from the smokestack flowed in through the open windows of that car. The whites sat in the rear car, more protected from the noise and the black smoke.

I am sure most Southern communities have at least one incident they would like to hide. This was surely true for Crossroads. It started when Tyrone, nephew of Cousin Eudie, arrived for a visit. Every inhabitant of the community was abuzz with talk about the good-looking boy from up North. Cousin Eudie took him straight away to Mama's house for introductions. She whispered to Mama, "You know I told you about my brother who lives in New York City, but I never told you he married a wealthy white widow, who said she came from old money; she was like a maverick. Well, this is their son. That explains his light skin color."

Tyrone was handsome and polished; there was no Southern drawl to that clipped voice. He told of how his mother put his father in charge of the clothing business she owned and that now at the age of twenty-one, he was made a full partner. So that clarified to me how he was able to dress so fine and drive a brand-new Cadillac Eldorado, the one with long fins and bulky grille.

The more he talked, the more I learned about Tyrone's real reason for being in Crossroads. He had been sent by the NAACP to meet secretly with the Negro community to champion equality for their race. I attended one of these meetings at Tyrone's invitation, and I must say, he was a rabble-rouser! He influenced me to join in with the movement. There was one occasion he was traveling to Raleigh to speak, and he asked me to go along. When he stopped by to pick me up, I eagerly jumped in the front seat beside him.

His eyes flew wide open, and his jaw dropped. "Are you trying to get us both killed?" he asked with much astonishment. "You can't ride up here with me. You must sit in the back so Jim Crow will think I am your chauffeur!" I got out and positioned myself in the rear, and we laughed about that most all the way to the capital.

The Civil Rights movement spread across the state with Tyrone playing a significant role. He was a familiar sight in Crossroads driving up and down the back roads going to and from meetings and rallies. Quite abruptly, he was nowhere to be found. He just up and disappeared. Aunt Eudie and Uncle Charlie were beside themselves. She talked to her brother, but Tyrone had not returned home.

I got the cold shoulder when I asked neighbors of his whereabouts. Like leaves blowing in the wind, the murmuring started. The whispering stopped when I joined the group and conversation would turn light and gay. I walked away, the whispering resumed. The headlines told the story. A burned-out Cadillac Eldorado was found almost totally submerged under the bridge in the Little Scissor River.

There was an investigation by the high sheriff, Edward Underwood, my cousin, Ned. A deputy and his bloodhound were dispersed from the Wake County sheriff's office to aid and assist in the search for Tyrone, but nearly a week had gone by since he was last seen. Hopes of finding him alive were slim to none. We watched as the bloodhound sniffed some clothing Ned had retrieved from Aunt Eudie, and the search was on. It continued on the east side for two days. A few local folks stepped in to help with the searching. On the third day, they moved to the west side to continue. Late in the day, we heard it; the predetermined gunshot rang out, signaling the search was over. It was nearly dark when the volunteers and the deputy and the bloodhound emerged from the woods. "Yep…found him about three miles back…there in a little clearing…hanging from his neck in a tree…not a pretty sight," the deputy reported. "There were charred remains of a burned cross about twenty feet away. I'll turn it back over to you, Sheriff, and head back to Raleigh."

The KKK along with other ignorant people resided in the Deep South. What a dark, murky era; evil, subversive men hiding behind white hoods, white sheets. Cowards they were, burning crosses, torching homes, staging rallies, furling hate from every direction toward Indians, Jews, Catholics, Negros, and immigrants. Maiming, hanging, wanton killing—fighting for white supremacy!

> For the Scripture saith, whosoever believeth on him shall not be ashamed. For there is no difference between the Jew and the Greek: for the same Lord over all is rich unto all that call upon him. For whosoever shall call upon the name of the Lord shall be saved.
>
> —Romans 10:11-13, KJV

I thought about Daddy, and I shuddered to think what his actions and behaviors would have been during the Civil Rights movement across the South and the resurgence of the KKK. Bombings of schools, homes, the killings; all the violence against Black and white activists were rampant. I thank God for courage and leadership of people like Rosa Parks and Dr. Martin Luther King Jr.

Whiskey Still

One Friday afternoon, I watched, with no small amount of concern as Cousin Freddie drove down the path to the tenant house where Douglas and I lived. He parked and got out of the car. Removing his hat, he said, "Your mama says you need to go to her as soon as you can because she has a problem. Says she needs your help with it."

It was late September, just over three months since Daddy died. I worried about Mama and Pam. Mama was helpless to ordinary everyday activities. I never realized she depended so much on Daddy for day-to-day undertakings. Pam was ineffective in making decisions; I reckon she was thinking ahead to her wedding and leaving Mama alone. Now that was one gigantic adjustment in the making.

"Is she okay? I mean, do I need to go now, today?" My fears, deep-seated in childhood, would probably go with me to my grave. Uneasiness quickly rose to the surface with even the smallest problems.

Cousin Freddie caught the anxiety that had crept into my voice. He patted me on the shoulder and said, "No Mam, Ms. Kat. I speculate it has to do with that young upstart Ernest. I saw him on the front porch, talking to Ms. Savannah yesterday."

Thank you for delivering the message Cousin Freddie. Would you tell her for me that I will be there early Sunday morning?" I asked.

"Yessum, I certainly will, Ms. Kat. It was good seeing you again. Place is kinda quiet these days what with no yelling and cussin' from Mr. Barnabas," he said jokingly. "And, Ms. Kat, when you gonna get a telephone?"

I laughed and gave him a bear hug, "Just as soon as I can get two nickels to rub together." I wondered what was so urgent that Mama had Cousin Freddie drive the thirteen miles to my house with a message. Why didn't Pam aid her or why didn't she ask

Larry to help her with the issue? Seems to me the oldest and the youngest get let off the hook when there is a difficult situation brewing.

Mama always liked Ernest, so I didn't think he was her problem. My thoughts turned to Tyrone and the senseless violence that took his life. "That cut Mama to the bone, and I suspect she still has bad dreams over it" was my reasoning. "Maybe she is still distraught with that and with Uncle Charlie and Aunt Eudie's grieving. Perhaps she only wants to talk it out." So early that Sunday morning, I went to see Mama.

Boy, was I off the mark! "You'll have to talk to him for me. It's only me and Pam. I don't want any problems with the colored folks, but I can't do what he is asking," she said to me. Mama seemed extremely timid and scared now that Daddy was gone, reclusive even.

"Who…what are your talking about?" I asked.

"Well, it's Ernest Sylvester, Willy's son, you remember him, don't you? He wants me to carry on with the contract he had with your daddy, to give him a right-of-way on my land to the back woods where the still is."

"Still? Whiskey still? The last time we were back there three years ago, it appeared to be abandoned. I thought they gave up making white lightnin' when Willy retired," I said lightly. Willy's was a sixty-gallon pot still, but the copper had tarnished to a blue-green color on the outside. I could only imagine what the inside looked like. There were always rumors of working stills around the county, but I didn't realize they had intentions of cranking that one back up.

"I won't sell him out to the feds, and I'll talk to him for you," I told Mama. Off I went in search of Ernest. We grew up together and were about the same age. As adolescents and teenagers, we barned tobacco and fished in Miller's pond together too many times to count. I considered us friends.

Ernest was short, athletic, and agile and brought to mind an image of Floyd Patterson, the youngest ever world heavyweight champion at twenty-one. He was just as much a charmer too, with his dimple-cheeked grin and his smooth man-talk.

He must have been watching because he walked out on the front porch and down the steps as I turned into his driveway. He opened the door for me; we walked over to sit in the wooden slat swing that was suspended by chains from a large curved limb of the sycamore tree.

"I'll bet I can guess what brought you to visit. When I saw you drive up, I thought, *Here comes trouble.* Are you bringing trouble, Kat?" he said with that arresting smile of his. I laughed out loud, denying this was true. "Ms. Savannah sent you, didn't she?" he asked.

"Earnest, you never were one to beat around the bush—just cut right to the chase," I laughed but then turned more serious. "You scared Mama, talking to her about making white lightnin' on her land so I…"

He interrupted, "I was offering her a better deal than my daddy gave Mr. Barnabas. Listen. This is what I told her. One, I would never operate on her property in daylight hours. Two, we will only start it up at night so people won't be able to see the smoke through the trees. Three, I offered her 2 percent of sales, and you know I am good for my word."

I looked past Ernest at the peeling bark on the trunk of the sycamore, listening as he gave his sales pitch. The seedpods under his feet snapped and crackled as he pushed the swing a little faster.

"It's a lucrative business today, Kat, because there is only one still running in the whole county. Ms. Savannah would never be suspicioned as having any dealings with a bootlegger…"

"Ernest, if you will allow me—" but he interrupted me again.

"Last week, I made a deal with a fellow in Richmond who said he would take five thirty-gallon cases every two weeks. He didn't even bat an eye when I told him it cost $125 a case! Kat, do you know how much money that is?" The more he talked, the more animated he became; the faster the swing surged through the air. He continued, "No one in Crossroads has ever even seen $1250 in a month. Ms. Savannahs cut would be $25 with that one customer. Imagine how it would become as I added more!"

"Ernest! Wait—" was all I could squeeze in before he cut me off again.

He pointed toward the back of the house to a one axel livestock trailer hooked behind his pickup. "See that? I've already built a mock floor in it with compartments in front and behind the axel, so it is well-camouflaged. I'd just load that heifer up and take off for Richmond and, Kat, you've got the power of persuasion too and—"

"Stop right there, Ernest!" I said so forcefully it startled him. I would never try to influence Mama to do something she is so against. She won't break the law for love nor money, you know that. You just need to find another place and move your still there, and that's the end of it. Don't go bothering Mama anymore. I will tell her you have to go back there to move your still out, but once that is done, you won't be back."

Ernest continued to argue but to no avail. "How did you get to be so stubborn in less than twenty years, Kat?"

"School of hard knocks, Ernest. School of hard knocks."

CHAPTER EIGHT

PAM

PAM WAS THE only one of her siblings to have a church wedding; Larry gave the bride away. The wedding was a lofty one indeed with a conventional white gown and veil, with attendants, with lovely music. I don't remember exactly how or where she met Levi, but he was a cute as a brand-new copper penny; his skin color fit that same description.

I remember Daddy took an instant dislike to him. "No, I don't like him because he's a Jew. Indians, niggers, and Jews, I hate 'em all. Them Jewish son of a bitches, they don't even believe in the Bible." How ignorant, inaccurate, and slanted the views of uneducated Crossroads dwellers.

Pam was married to Levi Rothstein some months after Daddy's death. Levi's parents came down from the North, for the occasion. That was the first time I ever saw a Mink coat up-close. Levi's dad, as he called him, removed his black Mink fur Russian Cossack hat and gave a slight bow when introduced. Mrs. Rothstein was all decked out in her diamond cluster ear-bobs and a full-length genuine black Mink fur coat. She gave a curt nod in our direction. Neither of them was smiling; I had a suspicion she was grinding her teeth.

Cousin Frankie and Cousin Tillie hosted an extravagant prewedding dinner in the fellowship hall of the church to honor the to-be-wed couple. The entire community was invited. It was such a sumptuous banquet with roasted prime rib with red potatoes, yeast rolls, garden salad, and sweet tea.

Pam relocated with Levi to his hometown, only to stay a few short months. She soon returned to Crossroads, a more familiar way of life with her mama. I remember her saying it was mostly because of isolation and cultural differences in the lifestyle of Levi's family. I reckon she was just plain homesick.

The Rothsteins were second-generation Jewish immigrants from Eastern Europe and settled in New Port, Rhode Island. Pam said his grandmother rocked the day away in the dimly lit parlor while muttering to herself in Yiddish, reading from her prayer book. The thing that made Pam most uneasy she said was the conversation with the rabbi the first time she went to the Touro Street Synagogue. "He was talking away about when Levi turned thirteen becoming a bar mitzvah and how grand the parties and gifts were. I was so embarrassed, I couldn't say a word. I didn't even know what a bar mitzvah was," Pam recalled. "And, Kat, his grandmother was a colored lady, just like Cousin Eudie," she whispered to me. Wouldn't Daddy have turned over in his grave had he known his lovely beautiful, perfect-in-every-way daughter had married a Jew whose grandmother was colored!

After returning home, Pam took a job as a salesclerk at a local department store in a nearby Winfred. She developed a unique connection to my firstborn daughter who must have been about three months old at the time. Pam spent most of the money she earned on pretty dresses, colorful tights, and ruffled panties for Megan. It was indeed a fact she developed a distinctive attachment to my husband, Douglas. Somehow, the timing of the birth of her first child, blue eyed and blond, just didn't add up to the arrival of her own brown-eyed, black-haired husband a number of months later. But you know how suppositions go…

TRANSITIONING

Megan was in her terrible twos when Angela arrived. Douglas and I were deep into our church, thus most of our social events were focused on that. There were many highlights to our church calendar. The Christmas Story was a big one with all the children of the Crossroads participating in the annual play that depicted the birth of Christ. Another was the Easter egg hunt on Saturday before Easter sunrise service. We held Vacation Bible School for two weeks in the summer, then the fall Harvest Day Dinner and Craft Show with the entire community participating.

The Harvest Day Dinner and Craft Show was where we raised money for big projects for our church: new roof, new windows, and such. We gathered in the fellowship hall at the church early that Saturday morning and began preparing the meal. Roasted turkey, white rice, giblet gravy, candied sweet potatoes, green beans, sweet tea, and rolls were the traditional menu. Ladies of the church-baked cakes, cookies, and pies to be served with the meal. Hence, this was the scenario the Saturday of October 15, 1967.

The fellowship hall was packed with family, friends, and neighbors. Everyone was lighthearted, cheerful, and filled with levity. The wood in the fireplace sparked and crackled as the yellow-orange flames reached up toward the chimney. Each time the door was opened, a slight draft was created, drawing a tiny bit of smoke into the room. What a hearty nutty fragrance, that of wood smoke. I was standing by the fire deep in conversation with friends and neighbors when I became aware the door had opened then shut. I looked in the direction of the door, and I just could not believe my eyes!

There, standing by the doorway, was Cousin Wallace, shoulder to shoulder with Mark! The last time I had seen Mark was in 1956 or 1957 when we were adolescents. Well, he was no youngster now. *What a looker*, I thought. Mark was stylishly dressed and virile indeed; his movements graceful as he approached me. He was most attractive, obviously athletic with his impressive physique. His square jaw gave him a noble, aristocratic look. Flashbacks of childhood days washed over me as I remembered my first starry-eyed crush.

"Well, you have grown up to be quite the eyeful," Mark said with a slight nod and a half wink. It would be a misnomer to say my cheeks turned rosy; my entire face was turned crimson. "Surely my eyes do not deceive me because…I must say…I meant to say…you are beautiful…gorgeous…my, my, my!" He continued with a more intelligent dialogue, and I was entranced by the sound of his voice…and his strong physical makeup. At that moment, I decided it would be disaster waiting to happen…just a matter of time…if we lived in closer proximity. Washington, DC, was about the right distance to put between us, to keep us apart.

Mark intermingled with those present, renewing old acquaintances, but his eyes frequently found mine. That evening, the occasion presented itself that we held many conversations, drawn to each other not unlike magnets. I was sad when the event was over, and we went our separate ways. Stuff dreams are made of…

WHEN PUSH COMES TO SHOVE

Life takes some crazy turns, especially mine. It certainly was short of a bed of roses, but it did capture some good times and produced three of the most adorable children any mother could ever wish for. Still, it was not the natural, quiet life of which I had dreamed. After six pregnancies and three miscarriages, I had the perfect family—two daughters and a son! No mother could be more ecstatic. We grew up together, in a manner of speaking.

Megan, the firstborn was a daddy's girl. She loved her Marmie as she so fondly called me, but her heart belonged to Daddy! Her eyes were almost jet-black and the color of her hair was just as dark. Then Angela arrived with a shock of blond hair and blue eyes. Her affections were neutral, but her keen eye contact started the day she was born. Even then, she would stare unblinking into your eyes as though she could read your very thoughts; she still can. After Angela, Aaron arrived, with blond curls and green eyes. He was quite attached to his mama. He had the tenderest heart of all.

Douglas and I were successful at the façade our lives had become. To the world (with the exception of his family), we had the text-book-perfect life: wonderful children, beautiful home with perfect accoutrements, perfect partnership. Even our closest friends were unaware of the strife within; they thought we did everything but glow in the dark!

On the bleakest of days, I allowed myself to think of Mark. And I remembered something he said back in 1967 at the church harvest sale. In parting, Mark gave me a quick hug and whispered in my ear, "I have learned, the things you least expect to happen do happen." Strangely enough, those words gave me a feeling of hope.

My family was complete; however, there was mounting contention and disagreement between Douglas and me. His family continued to act as though our children, and I didn't exist. I was never notified of or invited to their events: birthday parties, family reunions, Christmas parties, and the like.

The sands of time marched forward; the years 1970 through 1973 were almost a blur. The infighting continued, and the divisiveness became more severe. We had become strangers living under the same roof. Assuredly, God would smile on a happier union than Douglas and I now shared. I felt as though my life had evolved into one long assembly line; work on the farm, clean the house, care for the children, work, clean, care…

"Lord," I would pray, "Give me strength and courage, give me guidance. Point me in the direction You would have me go. Lord, show me the way." Sometimes, when I could not find the words, I would pray the Lord's Prayer over and over. And God was listening.

THE FARM

Douglas and his brothers were considered trendy agribusiness men. As was customary, wives and children carried their share of the workload as well. There was such an imbalance of productivity among these three families. At the top of the totem pole were his brothers with Douglas at the bottom. I felt oppressed, as though my children and I were descending into a bottomless pit of endless work. Looking back, I suppose I was to blame; my work ethics being greater than theirs. I obviously had more ambition than the other wives; my children were held to different standards than theirs.

Determinedly, I focused on positives with short phrases such as "Let's do it together." "Let's start early so we will finish early." "Let's do the long rows first then the short rows will be easy." I wanted to instill in my children the same values I had learned: respect, independence, love, patience, and giving. There is a thing about earning your way; call it freedom, satisfaction, or chose your own word. "So let's get the hard part done first, and the rest will be easy," I would say. In this little work group, the apathy of the other two wives and their children left me feeling quite dispirited.

Back in those days, farming tobacco was labor intensive. Tobacco beds had to be prepared then seeded. The fields had to be tilled, rows plowed, and the tobacco plants spaced evenly in the rows. Then as the plants grew, grass had to be chopped away with a hoe, more tilling of the soil, breaking out suckers and tops, then finally harvesting, grading, packing, and off to market. This crop required physical labor from January until November year after year in a never-ending cycle.

Ask any running back carrying the football and he will tell you one hundred yards *is* a tiring run! But if you are inching your way all day down those three hundred–foot long rows that span acres and acres, it is truly exhausting. The day with my children started at the same time, as it should, that the men started. A few hours later, one of the other wives and their children would appear; some time later, the other wife and children would show up. Lunch break was an hour then back to work. Not so for the wives and children of the top of the totem pole; they meandered back to the fields two to three hours later, if they showed up at all.

I was resentful of them; however, I did not change my behavior or expectations. I could have parroted their behavior but to what end? There had to be a way out of this unfair and imbalanced predicament. What could I do? How could I do anything?

HAZEL REMARRIES (1972)

Hazel joined the Pentecostal Church of God where she met her second husband Manley. He was twenty-three years her senior and had been a widower about that many years. As an affluent banker, he had accumulated much wealth and many possessions. He owned a summer home in Hilton Head in addition to the home he owned there in a gated community. Leave it to clever, underhanded Hazel. Manley didn't know what hit him.

Hazel poured over his financial statements discovering he had limitless assets and no liabilities—well, except for his ageing. In less than two months, the two were married, and within the year, her name was attached to everything he owned—fifty-fifty. She was now able to live the life of leisure she so adamantly desired. Now her teenaged daughters could be sent to that private boarding school, and she could act the part of a moneyed aristocrat.

Hazel, Manley, and her children visited Mama routinely. Upon arriving at "the peanut farm," as he referred to the community of Crossroads, Manley would immediately be reduced to a level of stupor as a result of the copious amounts of Maker's Mark he consumed; he remained in that drunken stage of suspended sensibility until their departure.

On one visit in particular, I closed the door of the bedroom where Manley lay passed out from too much booze the night before as I made my way to answer the knock at the front door. Cousin Frankie stood in the doorway as grand and stately as the ancient oak trees casting massive umbrellas of shade over Mama's house and lawn. He was wearing his best Sunday-go-to-meeting dark navy blue gabardine suit.

It was Sunday, and the event was Mother's Day. "Good morning, good morning, good morning, everyone, and Happy Mother's Day to you all," he said quite cheerfully as his outstretched arm swept the room to take in all the mothers gathered there. He had such a winning smile and the lines of his face became deeper as the dimples appeared beside the upturned corners of his mouth. His hearty laugh was so gratifying to everyone he encountered.

"Cousin Savannah," he said to my mother as he put his arm around her shoulder, "I have come for my white rose." My mother, Cousin Savannah to Eldon Franklin, was not surprised by this visit and was subsequently prepared just for this as she had a beautiful white snowball blossom waiting to be pinned to his lapel. This Mother's Day ritual had been in place for a good many years now.

My sister, Hazel, and her two daughters were there, all dressed in their finest. Larry, my brother, leaned against the doorjamb leading into the kitchen, quiet, watching, and listening. I was busy helping my youngest of three children put his jacket on over his white shirt and bowtie.

Everyone that morning wore a flower pinned over their heart, either red or white, signifying the status of their own mothers' existence: red for the living and white for those gone on. Larry was joined by his family, and we all made our way a mile or so down the road to the little country church to celebrate our Heavenly Father and show respect to our mothers. When undercurrents of Crossroads hid its ugly face, life appeared simple—on the surface.

Heavy drinking was not the norm for Manley when they first married; subtly, he added a cocktail, then another and another when Hazel wasn't looking. Being married to Hazel probably drove him to this. At the age of seventy-nine, he developed congestive heart failure and his heart simply wore out and stopped beating. Hazel was a wealthy widow, and she wasn't even fifty yet.

Chapter Nine

Me

MY DILEMMA PERSISTED. "You need to get off that farm and out of that tobacco field so you can build a decent life for you and your children," Dr. Patrick said to me at one office visit. He was a sharp-spoken, cussing, cigar-smoking, opinionated, and independent—did I say arrogant?—individual whom I loved deeply. He was my personal physician, who took care of me and my children through their toddler years.

"What on earth will I do? I am thirty years old with three small children. I only have a high-school education and no financial resources of my own..." was my initial reaction to him. That was it; he had planted the seed that would set me on the path to personal freedom.

Dr. Patrick made such a tremendous impact on my life. Over the next couple of years, we discussed occupations I might possibly pursue. "Kat, you've got to stop wasting time. We've finally got a technical school in our county now. Go out there and talk to the advisor. Find something you can enjoy and that will make you feel worthwhile." I didn't have a clue, didn't even know what was available. I finally made up my mind and took the initiative to go on campus and talk with the guidance counselor. It was a bold step; intuitively I knew it would widen the gap between Douglas and me.

She had many questions for me. "What are your interests? What do you enjoy doing? What experiences have you previously had?"

For her, I only had one question, "Which field of study that is offered has the most job security?"

She said without hesitation, "That would be the associates degree in nursing program."

I said with great emphasis, "Then, that is what I want. I want to be a nurse, a registered nurse!"

The reaction I received from Douglas was as expected. "No, I won't give you any money to go to college. If you go, you will have to get the money from somewhere else!" So that is what I did. I met with the guidance counselor, obtained forms, and filled them out in detail requesting grants and scholarships for tuition. Fortunately for me, I was qualified for a Pell Grant; one that covered all my expenses for the ADN Program in which I enrolled. In September of 1974, I spent my first day on the campus of Concord Technical Institute, which is today known as Concord Community College.

Dr. Patrick gave me my first PDR (Physician's Desk Reference) and more encouragement than you can imagine! He was overjoyed over my choice of careers! "My wife is a nurse, a nurse anesthetist, and she works right here at Concord General Hospital. You get your degree, and we will see that you get a job there too!"

The children and I gathered around the dining room table in the evenings for two years, with our textbooks spread out before us, each doing our homework, each supporting the other. Megan was eleven, Angela was seven, and Aaron was five. These were extremely challenging years. I had been ostracized from the beginning by Douglas's family, coming in last with him, behind the siblings and spouses, nieces, nephews, even cousins. By the same token, my children were not accepted by his family, as well. For the span of these two years, remarkably few words were exchanged between Douglas and me. We became two families living under the same rooftop. A dark emotional cloud hung over us; you know what the Bible says about a house divided... "And if a house be divided against itself, that house cannot stand" (Mark 3:25 KJV).

I had no choice now; my determination to succeed prevailed, and in the late summer of 1976, I was awarded a license to practice as a registered nurse! I applied for and accepted a job at Concord General Hospital in September of that same year launching what I prayed would be a long and rewarding career.

EARLY CAREER

Although I initially had no deeply embedded or strong desire to become a nurse, I threw myself into my new career. I had learned so much yet knew so little. Medicine was a strange bedfellow, and this avenue was as strange to me as world travel. Sometimes I felt like a sponge, soaking up every morsel of new information. With great anticipation, I awaited the arrival of Dr. Newton, the first physician specializing in pediatrics in this area.

We developed a wonderful and productive working relationship. "Let me share with you a Pearl for the Day," he would say as he imparted unfamiliar knowledge to me. He had his peculiarities, though. For example, he would not allow any nurse to start an IV on his patients. It did not matter the day of the week or the time of the day, he insisted he be called in to the hospital to perform this task.

We had a meningitis scare to erupt in our community, which resulted in a deluge of admissions of infants and toddlers. Dr. Newton was aware I was most adept at starting IVs in adolescents and adults, so one day he came to me. "Can I persuade you to become my assistant in starting IVs on these little ones? I am drowning in work, and you are the only one I will trust with the little darlings."

This gave me pause for thought, *What a tremendous compliment, to become this new specialist's right hand.* I accepted this new challenge knowing it would be a demanding yet stimulating situation. Almost immediately, I was able to contribute to the fulfillment of Dr. Newton's needs. I must admit I became moderately self-conceited for a brief time, just short of strutting like a rooster in a henhouse. Before I knew it, I was buried in the task, receiving calls from the nursing staff or the ER physician, "We need IV access on a six-week-old STAT!" This may have been the beginning of the end.

The hospital was in a massive transition early in my career. I was fortunate enough to be a part of history in the making. A new director of nursing, Sandra Jones, had come to town bringing with her a wealth of education, experience, and know-how. We shared some personality traits, shared the same astrological sign, and got on well at the beginning.

In wonder and awe, I watched Sandra in her rise to power, practically terrorizing subordinates, stealing their ideas; mine in particular, while gaining kudos from the administrative personnel. Sandra was a true people person, short on empathy but long on charm. She constantly lost her temper with those under her supervision but was irresistibly charming to those from whom she could gain favors leading to more power. She was the master manipulator!

Her many innovative ideas raised the bar tremendously at that hospital. Sandra miraculously found monies for improving our training and education. All members of the board of directors were captivated by her, acting much like lap dogs in her presence. Training began for a Code Blue Response Team, which at that time it was called Code 99! Hauntingly and seemingly heralding potential death…It still sends little shivers up and down my spine when I recall that blaring call over the intercom for all to hear; the operator's voice sometimes rising in octaves from her excitement. Code 99, room 425! Code 99, room 425! Code 99 room 425! Doors were flung open wide, the elevator was bypassed for the stairways, first responders from every department running flatfoot, without reservation down hallways to reach room 425.

Code 99, hereafter identified as a Code Blue is a term used in hospitals by medical professionals to alert the team a patient was in a life-threatening situation. If more than one physician arrived, one assumed the role as a leader of the team, and others were excused. The same held true if more responders arrived than were required to carry out the code. Generally, the team consisted of one RN to record, one to administer medications ordered by the physician, a respiratory therapist to intubate the victim and two people to perform CPR. It was not a requirement that these two were licensed, still they had to be certified in cardiopulmonary resuscitation. An ancillary employee would place a call to the family if none were on the scene; another would stand by the closed door to act as a runner should more items become necessary. In later years, as the hospital grew, a pharmacist was added to the team.

It was the responsibility of the charge nurse to appear on the scene with the Crash Cart in tow. She was always the designated recorder. The cart was a red Craftsman rolling five-drawer tool cart. Any similarities to the original tool cart stopped there. This cart contained lifesaving equipment and emergency medications. The electrical defibrillator sat imposingly on top with a clipboard containing check-off forms and inventory lists for the individual drawers. The first two drawers contained all the life-saving drugs: atropine, epinephrine, sodium bicarbonate, lidocaine, magnesium, and a host of others. Other supplies needed to carry out the resuscitation efforts were stored in the remaining three drawers: IV fluids, laryngoscopes and blades, tubes for intubation, sterile cut-down trays for the inevitable loss of IV access. A cylinder of oxygen was attached to one side of the cart. An ambu-bag, a handheld device used to provide positive pressure ventilation to a respiratory arrest victim, hung on the opposite side. All Code Blue situations were different, having their own diverse outcomes. Some responded favorably to the efforts of CPR and medication administration; some did not.

At this hospital, I learned the basics of cardiac life support and cardiopulmonary-pulmonary resuscitation and became certified as a CPR instructor. I trained at the UNC-Chapel Hill School of Medicine in how to accurately read and interpret EKGs. I learned that all who claimed to be your friend were not; wolves in sheep's clothing, Mama would classify them. I did get to know some exceptionally talented people who were honest and well-respected for their integrity. Among them were my dear Dr. Patrick, of course; Dr. Carver Nelson and his wife, Jean; Dr. Newton; and Dr. Owenby Willis. They had great faith in me, and I had unquestionable trust in them. Initially, Sandra and I were friendly enough; however, time took its toll, and friendship started going south.

It was with immense sadness and a heavy heart that I eventually became the caregiver of dear Dr. Patrick. He was diagnosed with terminal cancer with only a few short weeks to live, and toward the end, he was admitted to the heart unit of which I was the supervisor. As gently as I possibly could, I inserted the plastic catheter into his fragile veins, connected this to the morphine drip that hung just at the head of the hospital bed. He suffered excruciating pain those few weeks.

We had lengthy conversations as I sat on the bed beside him and held his hand. He told me how proud he was of me for all my accomplishments; I told him how humbled I was by his faith and trust in me. I am grateful for the opportunity I had for these conversations. I can't remember the month, but the year was 1979 that he passed on.

SLEEPWALKING

The screened door on the back slammed loudly, jerking me awake. The lighted dial on the bedside clock revealed it was half past midnight. "Here we go again," I thought as I donned my bathrobe. The night was friendly, and all the windows were open, allowing the light breeze to circulate. Sounds from the outdoors were sharp and clear.

I put on my slippers and padded my way to the back door, naturally knowing what to expect. As I pushed open the door, I heard his voice saying, "Brick men! Brick men. Down…" He grabbed my hand and with some show of force pulled me over to the floor of the deck. "Throwing daggers!" he spoke, words jumbled and choppy; however, I got the idea. Indicating I should follow, he crept behind the glider; I followed. "Destroy…world… Brick men." The next morning, Douglas added a second eye-hook latch to the screened door.

On another occasion, I was awakened with noises from the kitchen. The face on the clock said midnight. There, he stood fully dressed, making a ham-and-cheese sandwich. As though he were awake, he returned all the items to their proper place. He sat down in the breakfast nook and ate his sandwich. His eyes were glazed and expressionless as he spoke unintelligibly. When he finished eating, he walked back to the bedroom and crawled under the covers. When he awakened the next morning, he was embarrassed, unable to remember why he was not in his pajamas. A third latch was added—center, top, then bottom of the door.

It was when Aaron would sleepwalk without my knowing that I became alarmed; I sensed his apprehension as well. Even in his sleep, Aaron was able to extend his arms up high enough to unhook the top latch Douglas had placed. Sometimes I could hear the door closing with his exit, other times I could not.

Early one morning just before breakfast, Aaron came to me, "Mama, look how dirty my hands and feet are, and I've just gotten out of bed! I know you're going to tell me that I've been sleepwalking again, but, Mama, I can't ever remember if I've been sleepwalking."

With gentle coaxing, I was always able to get him back to bed without ever awakening. He was right; he never remembered any portion of the sleepwalking. He always found his way back to bed with no injuries thus far. However, the night Aaron peed in his closet was the most embarrassing for him.

He and I talked about this oddity, and we agreed to make an appointment to see Dr. Patrick. Neither Douglas nor I had a history of sleepwalking so that cause could be ruled out. "What about the head injury from the motorcycle crash?" I wondered. "Could it be related to all this hostility between me and Douglas?"

Dr. Patrick assuaged our fears. "The sleepwalking may have been triggered by that lick on your head, Aaron and will disappear, without notice, just like it started. Young man, I don't like you worrying about this. It doesn't show you have any other disorder. Time will take care of it all."

Eventually, Aaron stopped walking in his sleep and nighttime returned to more normal.

THE LETTER

Mama always said to me, "If you can't say anything nice about anybody just come sit by me and be silent." So how much do I dare say about Hazel? As is true with most of my account, the events are based on hearsay, selective memory, and whispers from others. I can say with assertion she was the epitome of selfishness and a real extrovert in every sense of the word. I think if she is still alive, she remains the same today. This still doesn't keep me from praying for her soul.

It must have been around 1982 when the letter arrived. I glanced at the return address, noting that it was a letter to Mama from her most beloved grandchild of all. She was seated in her favorite overstuffed chair in the living room when I returned from the mailbox with the mail. I handed Mama the letter and a *Southern Living* magazine, and I walked down the hallway to the study. I thumbed through the rest of the day's mail then tossed it in the to-do tray on my desk. I poured us another cup of coffee; mine black and hers with lots of cream and four sugars and carried them back to the living room.

Mama sat staring blankly at the lined and creased notebook paper, her gnarled fingers tightly gripped. Her hands were trembling. "What is this?" I asked her softly, pointing to the opened legal-size envelope lying in her lap. She didn't answer me and rather continued with that peculiar expressionless look on her face. Putting both cups of coffee down on the side table, I reached out and took the papers from her hand.

Dear Nana,

I've worried long and hard before writing this letter. There just seems to be no peace where this family is concerned. I can only say I do regret that I called you, making that first step to try to reunite this family. You talked with me as if we had spoken with each other every day over the years. I couldn't honestly feel quite that pleasant as three years without talking or seeing you had done something to my feelings concerning all of you. I will never forget the many times that I begged Mama just to call you – because you told me that if she would just call you first you would talk to her. So finally she did and you hung up. It was as if I lost all trust in you. Maybe you were just trying to impress Kat or Megan because they were home at the time. You'll never know, how in the past, I have cried over you to Mama. The only comfort I can have over any of the entire mess is that you've been brainwashed. It seemed from the day Mom remarried there was always some resentment towards us because of Manley. Well, he's gone now so I guess all of you celebrated…

Let me go back four years or so.

In the deep country, in rural North Carolina, there are many communities that still depend on private wells to provide water for consumption, and such was and still is the case for Crossroads. The water supply for the well at Mama's was exhausted and she was in dire need of having a new well dug. The problem was funding. She depended on a $92 per month pension from the government and a small amount in land rent paid to her by a farmer for the use of her land; just enough to keep abreast of buying clothing, food, and paying the electric bill.

From time to time, Hazel and I would give Mama a variety of gifts: clothing, bed covers, side chairs, and such. This meant a lot to her as she could not financially provide these things for herself. So when the well dried up, I contacted Hazel with the notion that she and I share the expense of having a new well dug, and she agreed. The well-digger was notified, and the mission was accomplished in short order. I paid half; she paid half—deal done.

Some months later, on a Saturday morning, I was making my rounds with my children in tow. My first stop was at the home of a shut-in to shampoo and roll her hair; second stop was to repeat the process with another elderly lady. There was no such thing as a "beauty parlor," as they were called then, in Crossroads. And after all, it was a little selfish on my part: do the task of the expected visit and help the ladies to look their best when they showed up at the Baptist church the next morning for services.

The plan was to arrive at Mama's house last, shampoo and roll her hair, then we would make lunch together. Megan, Angela, and Aaron dashed in ahead, bounding up the steps and through the back door with me following. She was sitting there, staring into space, breathing, eyes open yet not responding to my commands.

Instinctively and because of my training, I thought initially, "She must have had a stroke!" After what seemed like an eternity, she began to arouse. Obviously, she had suffered some memory loss and even stated she was frightened by it all. That very day, I took her to stay with me, and she never returned to her home to live independently again. On a visit to her doctor the Monday after this episode, it was determined the oxygen circulating in her system was dangerously low, and she was placed on oxygen by nasal cannula continuously: when she slept, when she read, when she ate, removing it only to wash her face.

Larry, who lived about three hundred yards away from the home place, was sorely missed by Mama because he visited with her daily when she lived in Crossroads. Now, he visited Mama at my house every week or so. They would spend hours sitting, chatting quietly, over hot tea or coffee, each enjoying the other's company.

I approached Mama one day and asked, "Mama, why don't you give your house to Larry and his family since you are not going to live there any longer." His home was in such disrepair, needed a new roof, floor falling in, plumbing that had failed… What better idea than for her oldest and most favorite child to be given the home place. After much deliberation Mama agreed to do just that and the legal documents were signed. She gave Larry the house and two acres of land surrounding it, keeping the other thirty or so acres for herself. Time moved forward in our new living arrangement. Mama was now living with me; Larry moved into the old home place in Crossroads.

Unexpectedly and relatively early one Saturday morning, there was a knock on my door. There stood Hazel, on the stoop while Manley, her husband waited in their car.

"What a surprise! It is only nine o'clock in the morning. It is an eight-hour drive from your home to ours. Where did you stay last night? Why didn't you spend the night with us?" I stammered to her.

"I've come to visit Mama," she said curtly and offered no further conversation. I sounded like Chatty Cathy as we made our way through the mudroom, kitchen, and into the hallway. She followed me into Mama's bedroom where she was sitting, reading from one of the many lifestyle magazines stacked on her bedside table. I asked why Manley didn't come in; Hazel replied that he was reading the paper and would be in shortly. Hazel stepped inside Mama's room, closing the door behind her. I left them to visit busying my hands elsewhere to keep them steady, trying to slow the flow of information from the neurons in my brain across the synapses, intuitively understanding something had gone awry. *Ticktock, ticktock…*

I was in the laundry room when I heard the side door slam with a jarring heavy smashing sound. Looking at my watch, I realized twenty or so minutes had passed since Hazel's arrival. Was the slamming of the door Manley's entrance or her exit? I went to Mama's room and found her leafing through the same magazine.

I asked, "Where's Hazel?"

"She's gone, and she may never come back," Mama said with a relatively flat affect.

She explained the sole purpose of Hazel's visit was to relay loud and clear she wanted all the things she had ever given her returned. She marked them off on her fingers Mama said, "The six ladder back chairs for the kitchen, the Naugahyde upholstered side chair in the living room, the salt and pepper shakers, the Abercrombie & Fitch pair, the electric water pump, and reimbursement for the well-digging portion she had paid." It had been years since I had seen anger flash in Mama's brown eyes.

"Why would she do such a thing, Mama?" I asked.

"She is angry because I gave the house to Larry, angry that I didn't sell it and give a portion of the sale to her. She doesn't want him to have any of the things she has given me over the years. Hazel said they are hers, and she wants them back." The slamming door did mark Hazel's exit; an exodus from the family that would span several years.

But back to the letter:

> When I told Mama that I called you I could sense in her reaction some signal of betrayal. I'm still not sure why I

even called…but YOU said YOU wanted the family back together again… There is nothing I would ever do to intentionally hurt her which leads me to wonder how you could live with yourself. What could she have ever done that she would deserve to be disowned? I never realized before, until now when I think back over the years but you have never loved her the way you have Kat or Pam. Is it because of their father? Yes, Mama told me Granddaddy wasn't their Daddy… It wasn't until then that I found peace within myself over all of this…

And it wasn't just the affair you had or the children you had by another man. It was the facts that when she was eight years old and sleeping with you that you let this other man also sleep with you. The affair with another man in front of your own children… What kind of mother were you? If anyone should be disowned, she should have done it to you a long time ago."

The letter was signed, "Insincerely, Amy."

Whether it is true or false or somewhere in-between matters not today. Even if the entirety of the remarks in the letter from Amy to her grandmother is correct, what triggered Hazel to tell it all to her youngest daughter? Did she hate her own mother that much to damage her in this way, unleashing her emotions, driving her own daughter, the saboteur to putting this on paper and mailing it off for her grandmother to read? Or was it essentially just another underhanded sinister episode conjured up by my sister Hazel? That was the icing on the cake!

It is hard to believe, the complexity of it all, and I probably will never quite understand Hazel. She was somewhat the looker: thick strawberry-colored hair; see-through, pale blue-gray eyes; and open impish smile. When she was younger, seems to me, she might even have had a hint of dimples. You would never know she lost four upper front teeth, two incisors, and two canines as a result of a car crash in the wee morning hours one Sunday, when she was a teenager still.

Malevolent is not entirely descriptive of my sister Hazel. She was ruthless, vindictive. She was the snake, not the snake charmer. She was mean-spirited and sinister—successfully sinister. I imagine, in looking back if she were studied by a psychologist, she may fall in the category of having borderline personality disorder or, more simply put, emotionally unstable. She exhibited no comprehension of her behavior in relation to others. She displayed all the characteristics: chameleon-like, interpersonal insensitivity, blame-shifting behavior. Or could her behavior solely be described as *like mother like daughter?* Was she genetically tagged with this behavior from her father? I have always believed the cells hold memory independent of the brain and that is transferred down generation after generation after generation.

WHEN THE SCHOOL BUS RAN OVER LUCY

Mama's company was pleasant and comforting. We talked about old times and olden days. She talked about many events that occurred before Pan and I were born. Strangely, she never discussed her relationship with Daddy, and I never asked. Maybe she wanted me to…to ask.

Mama talked about the incident of Lucy being run over by the school bus. "It was in the spring of 1933 or 1934,"she began, "and it had been raining for days. The bus routes in rural Bakers County were not graced with pavement or stones, rather a mixture of sand, black mud, and red-orange clay. These buses were notorious for getting stuck in the muck after heavy rains, and there was little recourse other than the passengers get out and lend a hand physically pushing it out of the mire."

We folded laundry as she continued, "On this particular day, the bus on which Lucy was being transported got stuck on a

sloppy wet hill on Redfern Road. Dutifully, the passengers dis-
embarked, lining up behind the bus. As directed by the driver,
they attempted to push the vehicle forward. At some point, it
started sliding backward, and the children quickly scampered out
of the way, all except Lucy. She lost her footing and fell into
the deep ruts cut by the bus's tires. Mama said the wheels did
not actually run over Lucy; her tiny, frail body got caught up
between the dual wheels on the back! The older school children
pulled her from her entrapment. She was covered from head to
toe with gummy mud and clay. Miraculously, she suffered not a
single bodily injury."

What a close bond we developed as time slipped by. I held
these moments close to my heart.

CHAPTER TEN

MR. ALBRIGHT, CEO

HE APPEARED TO be an extremely reserved gentleman, wore silver-rimmed designer reading glasses and had an enigmatic smile. Mr. Albright dressed immaculately in suits tailored to flatter his tall, lanky physique. He would wander upstairs to the fourth floor of the hospital where I was assigned as unit supervisor; coincidentally, our paths would cross. Well, initially that is what I thought. His was an inscrutable smile, which would cause me to catch my breath with strong, exciting, and pleasant emotions on many occasions. My face would flush, and I would turn away for fear these stirrings would be found out.

One day, I was buried in thought as I busied myself at the medicine cart. I was startled by the arm that reached around from behind me. I watched as the hand placed a ring of keys on the top of the cart. I turned around and found myself in a near embrace with Mr. Albright. "I wondered if you would go for a little drive with me," he spoke softly. Visitors and other staff members strolled by, taking in the idea of the CEO flirting with a nurse supervisor. I was intrigued by this man and obviously him with me. At forty-two years old, I was vivacious, the right amount of curves in just the right places and quite pretty to look at too.

Countless times, Ellen, the secretary, answered the telephone then motioned that the call was for me. She would place her hand over the receiver, and mouth the words, "It's him."

"Yes?" I queried into the receiver.

"May I take you out to lunch?" he asked.

"Of course not, Mr. Albright," I responded in a pleasant voice.

"Then I will join you in the cafeteria for lunch," he said and hurriedly disconnected the call before I could respond.

Thereafter, we enjoyed lunch together once or twice a week. We held interesting conversations, bantering back and forth and really delighted in each other's company. Although I was never approached about our relationship, it was evident in the body language of coworkers, giving me that look of knowing. However amorous his intensions were, I still did not take the bait. If you play with fire, you are apt to get burnt.

Always, Mr. Albright made a point to sit in the chair beside me in executive meetings. This came to be quite a natural occurrence as the chair next to he or I would always be left vacant by other attendees. Quite obviously, the participants were players in the game as well. One particular meeting, though, the chairs beside him were taken, thus I was seated several places down from him at the round conference table. I watched as he tore a scrap of paper from his legal pad, watched as he wrote hurriedly on this paper, observed him fold it in half, then in quarters. He passed the note off to his left to the person sitting adjacent to him, motioning for the note to be delivered to me.

All eyes watched the hands that passed the note forward to its destination. It reached my hands. At that moment, all eyes were on me. The blushing that began at my neck became a confluent bright red spreading upward, covering my entire face. There it was! His true intent! The note revealed it all… "I have a seminar next week in Danville. Will you meet me there?" Reflexively, my eyes met his across the room; I gave an ever-so-slightly nod to the negative. Most certainly the meeting continued to its completion, assuredly the atmosphere returned to normal for those present, except for me.

I wondered if he had written the note in an effort toward distracting Sandra the DON from her elaborate, nasal filibuster, preventing others to contribute ideas or suggestions. Maybe it was a combination of the two, for now, I'll just call it a flirtatious disruption!

SANDRA JONES, DON

Nine years passed like a blur, and precipitously, it was 1985. The already strained relationship I had with Sandra waned and became quite contentious. The handwriting was on the wall, and I had this ominous feeling of doom and gloom. In my imagery, I envisioned King Belshazzar from the Book of Daniel in the Hebrew Bible, at the banquet he hosted, watching the disembodied hand appear, writing on the wall. I shuddered; I felt that rabbit run right over my grave.

As time moved forward, our affiliation dwindled, becoming additionally antagonistic. In her attempt to destroy my reputation, an event occurred, propelling me to the end of my tenure. A dear friend and confidant said to me with some urgency, "You are becoming too powerful in this organization, and Sandra is working on a plan to frame you." I had not a clue as to what he meant. "I am telling you, there is a plan to sabotage your reputation. There is a document in her hands, accusing you of overstepping your job description. Sandra showed it to me. I read it and it's pretty inflammatory." Sandra should have been warned. Little did she know I cut my teeth on conflict management and problem solving skills.

Needless to say, I was in Sandra's office, being held at bay by her assistant, waiting for her to arrive the next morning. She brushed past me into her office, and I followed. I requested to see the letter I had been told of. Initially she denied one existed. I demanded to see my personal file. After much confrontation back and forth between us, Sandra handed my file over. Sure enough, in the front of the manila folder was a three-page, hand-written document. It was written by an evening supervisor who claimed her staff would not follow her directions while she was on duty, preferentially calling me at home for advice and direction, circumventing her authority. The document went on to include many other instances of the staff sidestepping her for guidance from me. The entire letter was fabricated, malicious, and backbiting.

I placed my file, with exception to the document on Sandra's desk, and said to her, "You and I need to go to the CEO's office, now!"

She remarked that was impossible without an appointment. Naturally, I turned and walked out of her office and rapidly down the corridor to the administrative suites, walked past the executive secretary, and pushed open the door of Mr. Albright's office without knocking.

All the while, the director was behind me, high-heeled shoes going *clickity*, *clickity*, *click* on the marble floor, frantically exclaiming, "You can't do that! Come back! Stop! Give me those documents!"

Mr. Albright was startled to say the least! He pushed his chair back from his desk, half standing then falling back into the chair in a sitting position as the two of us stormed in. I was livid, as was she. "Will you two ladies take a deep breath, calm down, then explain to me what exactly is going on," Mr. Albright asked, looking over the rim of his glasses.

I explained as best I could then, seeing an even more puzzled look on his face, I said, "Mr. Albright, if you will allow me to read this—*this document*—to you, it will make more sense."

Over her much blubbering and protesting, I was permitted to read the complete document out loud. A lengthy silence ensued. Mr. Albright removed his glasses, polishing them with a handkerchief he withdrew from his back pocket. He rose and walked to the expansive tempered-glass wall, pensively looking out at nothing in particular.

I waited. Sandra coughed and cleared her throat, trying to signal his attention. More time went by. He turned and then walked back to his desk. Replacing his glasses, he assumed a comfortable position in his chair then asked of me, "Kat, how much of this is true?"

"Not one single solitary word of it," I said to him, quietly but deliberately. With a questioning look on his face, he turned to Sandra who was standing a pace or two to my right.

"Well, it is the supervisor's word against hers," she snorted in antipathy, nodding her head toward me.

"The three of us know all of this is a lie and an attempt to discredit me," I said in my own antagonistic voice. That look on her scarlet flushed face sealed the deal for me. She was caught like a rabbit in the headlights.

I reached into my lab coat pocket, extracted a cigarette lighter, and set fire to the document in my hand. Replacing the lighter, I overturned his trash can, emptying the contents on the carpeted floor of this extravagantly decorated office. I watched the final ashes of the document fall into the trash container, watched as the gray plume of smoke made its way toward the ceiling. I inhaled deeply and caught a whiff of the sweet odor of burning paper then turned and walked out of the room.

This event was never mentioned by any of the parties involved. About two weeks passed and the supervisor who had falsified the document resigned "for health reasons." Another thirty days later, I resigned, knowing it would be only a matter of time before another contrivance occurred. You don't need a weatherman to know which way the wind blows.

Sandra held a grand and pretentious catered going-away party for me on my last day; I was a no show. My real friends held a party at the same time in a different location, which I cheerfully attended. I still have the Silver Serving Platter inscribed on the back with all their names. A most appreciated farewell...

SOJOURN

"Well, this is as good a time as any to start over" was my thought process at the time of my departure from Concord General Hospital. My personal life was nothing to brag about either. My children's dad, Douglas, and I were what seemed to be millenniums apart in every sense of the word. For a few years now, we had been transitioning from raising tobacco, corn, and soy beans to raising horses: quarter horse and appaloosa breeds. What had started out as a hobby had grown into a full-fledged horse farm with twelve brood mares and a couple of stallions. The farm now had a name—Remanaran Stables, named after our children, using a combination of letters from Megan, Angela, and Aaron's names. Pretty creative, I thought! Interestingly enough, I did not include any portion of my name. Freudian slip perhaps? Had I already subconsciously moved on?

We did everything that was routine to raising horses: broke green horses to halter and saddle, boarded horses for clients, and gave basic Western riding lessons. We showed beautiful quarter horse weanlings at halter and showed stallions across the states. We also offered to breed our stallion to select equine enthusiasts; those ever striving for that first place win, the Blue Ribbon. I showed some horses at halter, but Angela was the pretty young thing the judges kept their eyes on as much as they did the show horses. The rest of us were stable crew working together, trying to make it happen.

The appaloosa was my favorite, more fluid and refined in their movement. The breed is easily identified by the leopard-like spotted coat pattern they exhibit, and they are one of the most popular in the United States. I read somewhere that the Nez Perce tribe developed the original American breeds. Early settlers referred to this breed as the Palouse horse, possibly deriving the name from the river by the same name. The Palouse River is a tributary of the Snake River and flows for 167 miles from northern Idaho into southeast Washington through the Palouse region. History tells us most of their ponies were lost in a stampede during the final stages of the Nez Perce War of 1877. However, a dedicated group of horsemen preserved this breed from which the name Appaloosa eventually evolved.

Foaling season was the bright spot of the year. Mares were bred to foal eleven months later, preferably on New Year's Day or as soon thereafter as possible. The older foals had the advantage of time; more time for the trainer or handler to work his magic in getting the weanling ready for show. There was always rumors and gossip of certain owners' mares foaling as early as the first week of December lending a distinct, albeit dishonest, advantage to the foal. It must have been unnerving to constantly be on the lookout for visitors: to hide the mare and her foal away from public view, to prevent the truth from being found out.

The training process began as soon after foaling as possible and certainly before separating it from the dam. We began touching, stroking, picking up feet, and putting them back down, building trust between the foal and the handler. Haltering, which is no easy feat followed. This too must be done prior to foal-dam separation, then on to training him to walk and jog just at your elbow. With this, we were building confidence and showmanship.

My hopes were this venture would improve our marriage; instead, it sent it further south. We were still a camp divided. My sojourn was over, the "stay" had come to an end, and after a year, I returned to the professional workforce in which I was educated, that of being a nurse. Thus I applied for and accepted a position at a small community hospital in a town nearby. The year was 1986 and brought to an end my marriage to Douglas.

ANTIQUATED

I was utterly dumbstruck, astonished at the outdated and anti-quated condition of this hospital facility. It was difficult to believe a hospital could be so out-of-date. The paint on the walls was a depressing gray with a hint of forgotten yellow that had faded over the years. It was suspended in time; the manual hand-crank beds were dilapidated and narrow with a worn thin mattress topping each. Absent were piped in oxygen or wall-suctioning devices. Oxygen was kept on the back loading dock in various size cylinders: C and D are all I can remember, and they were the state-of-the-art portable O2 tanks for that facility.

The emergency room equipment was obsolete, yet the staff was quite proficient in doing what they did best—performing as a Band-Aid facility and transporting critical patients with acute crises to neighboring hospitals that were better equipped to handle life-threatening emergencies. There was no intensive or critical care unit, but there was an observation room outfit-ted with two beds on the second floor near the nurses' station; that is where critical patients awaited transfer to a medical center equipped for such.

Early on, I met with the director of nursing and the CEO and urged them to consider the necessity of upgrading this facility with more modern equipment and initiating a continuing educa-tion and training syllabus that would correspond to use of the equipment. I was given permission to proceed with setting up the first crash cart and training of the staff in its use. How pleased I was to be pioneering a new endeavor for this facility!

Here is a prime example of utilization of the observation room. There was the incident of a dissecting aortic aneurysm, suffered by Rex Thurmond, the town manager. This is a fatal condition should it not be recognized and treated promptly. Mr. Thurmond presented to the emergency room complaining of severe chest pain and difficulty breathing. Blood tests and EKG ruled out any cardiac involvement. However, he was admitted to the observation room to assure no signs or symptoms would go unnoticed.

It was two in the morning. Mr. Thurmond was swathed in perspiration, writhing in pain, skin color mimicking the ashes from the too many cigarettes he had smoked throughout his life. The nurse, very apt to handle such events, notified the primary physician.

"I believe Mr. Thurmond has a dissecting aortic aneurysm and must be transferred STAT," the nurse reported rapidly to the attending physician. She continued hurriedly, "His blood pressure has fallen dramatically, his skin is cold and clammy, and he is unable to take a deep breath because of the severe pain."

"Okay, let's get a chest X-ray, repeat the labs for cardiac enzymes, and…" the doctor ordered.

"You don't understand. I don't believe we have time for that. Honestly I am 90 percent sure this is a dissecting aortic aneurysm," she shouted into the telephone, cutting the doctor off in mid-sentence.

"Then arrange for an emergency transfer. I want you to accompany Mr. Thurmond in the ambulance with the EMTs," he said, now with some urgency.

The rescue squad was notified, and the patient was transferred to a regional medical center where he received emergency surgical intervention—a procedure this hospital could not provide. The outcome for this individual and all involved was the most successful. I was humbled by this example as I was the nurse caring for Mr. Thurmond that night.

But let me go back to the inception of this small rural hospital. From the archives of their recorded history, I find that "Many years ago, the Honorable Jonas I. McAdoo, a native of York County represented this district as a congressman of the United

States. Mr. McAdoo left a large tract of land to York County to be used for the poor, the widows, and orphans of York County. For many years, the county operated the land as a county farm; however, it was eventually sold at public auction, and the money derived from the sale was put into a special fund.

Around 1947, a hospital movement was launched in York County. Finally in November 1949, an historic election was held, wherein the voters approved the construction of a nonprofit hospital. The county received matching federal funds, which coincided with county funds. Construction plans were soon underway. As the matter of site selection came up, the county commissioners decided to use the McAdoo funds for the land purchase. Almost one hundred years after the death of Jonas I. McAdoo, the money he left the county was put to its intended use.

The dedication service for the first York County Hospital, made possible in part through the generosity of the Honorable Jonas McAdoo, was held on a Sunday in September of 1951. Through the years, York County Hospital was able to expand and grow without any additional county funds. By 1987, the needs of the hospital were extreme, and the citizens approved a $4 million bond issue."

The excitement was unimaginable as the new construction began, anticipating the first-ever intensive care unit. I was tasked with the layout and design and procurement of all equipment and supplies. Further, I was designated to be the supervisor of this unit, to select and train the licensed and ancillary staff.

Dr. Drake, an internist, and I attended a ten-day grueling seminar at Bowman Gray School of Medicine for training and certification in advanced cardiac life support. It was pretty intimidating for both of us. Upon our return, we developed a training syllabus and trained other physicians, ER, and ICU RNs.

No longer would we have to retrieve cylinders of oxygen from the loading dock or go to the storage area for a portable suctioning unit. Such items would actually be located in a separate mechanical room with piping routed and controls provided throughout the facility in each patient room and care unit. We would have new cardiac monitoring equipment, electrical mechanical pumps for delivery of intravenous fluids and medications, administration of packed red blood cells, and pumps to monitor enteral nutritional supplementation. We made a giant step in care delivery for the area.

CLEMENT'S GRILL

On my way into work one morning, I stopped at Clement's for a breakfast biscuit. It was April and the weather was mild, the breeze gentle. The aromatic foliage of the clumps of rosemary combined with the sweet fragrance of gardenia blossoms filled the air. I stepped inside and took my place in line at the counter where orders were placed. Where in this universe can you order a fried bologna sandwich with mustard at eight in the morning except at Clement's Grill, smack dab in the middle of Gibson?

Gibson is a sleepy little town located in the coastal plain region of North Carolina, only fifty miles from the beautiful Atlantic Ocean beaches, with easy access to the larger towns of Brookville, Raleigh, and Wilmington. Gibson is best known for its many natural lakes. Every summer, the Goose Lake Water Festival is the talk of all the surrounding towns and "the" place to go.

I chatted with townsfolk as I waited for my order. I took my little white bag that held the smoked sausage-with-mustard biscuit, a medium black coffee, and headed for my car. Exiting the restaurant, I followed a decidedly disgruntled couple out the door.

I pressed the button on the remote car door opener on my key ring. The door unlocked, and I swung it open. As I was putting things in place, the gentleman whom I had followed out of the grill, came storming over to my vehicle. "Excuse Me! Hello. Hello! Excuse Me!" he said with obvious irritation. "Can you tell me where I can find a restaurant in this rinky-dink little town so I can have a nice sit-down breakfast that we can order from a menu, and I can read the *Burlington Free Press* over coffee?" The woman stood submissively by their shiny champagne-colored Mercedes Benz. I am sure they spent quite a pretty penny for that. In fact, I would bet you the necessary minimum maintenance of that import would provide for three hungry families for a year. Clearly, this man was accustomed to more elegant dining than this little fast food grill had to offer.

"We are from Vermont, traveling to Wilmington to visit relatives and can't find a respectable restaurant for breakfast in this little…uh…settlement," he quipped sarcastically in such a clipped tone. "Why, there is not even a hotel in this town. We had to sleep in that dreadfully old-fashioned Jordan's Inn," he continued. *Old-fashioned Jordan's Inn*, I thought to myself. A better, more accurate description would have been quintessential and idyllic with a Currier and Ives ambiance. The tin roof, the antiques, the turned moldings, and other accouterments brought back an imagery of yesteryear. It was the place that the present and past governors along with other dignitaries of this great state chose to spend vacations from time to time.

So I said to this fellow, "You know, they have truly fabulous food inside Clement's and their health department code is Grade A. They do have a menu that you can order from…"

He puffed and blustered. "I mean no disrespect, but I do not want to eat breakfast this morning at a fast food place!"

I thought about it for a moment then responded, "Your best bet is at your destination, Wilmington, which is only about an hour's drive away."

I felt a certain sadness for this man. How could he be so presumptuous as to think himself so much better than the anesthesiologist, Martha, whom I kissed on the cheek when she greeted me as I entered the restaurant? "How truly grand to see you again," she said. "And are you working still?" I felt a gentle touch on my left shoulder, and I turned to see Dr. Martha Adair, just standing there, stroking my back and saying how much she missed seeing me around town now that I had taken a job with the "city folk."

In the corner booth sat the postmaster, Wilbur, with his wife. She was leaning over the back of her booth to whisper something to a friend who just happened to be the mayor's wife. The mayor didn't seem to mind as he was engrossed in conversation with Rex, the town manager. The tobacco and peanut farmers too were casually standing about, sipping their coffee, and having a conversation with Ronald, the county attorney, and with each other. Little did this man from Vermont know of the riches he had just denied himself in his search for fancy...

CHAPTER ELEVEN

MY SECOND MARRIAGE

I HAVE SPENT A great deal of time in my quest for understanding the multifaceted personalities of people in my life. I have especially searched for the personality traits of such a person to whom I was married for twelve years, searching for answers, comprehension.

It was in 1987 that I met Phillip. He was textbook charming, spouted grandiose ideas, yet was lacking in remorse or shame. To those on the outside looking in, Phillip was entrepreneurial and innovative. I learned a different side; one in which he exhibited hostility, dishonesty, and a strong lack of respect to the laws of nature and to the laws of man. He was irresponsible and unreliable. Unquestionably, he lived a life of infidelity. To hear him tell it, he could turn geese into swans. His was no Ponzi scheme, but he could have competed for con-man of the century and won. Without a doubt, he was a legend in his own mind.

He would become outraged at seemingly ordinary things, yet steely calm and unmoved in events that would upset a normal person. My first insight into this was our first New Year's Eve together. We had planned to attend a celebration beginning at eight o'clock that evening in a town about twenty miles away. Six o'clock came, then seven, then eight. Wondering whether he was in harm's way, I began paging him. Nine o'clock came, another hour ticktocked away, and still no Phillip. He came hurriedly through the door, at ten thirty that evening, with an off-hand statement that his car had been stolen. "I had to borrow a car from a friend to come home. Listen to this," he said calmly while donning black tie apparel for the formal event to which we had special invitation. "I parked in front of the jewelry store, left the engine running, jumped out, and ran inside to pick up the gift I had ordered for you. I was only in the store a minute. When I went back outside, the car was gone. I even had my two timber checks on the front seat—one for $9,000 and the other for $12,000. I have been at the police station filing a stolen vehicle report." He relayed this turn of events in a remarkably calm and nonchalant manner where a normal person would have been sweating bullets, a stolen vehicle, and the theft of $21,000! Amazingly enough, I believed that cockamamie story! Roughly two weeks later, Phillip drove the "stolen" car home saying he had received a call from the police, and they had recovered the car. And yes, the checks were exactly where he left them.

Then there was the time a piece of logging equipment caught fire and burned in the woods: a $50,000 Franklin Skidder. "It was just vandalism," he said coolly and evenly. "I reported it to the sheriff, and he is going to investigate." Phillip did file and was awarded an insurance claim. Since that time, I have wondered, *Vandalism by whom?*

On another occasion, someone broke into our home while I was away at my job. The thief made off with five antique shotguns and rifles and several less expensive handguns. Phillip described the scenario to me rather indifferently, "The French doors were locked but somehow they were able to shove them open and entered the great room from the patio. See where they broke the glass on the gun cabinet? I filed a report with the sheriff and also the insurance company."

The inventory list of the stolen guns was impressive:

1 1886 Remington Carbine Rifle excellent condition, no chips or bruises. Value $2750.00

1 1894 Remington Eastern Carbine Rifle excellent condition, finish original blue. Value $1595.00

1 1928 Baker Black Beauty Double Barreled Shotgun 30" blue barrels. Value $1950.00

1 1927 A.H. Fox Stirlingworth Deluxe 20 gauge auto ejectors and walnut stock. Value $2595.00

1 1912 Pigeon Grade LC Smith auto ejectors and double triggers like new condition. Value $5500.00

1 1864 Allen & Thurber Pepper Box Dragoon size Cap & Ball 6" revolver, wood grips. Value $2495.00

1 1878 Colt US Artillery 45 Caliber 5 ½ inch barrel, excellent bore very good condition. Value $4400.00

The market value of this inventory was submitted as $21,285; the insurance claim was filed and settled at 85 percent of the value with a check in the amount of $18,092.25. "Not a bad day's work, huh, Phillip?" I thought to myself as he gloatingly showed me the check. "I guess now I understand why your insurance premiums were so costly." This was another of his absurd stories, but I believed it. Ironically, one by one, the guns reappeared over the next few months.

"Oh, I have friends in high places and was tipped off to their locations," Phillip responded. "It is in your best interest to keep your mouth closed about my business. Don't act the giddy goat! I hope you understand what that means."

I never did tell of this insurance fraud. Who would I tell anyway? The insurance company that Phillip no longer had? What would be the point?

How can I accurately describe the character of Phillip Roberts, the person to whom I was married for twelve years? If I were to use one descriptive word for him, it would be *Machiavellian*. One source the web site ask.com defines this word as "the employment of cunning and duplicity in statecraft or general conduct." It is descriptive of one's tendency to deceive and manipulate others for their own personal gain.

It is also possible he may also have been the victim of the Hubris-Nemesis complex. "Hubris" means excessive pride, arrogance, and self-importance while "nemesis" refers to a vengeful desire to confront, humiliate, and defeat another. Marry the two words and that labels most of Phillip's behavior. Adolf Hitler has been diagnosed with such a disorder. All I know is Phillip's personality was a malicious and spiteful one.

He was a person I never honestly knew until after our union dissolved. He walked away from our twelve-year marriage with a young married girl as arm candy; she was half his age. She was from the Meherrin Indian Tribe of North Carolina. My daddy would have called her Croatian or high yellow. But perhaps I should start at the beginning... I seem to be waffling.

Phillip described himself as a shrewd businessperson, and it did seem so early on in our marriage. He told a credible story...

"I am divorced," he said. He was a deacon of the Presbyterian Church in Gibson, an elected member of the board of directors for the local First Savings and Loan Bank, a son entirely devoted to his mother, crazy as she was. He was exceptionally personable, charming even, and could have won first place in a Clark Gable look-alike contest. "There is just one thing I must tell you," he said. "My wife maxed out all my credit cards for cash, leaving me in big debt." *Not to worry*, I thought to myself. *Together we can get those paid off in short order.*

He dabbled in selling previously owned high-end vehicles and owned shares in one car dealership located in Brookville, North Carolina. He bought and sold timber and was the owner of a logging business. He had a large circle of acquaintances and spent large amounts of money. He entertained late-night visits from some of these friends and would be called outside chatting with them for hours on end.

I was outside hanging laundry on the clothesline one brisk sunny spring day. I could hear a single-engine airplane approaching. Suddenly it dived low to the ground over the seventy-five-acre soybean field we owned directly in front of our home. I knew it was too early in the year for crop dusting, so what was going on? The plane circled and made another dive over the field, and I could see what appeared to be bales of hay falling from the back of the plane. I immediately tried to contact Phillip, by phone and pager, to inform him of this. He did not respond.

It was after dark when he finally came home. He sauntered in, calm and relaxed. I relayed the details of the plane and the bales of hay. He responded with some ridiculous story about the bales being alfalfa hay for the horses. *Alfalfa hay delivered by plane? I could drive to the nearest feed store eight miles away and buy all the alfalfa hay I wanted*, was my immediate thought. Not long after Phillip arrived, three Jordan brothers appeared along with their sister Elaine. The bales disappeared that very evening. Perhaps it was not alfalfa hay at all. Later events would lead me to believe they were bales of marijuana.

On another evening, this same group of Phillip's friends lingered late into the night, hanging out just outside our garage. Multiple times, I went to the door and inquired as to when this meeting would be ending. Rumblings from the group indicated I should go back inside and mind my own business.

I did go back inside, but the more I thought about this, the more I felt like a prisoner in my own home. I became furious, "This is *my* home! Who do they think they are? I won't let them get away with threatening me," I thought as I retrieved my car keys from the hook by the back door, turned the outside flood-lights on, and stepped back outside.

There they were, still standing around LeRoy Jordan's brand new Hummer, a civilian version of the military Humvee. The vehicle was parked about thirty feet behind mine. They were drinking and toasting their beer bottles to who knows what, laughing, and apparently enjoying each other's company. "I am going to get in my car, start the engine, and put the transmission in reverse on the count of three. Anyone left standing can expect to be mowed down by this vehicle!" I yelled to them as the car door slammed behind me.

In the rearview mirror, I could see them scrambling into the Hummer. I could hear the screech of their tires over mine as both vehicles propelled backward. The stench of burned rubber on concrete enveloped me. To my annoyance, LeRoy's vehicle was more powerful than mine and their escape was not hampered. Angry was not an adequate description for Phillip's mood that evening. He kept to himself, though, saying not a word to me.

Later, the phone rang; it was Elaine. "I am on my way back to your house," she shouted. "I'm gonna kick your ass!"

With a resounding clack that she could hear over the phone, I closed the chambers on the shells I had just dropped into the double-barreled shotgun. "Come on, Elaine. I'll be waiting."

And wait I did. Phillip went to bed. I waited until dawn then it was time to prepare for work again. She did not appear, being the coward she was. A coward dies a hundred deaths, and I have no lost love for cowards and bullies!

Then raids on numerous car dealerships followed. Owners were arrested in Lafayette and Eldon counties. Apparently, a two-year undercover surveillance coupled with a sting operation identified a very sophisticated criminal group. Multiple dealer-ships were being used as fronts for drug operations and money laundering. This made daily headline news throughout the state during the trials and sentencing. Prison sentences were handed down to many including LeRoy, Elaine, and their two brothers. As usual, Phillip beat the system and came out smelling like a rose.

Maybe it was from his mother's ancestry that he inherited his evil genes. I won't say he was the textbook definition of a dual personality; however, that is what he came to be. In the presence of others, his charisma filled the room, his good humor kept the mood light and entertaining. The last years became stormy; he reacted in fits of rage, verbally threatening to cause me bodily harm.

Late one afternoon in particular, I was in the kitchen putting away the last of the eggs I had collected from the dozen or so free-range hens I had. The egg bucket was a forty-eight-ounce tin coffee can with two holes punched near the top with a length of wire inserted to create a bail.

I was questioning Phillip as to why it was necessary for him to be gone from home every Saturday. He became extremely furious, and the conversation turned into a heated and dramatic altercation. The argument raged on as he grabbed my upper arms and began shaking me violently. I wrenched away from him. He backed away then roared like a madman and headed toward me again. His face was contorted like a bulldog chewing on a nest of wasps. Reflexively, I grabbed the egg bucket from the counter and swung it in front of me, striking him on his left temple and opening an enormous laceration. Blood spurted, ran into his left eye, the corner of his mouth; it was everywhere!

He stopped in his tracks then went barreling outside. I slammed the door behind him, trembling, gasping for breath. Several hours later, he returned muttering that he went to the local emergency department, that he told the doctor a horse kicked him, requiring the need for medical treatment. If I correctly remember, the laceration required twenty-six sutures to close. That undoubtedly put a dent in his narcissistic ego.

Phillip's mother passed away and I think that may have been the catalyst that sent him over the edge. To say the manner in which she died was unsettling is an understatement. There is some backstory of her behavior during the two years leading up to her death. She locked herself in her home, refusing to let anyone in, even her son. The roar of the blower on her oil heater could be heard from outside during summer or winter, and you could hear her singing, shrieking the words at the top of her voice. She began wearing her late husband's clothing, including his socks and underwear. She was unclean and unkempt, and she would not eat.

Reports from visits when I took her to talk with the mental health professionals in Gibson failed to show she exhibited any mental issues, that she had a right to wear what she desired, bathe when she wished, etc. I did not agree. And she walked…she must have walked twenty or more miles a day, in circles, going around and around that 150-year-old home in which she lived, all alone. Hers was the type of house that was built on elevated pillars for support but no underpinning. A toddler could have walked in and out from under the house without ever bumping its head. The circular path in the grass her many steps left behind is probably there still.

On the morning of her death, I was summoned to the director of nursing's office in the hospital there where I was employed. A colleague took me by the hand and led me to a chair. "Let's sit down, Kat. I have something to tell you." A hundred tragic events flashed before my eyes, not one of them being the death of my husband's mother. That was her revelation, though; I gathered up my things, left the building, and drove to her house.

As I turned into the driveway, I could see the flashing lights of a rescue vehicle; the blue lights of the sheriff's deputy's car blinking in that swirling fashion creating a feeling of trepidation that welled up inside me. Approaching her home at the top of the hill, I spotted Phillip as he came walking toward my car. He was devastated; his body shaking with the sobbing. Eventually, I was able to understand the scenario he was presenting. As was customary, after I left for work that morning, Phillip went to his mother's house to check on her. He never made it inside.

Lying just barely under the edge of the house, near the side door, is where he discovered her body. She was totally naked; all her clothing was neatly folded and carefully placed by her side. Her hands were folded across her bosom. I thought how heartbreaking and horrifying it must have been for him to find his mother dead in such a state as this. We questioned the deputy who would not let us near her body. He said it did not look like foul play, but an autopsy would be performed as required by law. The report from the autopsy said she died of "natural causes." I still have questions; however, I suppose stranger things have happened.

Time passed, and our lives settled back into some sense of normalcy. Phillip had sold all his logging equipment and was totally out of the timber business. The shenanigans with drug dealing were too risky, so he was in limbo. Phillip decided to take a job installing satellite dishes for a company in Brookville. Abruptly, he became guarded and secretive, deceitful even. He started dressing differently, blackened his graying hair and mustache, spending more and more time away from home. Then came the nights when he did not return home at all.

It was the middle of August in 1996 that Phillip finally moved out of our bedroom and into the guest room, relocating all his personal items. We were coolly polite to each other, but that was the extent of our relationship. I was burdened with my daughter's progressively poor health and honestly did not want to focus on the reality of my marriage. I returned late one evening near midnight in at the end of the month from doing a follow-up visit with a patient. I was surprised that Phillip was not at home, but I was so exhausted I fell into bed and slept through the night.

When I awoke the next morning, it was with a strange feeling—surreal; something was just not right! I went from room to room and discovered that Phillip had removed every personal item he owned from our home while I was at work the day before. The only thing he left behind was a portrait of his parents hanging in the hallway. Day after day, I called his mobile phone, but he did not answer. I paged him on his personal pager inputting our phone number; he did not respond. Then, several weeks later, out of nowhere he called and said he just couldn't handle the pressure of Megan being so near death; he needed time to think. However, by this time, I had begun to realize that he had no legitimate remorse about anything or anyone, especially my daughter.

At that time, statements were arriving for monies owed; every account was delinquent by sixty to ninety days. The two gut-wrenchers were the pager account and the letter from the IRS. For whatever reason, we always filed for an extension each year and never paid our income taxes until August 15. Enclosed in the envelope from the IRS were our tax forms. The letter explained that even though the forms were signed there was no check for payment enclosed. The amount of $4,584 was due upon the receipt of the letter and was to be paid or severe penalties would accrue! The pager account was a staggering $905. The mortgage payment was in arrears by more than ninety days with the note holder sending threatening letters to foreclose. Thank God the utilities were my responsibility, so they were paid current, up-to-date. I would at least have gas, water, and electricity until foreclosure!

Panic welled up inside me! "What was I going to do? How was I going to be able to meet all these demands? Where would I start?" Immediately, I began canceling nonessential services. Daily newspapers were the first to go. I stopped purchasing high-end items; certainly I stopped name-brand buying. I arranged, with the phone company, to make payments on that enormous pager account. I met with a representative from the IRS, and after hearing my case, we reached an agreement that I would be allowed to pay $175 per month until the taxes were paid in full. The money left owed for the expense of his mother's funeral, and burial was left, still unpaid. I could not live with that. The owner of the funeral home allowed me to make payments on that $5,500 debt as well. I surely could live without satellite TV, so I called the company to arrange for the disconnection; the same company Phillip was working with when he snuck off like an egg-sucking dog.

The technician arrived as scheduled, performed the necessary tasks, and presented me with a form to sign. "I know you couldn't have been too surprised to learn Phillip ran off with that Indian gal. After all they've been running together for over two years," he said as I poised pen over paper. My hands began shaking uncontrollably; in fact, my entire body was in a state of palsy. To his dismay, the technician realized he was sharing something with me that I had not yet learned. He stammered and stuttered. He must have apologized. I couldn't hear because the roar in my ears was so deafening. I must have signed the paper; I must have made my way back inside because I found myself in the kitchen.

For the longest time, I remember standing, staring out the kitchen window, in a state of shock. I remember crumbling to the floor, not knowing how long I remained there. Slowly, I tied the loose ends together. I recalled the many times his pager would buzz, and he would step outside or into another room to make a phone call. I remembered all those Saturday mornings he would rise early, shower, shave, and dress in casual attire and wait for the buzz of the pager. He explained that he had to go to a training class for the day, and he would be late returning. I remembered conversations he would engage me in about what lovely people the Meherrin Indians were. I certainly didn't disagree with that. His affair with the Indian girl followed the same pattern of most, I supposed.

Apparently, the technician who removed the satellite dish notified Phillip he had been found out. The threatening and harassing phone calls began immediately. Phillip would ring my phone, awakening me in the middle of the night threatening, "If you don't leave that house, I will burn it down around you with you in it! You know the house belongs to me!" Or he would call me at work and say, "If you don't pack up and leave that house will be nothing but cinders when you get home from work today." I met with Sheriff Evans and gave him the details of these conversations, and he agreed to add more surveillance to my home night and day. He sent me directly to a magistrate where I obtained a restraining order against Phillip. Still, there was little comfort to be had, and honestly I was afraid.

The sheriff called, "I sent a deputy to talk to the owner of the company where Phillip is employed, but they refused to allow him to talk to him. He said, 'Talk to him on his time, not on mine' and refused to give the deputy a phone number or address for Phillip. He's a slick one, that Phillip, like trying to catch a greased pig in a contest."

"Pig…swine," I thought without humor. "A chauvinistic, insensitive, and disgusting pig was a perfect correlation to make."

"We have been looking for Phillip and have put out alerts to other agencies that we just want to talk to him. So far, he can't be found, but rest assured, we will continue to keep a close eye on your place, and we'll keep looking for him," Sheriff Evans said on another occasion.

I lived in fear of bodily harm and the fact that Phillip would somehow set me up, so to speak, and do further injury to me. What if he planted illegal drugs somewhere in my car? What if he hid narcotics in or around my property then made an anonymous phone call to the authorities? What if he caused me to lose my license to practice as a registered nurse? That would surely be an end to my independence!

Throughout all this, I was meeting with bank officials, trying to purchase the house they were ready to foreclose on. The Lord surely works in mysterious ways. It was with His help I was able to do just that, purchase my home from the bank and finally have it in my name.

God only knows the struggles of the next three years; I lived off grits and potatoes, kept a loaded shotgun by the door around the clock, and prayed for better times. For one final shock, I learned from one of Phillip's friends that not only was he not divorced when I met him but still living with his wife and daughter while I lived in a tiny apartment in Gibson. I was now wife number two as he had moved on to wife number three. I wondered at the possibilities of other infidelities.

When a year had passed, I filed for a divorce from Phillip. The marriage was dissolved, uncontested.

SAVANNAH WILLOUGHBY: COUSIN SAVANNAH, MY MOTHER

Today I am in such a pensive state of mind and am preoccupied with memories of my mama. Mama's life cycle was playing out, and she was nearing the end of her earthly years. Her fingers were gnarled and twisted from rheumatoid arthritis. She had remarkably few old-age spots because she rubbed them away with L'oreal Wrinkle Defense Cream. Mama loved her country, proudly displaying our American flag. Her eyes would tear, and her voice would become husky when listening to "The Star-Spangled Banner."

Her life was a tumultuous one; her son Nick held her at gunpoint, threatening her in a dispute about a dog. A granddaughter, Amy compiled then mailed her a letter so filled with hate, it would generate waves of nausea in anyone. She appeared impervious to these events and other adversities. Throughout her life, she remained resilient, and in her later years, her personality grew softer. She was a pioneer of a woman, though, and maintained courage and fortitude throughout her life.

I recalled the account Mama gave of her parents. She sipped her tea and reminisced about earlier days. She told of being born in Lafayette, West Virginia, in 1906, the fourth child of nine to a very successful plantation owner, Will and his wife Caroline Wainsworth. "Our home large and imposing, three stories high with huge white columns supporting the front. Nannies, butlers, cooks, and house girls scurried about, attending to the needs of their master and his family. House girls with skin as dark as the walnut trees from which the furniture was made, rubbed the banisters of the winding stairways till they shined. They cleaned the mirrors, polished the heavy silver frames. They kept the house clean and orderly as they whispered secrets to one another…"

She said her father, Will, was a Christian man, slow to anger and always deep in thought about providing for his family and the turn of world events, about getting his family to church to worship each Sunday.

She recalled with a smile what opposites her parents were. "Caroline, we will drive the Red Surry to Sunday meeting today." He would call out to her, and Caroline would be pleased because she *was* one to put on airs a bit.

"My mother was of a more fiery nature, adventuresome and frivolous, and was called to task by Daddy many a time when she got just a little too big for her britches." She recalled the cold winters with all the sleet and snow; she talked about sitting by the gigantic walk-in stone fireplace with the blaze reaching high into the chimney and the scent of wood smoke all around her. She remembered what a good provider her father was and how he nourished his family both physically and spiritually.

Mama remembered her own mother's beauty and intelligence and the wonderful education she and her siblings received from their mother's teaching. She recalled the good humor that was instilled in her by her mother and how there was always work to be done, but there was time set aside for play too.

Images of the plantation she described of many years ago came to mind. I could visualize the cane mill with the aged wooden beam going around and around…could smell the aroma of the sugar cane as it cooked in the huge vats and could almost taste the rich, sweet syrup that would be the end product of long labor.

She said her father tended the beehives; there were at least fifty of them, and she told in minute detail of the nectar on the bee's tiny legs as they went about making their honey. "You know, Savannah, bees are very hardworking, except for the drone bee. He is a lazy sort…you don't want to be labeled as a drone bee," Will would say to his favorite daughter. I knew for a fact this was a lesson Mama took to heart—never to be a drone. Mama became quiet and thoughtful. I waited. Perhaps she will continue the story another time.

Mama loved New Orleans… She adored Pat O'Brian's, Bourbon Street, the Raw Oyster Bar, and the lighted oaks at Christmas. She treasured the Riverboat Queen and the music in the streets. She enjoyed Colonial Williamsburg and showed her expertise in explaining to us what all the "old-timey" gadgets were. Mama loved Disney World and all the futuristic sights and the make-believe it portrayed.

It was just after Christmas 1992. I was in Granville, North Carolina, to discharge my mother from the hospital where she had been admitted a few days earlier. She was in this particular hospital because she was living with Pam at this time. Mama's time was spent, half with me and half with Pam. Many years before, she had abandoned her home, giving it and everything she had to her oldest son Larry. It was Wednesday late afternoon when we arrived at Pam's from the hospital. Her discharge diagnosis was "For Observation"; her doctor would not elaborate. But I knew it was more… her breathing was quick and labored; she required oxygen at two liters per minute continuously. She could take only a few steps without stopping to rest and catch her breath; her whole body trembled.

The following morning, we watched recordings of the political debates between Bill Clinton and George Bush prior to the November election. Then we made plans to go shopping in the afternoon. She was eager to go. "Let's go to the mall. That's where Lisa showed me that beautiful red coat. I wanted it so badly... I didn't know if you would like it." She spoke haltingly, taking shallow breaths throughout the sentence. Lisa was Pam's middle child and the youngest granddaughter. Mama was almost as attached to her as she was to my daughter Angela, but not as attached as she was to her granddaughter Amy those many years ago.

I had arranged for a handicapped tag to hang on my rearview mirror, but I just could not allow myself to display it. "I do have that tag Mama, you will let me hang it," I said to her as we approached a parking space labeled for the handicapped. However, the sadness in her face compelled me to park just one space over.

She hesitated only briefly when I made the statement, "I am going to the hospitality center for a wheelchair. I'll be right back."

In the most positive manner she could muster, she made jokes about the wheelchair. "Is this a five speed?" "Will it go as fast as Aaron's car?" "Will it perform a wheelie like his motorcycle?" I prayed she was not aware of the tears flowing down my cheeks as I rolled her around and about the mall.

Our first stop was at the cosmetics counter. Goodness, Mama loved perfumes and fragrances and splashes. We bought the perfume Poison by Christian Dior. She said she had sniffed this one in a magazine and liked it tremendously. Well, one for me and one for her, like always. Our next stops were at the small specialty shops: The Linen Room, the White House Black Market, and the Hallmark Shop, where she chose unique valentines for those special ones in her life even though we were still in December. The Art Gallery caught her eye. "I've never been in an art gallery before," she said as I wheeled her slowly past wildlife and still-life paintings and drawings—past paintings and sculptures of nudes, all so tastefully done.

That day for lunch, we shared a "Ziti for One," the two of us, along with Coke and lots of garlic bread. I purchased a coffee for each of us, then I sat on a bench sipping coffee and smoking a long Merit Menthol King cigarette while she sat in the wheelchair, consumed by our own thoughts and fears. Her head began to bob, and I could see how tired she was, how fragile she looked. We made our way back to the car. I returned the wheelchair to the proper place and then we were back on Columbus Avenue, winding our way back to Pam's. That night we packed her suitcase in preparation for the trip back to Gibson the following morning.

Suddenly, out of nowhere, Mama began to ramble. "You know, Aunt Annie is in a rest home there in Laramie County. She is only one year older than I am, and the only reason I call her aunt is because her husband, John, was my uncle and…well, that's not significant now. Anyway, Kat I just want you to know…I've been thinking…that until I die, I want to keep my right mind and do things for myself and"—she paused momentarily then continued—"I want to die in my sleep. Now where is that box? You know…the one from Angela. I want to show you what she sent me for Christmas. She sent me this Christmas present…a "box" like she's got and she recorded a message for me. I've been waiting for you to come so we could listen to it together."

From her birth in 1965, Angela was one of three of Mama's most favorite grandchildren. The why never truly mattered to any of us and most of all not to me, as Angela was a favorite with me as well! I can't begin to tell you of the many hours she would sit on Nana's knee (all her grandchildren called her Nana) by the fireplace reading Rudyard Kipling to that snippet of a little girl. Angela looked so adoringly into her grandmother's aged and wrinkled face. I wonder if she remembers those Rudyard Kipling readings.

Mama located the package, and we sat on the side of her bed as she removed the small portable boom box from its container. The plastic and Styrofoam and bubble wrap were carefully laid aside, and the electrical connections were made. I carefully inserted the cassette tape that Angela had enclosed into the chamber; I pushed the button marked "Play" and there was Angela, her presence in the bedroom with us. Her sweet voice saying, "Hey, Nana: I'm sending you this for Christmas because I know you wanted a box so badly, just like mine, and I know how you hate country music, but I know how much you like George Strait, and I know this is your very favorite song because I know how much you love our land and God's creatures and life and good things..." and she rambled on and on as only Angela could do. Poor Angela, she inherited those genes from her mama, you know the one—I call it the rambling gene!

Then the music began, filling Mama's bedroom; a little boy's voice began singing, "There's a place where mornings are an endless blue, and you feel Mother Nature walk along with you..." Then George Strait, with his warm and magnificent country classic voice took over the song. Mama threw herself down on her bed, covered her face with her hands, and wept and wept and wept. Never have I been so moved, felt so forlorn or forsaken as I did at that moment. I gathered my Mama in my arms and held her for such a long time. Words were not spoken nor were they needed. I knew at this exact moment and so did she that she would be leaving us soon.

We made the trip back to Gibson in the pouring rain, listening to Rush Limbaugh arguing politics and world affairs. After we arrived and when we were in, Mama wandered throughout every room, reacquainting herself with the contents, touching objects, turning on lights. "It feels so good to be here," she said. That was to be the last visit she would make to my home. I was never to see her again, sitting in her favorite chair by the fireplace with her feet resting on the overstuffed ottoman. That would be the last time I would see her puttering about the kitchen or "just piddling, Doll Baby" in the herb and flower garden. Never again would I arise in the middle of the night to stand by her bedroom doorway, with the soft nightlight burning, to watch her sleep and listen to her tortuous breathing and wonder how many more weeks, days or hours I would have her to hold, love, and cherish. And the preparation of the journey to the end began…

Mama's health deteriorated over the next few weeks. She was admitted to York County Hospital in Gibson and then transferred to the region's largest medical center. I stayed with her, never leaving her alone. This Sunday night was the night of Super Bowl XXVII. The game was boring even though we both were Troy Aikman fans. At half time, we turned the lights down low and stretched out on our respective beds. We chatted for a while, mostly trivia then drifted off to sleep.

I awakened several times throughout the night, leaning near to hear her breathe, watching the thin cotton bed covers rise and fall. Sometime around four in the morning, a nurse came in to give her a pill. She took it dutifully then went back to sleep. I arose around 6:00 am, checked on Mama, and watched her pull the light weight blanket up under her chin. Her breathing did not seem to be as labored.

I showered, dressed, and applied the necessary makeup. It was now seven o'clock. I sat on the bed next to her and softly spoke her name, "Mama?" She did not open her eyes to look at me; she sighed deeply, then she was gone. Her cheeks were warm as I gently kissed her good-bye. I told her how much I loved her and how much I would miss her, and oh, how much I wished she did not have to go. Her prayer had come to fruition; she kept her right mind and died in her sleep. We come from dust; we return to dust, and three days later, my mother was laid to rest.

The day of her funeral was pleasant enough even though it was the first week of February. The breeze was gentle; rays of warm sunshine peppered our bodies as we said our farewells to

Mama in the Baptist church cemetery after the funeral service there in Crossroads. Family and friends remained in small groups in the churchyard, after the service, to offer condolences, to share embraces and memories.

Someone touched my shoulder. I turned to see this was a childhood friend, and she directed my attention to my mother's grave. "Kat, who is that fellow at Ms. Savannah's grave? I've been watching him. He is no one I have ever seen before. He…he waited until everyone moved away from her grave and look! He just walked up and laid a single, long-stemmed red rose on her grave. Tell me, who is that man?" she asked again.

All my senses were focused on the man kneeling there. Unhurriedly, with the aid of his walking stick, he stood. He was quite tall and thin. His hair, moustache, and beard were as white as snow cutting quite the contrast against his olive skin. What a stately debonair figure he was, dressed in a custom-tailored black sharkskin suit. As our eyes made contact, suddenly I knew! We looked directly at each other for a long time, taking each other in. He and I exchanged brief, almost undetectable nods. Softly, I responded to her, "I'll never tell."

Rendezvous

Some months after my mother's death, I questioned her closest and dearest friend about the rumors and gossip connected to my birth-right. Even though Aunt Eudora was approaching ninety years old, her mind and spirit remained intact. The following is my attempt to put into words the story as told to me through the eyes and memory of that friend, Aunt Eudora:

"She was pretty, your mama, and spirited too. She had a mind of her own and maintained her independence back when women were not supposed to be independent. She was smart as a whip and full of good humor. I won't speak badly of your daddy, but your mama was lonely and, I guess, bored. That is when *he* appeared. You already know *his* name."

"Your mama was a dreamer, she was. She loved books, music, and fancy things. I recall one evening in particular..." Cousin Eudie continued. I closed my eyes and listened to her gentle quiet voice as this discerning mental picture of my mother unfolded. "It was almost dusk dark, with the sun setting prematurely behind a bank of silver-gray clouds, offering some relief from the humid, dusty, dank air that hovered about. Behind her, in the parlor, the Victrola—you know the one I'm talking about—the Victor Talking Machine was wound tight with Glenn Miller orchestrating his big band, playing "In the Mood." How your mama loved the sounds of the big bands. She told me of how she imagined herself, in ballroom dress, skimming across the dance floor in perfect step with a remarkably handsome beau."

Cousin Eudie's voice was entrancing, "Ms. Savannah told me she was leaning on the doorjamb of the open front door watching all the commotion occurring just a few feet away. I expect she was excited by the novelty of it all and rightly so. The usually quiet ten-mile stretch of sandy rutted road that led past her home was now lined with motorcars and horse-drawn wagons filled with unfamiliar people and unknown commodities. I could understand why she was particularly drawn to the tall, dark stranger Mr. Barnabus was speaking with, giving directions to. She told me their eyes made contact, and she felt a stirring inside that had been absent for so long.

"These folks came from up north way to finish laying some railroad ties that would connect our community to the next town," she talked on. "That was some exciting times indeed, what with all the hustle and bustle created by this activity. I even said that to Mr. Barnabas one day, but you knew your daddy and the mind-set he had."

"Just another bunch of damn Yankees come to rape our land and probably our women too" was Barnabas's reply.

Sighing deeply, Cousin Eudie wiped a tear from her eye with the corner of her apron and then continued, "She swore me to secrecy as her account of this forbidden romance unfolded. Ms. Savannah and that Mr. Isaac Matheson found many occasions to take long walks together in the fields and nearby forests. I saw them myself, more times than they knew. I could see she carried a picnic lunch, and he had a blanket thrown over his shoulder as they disappeared from sight."

I remember Cousin Eudie telling me the railroad project lasted only a few weeks, and then they left as abruptly as they arrived. "Nine months later, you were born. Ms. Savannah and I never discussed this again."

CHAPTER TWELVE

ALONE

IT WAS 1996; I was fifty-three years old and alone. Not necessarily lonely, just alone. Although I had my children and a multitude of friends, there was no possibility of a companion on the horizon. On September 6 of that year, about two weeks after Phillip deserted, Hurricane Fran struck the North Carolina coast, making landfall in Wilmington with wind gusts up to 137 miles per hour. In the little community of Gibson where I lived, heavy rain and high winds brought down hundred-year-old oaks and loblolly pines, leaving a multitude of folks without electrical power for many days. My cleanup in the aftermath was executed with the help of my children who lived in nearby Raleigh, the capital of our state.

The state of North Carolina, also known as the Tar Heel State has been the recipient of many a violent and destructive hurricane. A storm with the magnitude of Fran has a way of humbling even the most stalwart of men; thus it was in the aftermath of this deadly storm. Fran dumped torrential rain, causing river flooding. Damage across the state reached billions of dollars. What an economic disaster. Fourteen people lost their lives in that storm. The nickname, Tar Heel State, originated from the production of tar, pitch, and resin in the colonial era and befittingly so in the mid-1960s, the pine tree was designated as our state tree. There are quite a few species of pines here in North Carolina: the loblolly, eastern white, longleaf, and Virginia pine, to name a few. Carolina Pines are the oldest in existence.

But I digress… Most of the men I was acquainted with were husbands of my friends. However, that did not prevent them from making sexual advances toward me. Consequently my circle of friends dwindled. I was invited to dinner, to community theatre, and other events by single men whom I thought had interests similar to mine. I had an interlude with a man twenty years my junior. I enjoyed a lengthy rendezvous with an especially attractive and engaging African American gentleman. I became disenchanted with them all. I could blame working three jobs and being stressed over making all the ends meet. Most likely, I was embittered toward men in general. I laughed out loud when I internalized the vision brought about by the thought, "I need a man like a fish needs a bicycle."

As the clock ticked on, I could see some order returning to my life. The yearning for a partner was renewed so, as many people did and still do, I turned to the Internet to "findamate.com." I had conversations with some interesting people over that period of time; it was a welcome distraction from day to day worries. Especially the deep seated fear I held for Megan…

THE DEATH SENTENCE

It was ten o'clock in the morning as I answered the phone. The scream, the agonizing, piercing scream ran my blood cold. The sun turned black and the world stood still. "Mama…Mama… Mama…"And the nightmare began. It was to be the end of her life, her dreams, her forever. The screams continued, although now silently, but of sonic intensity and with indescribable pain inside my head.

"Mama, you promised..."

I went into my closet. I fell to my knees, and I talked to God. The pain, agony, and suffering that began in June of 1996, lingered through three seasons. Did the sun shine? Did flowers bloom? Did the rain fall? Did the earth rotate? I do not know for all I could hear was "Mama...Mama...Mama...you promised."

Over and over I kept repeating to Aaron, Angela, and especially to myself, "This is our faith walk. It is a test we must endure." It was difficult for us to even take a breath. We went through the motions: ate, slept, bathed, and made mindless conversation. We knew that God was watching and making notes and keeping score... Oh! Some say He doesn't, but we know Him better than most. We have had the opportunity to talk to and visit with Him more than the average person.

Guardian angels were assigned to us by the promise keeper to comfort and energize us through the endless wait. And they stayed...and they linger still. Then in January of 1998 came a miracle and the screaming stopped. The sun shone, the flowers bloomed, the rain fell, and the world became more beautiful than ever.

"Oh, Mama ... You *did* promise..."

In the throes of Megan's bout with cancer, the outlook was bleak and dismal. Now after two consecutive years, she was pronounced cancer-free. We gathered together, this family of mine to thank God and to celebrate this miracle.

Chapter Thirteen

Encounters

THERE IS AN unknown presence in this house. She is female, appears to be in her late thirties; however her chronological age is difficult to determine. I first met her back in May of 1989. Was she here when I came? Could I have brought her here with some of the timeworn splendid furnishings I brought with me? Maybe she inhabited this space before any of us. I sensed her, heard her long before she became a vision.

At our first encounter, it was clear she had no intensions of frightening me. Her audible hums and whispers, sounding like echoes have been quite subtle. The same is true of the rustle of clothing; papers being shuffled; soft, light footsteps down the hallway and…

In the periphery of my vision, I can see her. Sometimes she is sitting on the hearth or in a chair by the fireplace. I have seen her, standing in the great room then quite suddenly, disappearing into the breakfast nook. One particular day in May, she startled me by appearing quite abruptly in front of me in the mudroom …directly blocking my path. She is taller than I am and thinner,

I think. Her dress or skirt is long …down near her ankles with a long-sleeved bodice and some sort of sweater or shawl…it's hard to tell…could be colonial or contemporary dress.

She only comes into view when my life is a little unsettled, and I am not expecting to see her. She just appears. This morning, the key turned in the lock at the back door; I heard it very distinctly. I looked inside and out, but no one was there. I wondered if she was coming or going.

I still do not have a clear picture of her; should I be afraid? I have a peculiar sense she is in and out of every room, but I cannot really focus on her. Last night, I was sitting by the fireplace, making notes in my journal, when suddenly I was aware of her presence again; a much stronger feeling than I had experienced in a long time.

My pen grew still and I waited, when to my left and just behind me, she was there, just sitting on the hearth, still and quiet, making no movement. I sat transfixed for a moment, and then began to write again. Suddenly, I was lost in my journal once more, recording my fears and disappointments, and she unhurriedly moved from the hearth to the kitchen.

I placed my pen and journal on the weathered library table, and I followed her into the kitchen. There, where I had left the napkin under my coffee mug, I saw the slightest movement; the napkin shifted ever so marginally from beneath the mug. I was still. Then I stepped forward toward the movement and all activity ceased. How can I reach her? Communicate with her? She seems as lonely and lost as I feel. Was this her attempt to bring us together to chat, over coffee?

Time moved on, and some months later, I was awakened from a restless sleep. I arose from bed, walked down the hallway, through the great room, and into the kitchen for a sip of cool water. I was startled, for there she was, perched on the bar stool, trifling with a folded paper towel as though waiting for me to join her.

My senses keened. The air, which I was breathing now with some amount of effort, gave the impression it was thin from lack of oxygen, causing me to feel incredibly disconnected. I brushed the sleep from my eyes, and quite suddenly her image disappeared. Was this a sleep walk; was it just a dream? I know I felt… saw her there.

It is understood that fear, stress, and anxiety play a key role in our perceptions. To this I attributed the visions and sightings I continued to have of my own personal apparition.

This ghost, this spirit of mine, visited yet again. I did not move, could not move. I lay there in my bed, awakened from a troubled sleep, my skin damp and cold from perspiration and my hair standing on end. Someone was there but whom? Who, what was standing at the foot of my bed?

On another occasion, I am sleeping somewhat fitfully, when I am abruptly awakened by something, someone tugging at the black and gold brocade duvet that adorns my bed. I turn and toss and roll to my left, then to my right and turn some more. There, on the right hand side of the bed she is … She is manipulating the covers, tugging at them, attempting to make them straight, perfect.

She ever so gently tucks me in, with tenderness, care, and concern, offering me comfort and reassurance. I lay there, unmoving and silent. The perspiration is thick and heavy on my skin…and I wait, not sure for what. The vision dissipates, and she is gone once more. How can I influence her, connect with her, assure her it is okay for her to be here. Actually, I look forward to her visits very much. What lonely partners we make.

The millennium was coming to fruition. Such uneasy feelings I have had all weekend. Friday was New Year's Day. I prepared the customary Southern meal of black eyed peas for prosperity and collard greens for good health. The day progressed like any other day except…except, I knew I was not alone. She, my friend, the ghost, had come back to visit. Little things, like walking from one room to another and walking through a space that must have been twenty degrees cooler than the next step away. And seeing shadows where no shadows could have been cast.

Saturday, in the early morning hour around four, I was awakened by someone humming, sounding much like the old spirituals that Mama used to sing. But it was faint, and I was unable to identify the tune. I drifted back to sleep. Then, today, I have felt her *everywhere*! If I could only turn quickly enough I could see her as she made her exit. Or if I could walk a little faster, I would come upon her in the hallway before she disappeared again.

Now, it is Sunday night, and I will soon make my way to bed. Will she make herself more evident to me as the night progresses? Will this be another night that she tucks me into bed? And how does she know? How does she know when I have so much turmoil in my life? And does she know what a comfort she is to me at times like these?

CHAPTER FOURTEEN

CULMINATION

I THANKED GOD MORE times than I can remember for giving me a strong will and a good job. Well, I actually had three jobs. Monday through Friday, I did case management for a local home care organization; on evenings, I performed skilled nursing visits for another similar company, and I worked weekends as the house supervisor at a local hospital.

I also thanked God for giving me strength and the good health to make it through those dark days. Finally, I was able to see a glimmer of hope at getting out from under all the debt that had accrued during my marriage to Phillip. Although I was in good health, I guess the stress of it all took its toll. My hair thinned, I looked emaciated from all the weight loss, and my menses returned after being absent for five years.

Our divorce had been finalized almost a year now. I learned through the grapevine that Phillip had married the Indian girl some weeks earlier. "Perhaps this will bring an end to his menacing phone calls," I was thinking this Saturday afternoon. I was outside, tidying the lawn when a car pulled into my driveway.

A young man got out, and we exchanged introductions. "Good morning, my name is Richard Cottle and an acquaintance of your husband," he began.

"Before you go any further, I must tell you that Phillip and I have been divorced for some time now, so if you expect to find him here you are sadly mistaken," I retorted.

"I did come to find him because I have lost contact with him for about eleven months now. He is just impossible to find!" He sounded at wit's end.

I remembered the statement from Sheriff Evans: "Slick as a greased pig in a contest."

"Do you know about the Corvette he sold me two years ago? I mean, do you know the truth about it?" he asked.

"Yes, I remember he sold a Corvette, but I never knew to whom. The car sat in our driveway for months and months. I asked Phillip when it was going to be picked up or delivered. He said something about a problem with the title," I told Mr. Cottle. "About three weeks later, I noticed the car was gone, so I asked Phillip about it. He said he had delivered the car to the owner that day."

"That is just about timed perfect with the last phone call I received from him!" His voice became more excited. "The last thing he said to me is my Corvette, the one I paid him $10,000 for, burned up in this very driveway! I never even drove the thing, never even had a title for it!"

Thinking to myself, *Phillip, the pathological liar*, I said, "Well, I know for a fact that is not the truth because I have been told his new wife is driving that very Corvette everywhere she goes." I shared with Mr. Cottle the difficulties I had in locating him myself, the threats. I gave him the name of the business where I knew Phillip last worked. Our conversation ended, and he drove away.

Two or three weeks later, Mr. Cottle stopped by, again on a Saturday afternoon. "I found him, finally. I went to his place of work every day until I saw him drive away. I followed him, at a distance, of course. He turned into a driveway and got out of his truck. That's when I saw it. My Corvette! Things got pretty nasty, and I had to get the police involved, but it paid off as you can see," he said, pointing to his shiny red Corvette. Restitution is gratifying.

TEMPTATIONS AND DOG RUNS

Don't get me wrong. There were some intriguing situations that occurred after Phillip left. Even the old man, Jesse Hill, who must have been at least eighty-six years old, lived just down the street, stopped on one occasion, and tried to "cop a feel." Sorry, Jesse, you are out of luck!

Then there was the day I remember so vividly. It was January 29, 1998:

Today is one of those rare times when I take a day out of the office and stay at home to nurture myself. Even on these days, I rise early for fear of missing a part of the day. Simple, thoughtless tasks are on the agenda. One thing for sure, I will get dirty and sweaty, and my muscles will ache by the end of the day.

Even though it is the end of January, the weather is agreeable. The sky, scattered with soft billowy clouds, still allows frequent beams of sunlight through. The scent of fallen pine needles is released by the sun's rays. The wind is whipping about, just enough to make the sweat pants and sweatshirt comfortable. I gather the tools: post-hole diggers, yard rake, tool box, grubbing hoe, two rolls of chicken wire, and set out to erect a dog run. Just minutes into the job, a familiar vehicle pulls slowly into my driveway. I hear the engine, and I look up. It is the husband of a colleague, Susan.

I first met him when he accompanied Susan to hospital functions and events. Matt was such a handsome individual: six feet three inches tall, masculine, and sensuous in every way. He would cause any woman's heart to pound, to flutter with palpitations if she allowed herself to go unchecked...of which I had allowed myself in my imagination on many occasions since Phillip's leaving. I watched in apprehension.

"Why is he here? What will I say? What shall I do? I so longed for intimacy with a man, yearned to be held passionately..." Already, I was putting myself there in his embrace.

Like a bolt out of the blue, he was making his way across the lawn. My heart stood still. It must have been a lifetime before I could breathe again. He stopped only inches away, and I could see his hands tremble as he reached out, touching mine. The rich, erotic fragrance of his cologne filled my nostrils. The warmth emanating from his lanky figure encircled me. We stood in silence, wanting and wishing what can never be. A single tear formed, found the way down his cheek, and my eyes, too, filled with tears. Body language is so powerful, and much can be shared without effort.

"All these years, I have watched you, desired you," he said. I nodded in the affirmative, indicating I understood this to be true; I had sensed this on many occasions.

He pulled me into his arms, "Please let me hold you, kiss you just once."

With every ounce of willpower I possessed, I withdrew and took a step back.

"Do I have to leave? May I...and will you..." he stammered.

I interrupted him, "No. You can't unsay the words. You can't unring the bell."

He turned and slowly walked away. I followed him to his vehicle; my heart silently pleading with him to stay, my integrity insisting he must go. He entered, closed the door, then made another plea. My answer remained steadfast. We know we can't and never will, but the temptation is ever there. He touched my hand, I moved away—forbidden fruit. We did not speak again. The temptation lingered as I stood there, soaking in the warmth of the sun, watching him drive away. That is what fantasy is made of. And that is as it shall remain. But today, a dog run must be built.

CHANCE MEETING

It was spring of 1998, and we were here for a purpose, at the Brass Lantern Inn's dining room—fine dining room I should add. We were here to celebrate their dad's last radiation treatment for prostate cancer. I was happy and at the same time sad. I was happy for him that the treatments were over, and he had been proclaimed cured! Sad for Megan, who, in eight days, would have another surgery and another biopsy in her fight with cervical cancer.

Conversation bantered back and forth as we made our way through the entrance. Megan took my elbow and held me back. "Uncle Steven and Aunt Sally are here, but you don't have to speak to them if you don't want to." How kind Megan was, always trying to protect those she loved. I gave her a forced smile as we entered. We were greeted by the hostess of the evening, and she led us to our reserved seating. In route, we passed by the table where Steven and Sally was seated. "I'll catch up," I said to our group, excusing myself, pausing at their table.

My mind wandered back to earlier years of my life and marriage into this tight-knit clan of a family. I remembered the scornful looks I received from this sister of his; how she manipulated to keep her little brother tucked tightly under her bosom. I remembered the days of us setting up our first home together, there in the back fields of their property, down a quarter mile sandy path, to a ramshackle tenant house. It was obvious; this family felt I was not their choice for baby brother.

I remembered Douglas working closely with her husband as a grease monkey in Steven's garage; I remember happily preparing lunch meals for my husband. I would put the food on the table at exactly twelve noon and wait…and wait…and wait. Looking out the back screened door across the field, I could see people walking out of the garage, I watched as he and Steven went into her home… I ate alone and put the leftover food away. "Well, she invited me to eat with them, so I thought that was the thing to do" was his challenging response on the many occasions this act was repeated. "Besides, we live in their house for free!" I certainly couldn't argue that point.

I shook hands with Steven, then Sally and slid into the chair beside her, praying that I was convincingly covering the resentment that still swelled within my body. "Why, you look just like your mother!" she said, and I thanked her for the compliment.

I looked across the table to Steven. "It's been a long time. I just don't know how long it has been," and he repeated this several times while maintaining a fierce kind of eye contact with me.

"Well," I thought, "it has been at least thirteen years." As our eyes met, mine were misty as were his. My thoughts wandered back even further, thirty-five years, and I remembered…and I could see that he did too.

I remembered all the late nights we shared our secrets and our dreams during the time Sally was institutionalized in a private pay mental hospital; I remembered the long stretches of silence we two were so comfortable with. Sometimes, words were not the most important thing. I remembered all the aching and tears and fears that melded us together. Sally, being of fragile spirit I suppose, with a keen desire to climb the social ladder, suffered a mental breakdown early in their marriage, must have been in their fifth year. The real reason was always wrapped in ambiguity and only whispered among a few. "I just can't do enough to make her happy. She wants finer clothes, a more expensive car, a brand new house, and I just don't have the finances for that, not yet anyway. I am afraid…the doctor said it would be a long time before she can come home, and she doesn't want to come home to this." And he spread his arms wide to encompass his meager surroundings, meager only in the fact she had brainwashed him to see it through her eyes.

In the mental institution, she was administered electric shock treatments, which were meant for catatonic or schizophrenic individuals. This convulsive therapy was introduced in the mid-1930s, when scientists believed that by triggering a seizure with this electrical jolt to the brain, they were able to shock psychiatric patients back into a functioning state of mind.

Thus wide use of electric shock therapy began on patients with depression such as my sister-in-law, Sally reaching its peak in the 1960s. The same treatment Hazel's first husband received. Even if doctors stuck to the standards of the day, the experience was horrifying for patients. They were wide awake as they were dosed with these powerful shock waves, their bodies convulsing, sometimes so intense they would break their own bones.

Sally did eventually return home six months and a multitude of electroconvulsive shock treatments later and life returned to its torturous journey for this brother-in-law of mine. She brought to mind a wounded animal or a crushed, wilted flower on a weak stem, withdrawing, shrinking away from the real world, docile in every way. When she arrived home, she did have a newer car although it was not the luxury car she wanted. She did get more expensive clothes and she came home to a newer and finer house. Keep in mind, I did not say new house; I said newer house. The new house came about two years later but most likely five years and twenty-three months too late.

House-proud she was, idolized that new house and furnishings to a fault. I can still see the sheets of plastic wrap she kept covering the guest towels in the bathrooms. Over the years, she became a master at manipulation with roller coaster emotions feigning signs and symptoms of depression just to get the things she wanted. You can call it what you want to, the after-effects of electrical shock therapy, cognitive side effects such as mild to severe short- to long-term memory loss is still brain damage to me.

We stood and as I left their table, Steven's blue-gray eyes turned damp with wanna-be tears; I walked away, my back straight, my head held high with my spirit lighter. For the first time in all these years, I felt a certain freedom from the contempt Sally had always held for me, and quite honestly, I now held only pity for her.

Our dinner was superb, the fellowship was first-class, and there was lots of laughter. Angela chatted away with stories and stories of stories; Aaron kept us in stitches with his wit and dry humor. Megan was mostly quiet. She was aware, though, of the efforts at cheerfulness. The accoutrements were perfect—soft gas lantern lighting, tables topped with white linen cloths and fresh flowers. The maître d` appointed his best waiter to serve us. We enjoyed the variety of great food this elegant restaurant had to offer: Surf and Turf, amandine stuffed trout, smoked duck with shaved imported French truffles, all served with red or white wine. Then coffee with slow dessert of baklava and other assorted pastries. What a grand feeling that we could still be a family, although broken of sorts.

Megan nudged my knee and leaned in toward me "Uncle Steven and Aunt Sally are walking toward our table." I placed my porcelain coffee cup back onto its delicate, gold-rimmed saucer. Steven was standing with his hand on the back of my chair, giving it a slight tug.

"You have to stand up so I can have a hug. I haven't had one of those in a long time." And I stood and embraced Sally first then turned toward Steven. We held each other tightly, and he spoke softly, "That feels good. I haven't had one of those in such a long time."

That great big lump in my throat prevented me from saying more than "I know. I know." Dear, old friends, clinging to each other for possibly the last time.

Just as I pulled away from his arms, he whispered into my ear, "It's been such a long time. I miss you, girl." There were tears in his eyes and wistfulness in his voice.

Bootsie

Lucy was visiting me for the weekend. She was alone and so was I, so we took advantage of get-togethers as often as we could. It was Saturday evening, and I was preparing our dinner. She was sitting on the bar stool, drinking Johnny Walker Red over ice, and her tongue was getting as loose as a goose. She started talking, bringing up the good old days. I sipped my wine and listened...

"Bootsie was Aunt Eliza's son and brother to Cousin Frankie and Pogo Underwood. His given name was Earl Allen Underwood. He was a very...debuna...what was that word you used the other day?" she asked.

"You mean the one I used to describe Phillip when I first met him?" I laughed at her and said, "*Debonair*, the word was *debonair*—you had it right."

"Well, he was that word that well-off cousin of ours, dressed real pretty and drove a fancy new car. It was a summer evening in 1948 when it happened," Lucy said. "Me and Hazel disobeyed Mama and accepted the invitation from Bootsie and off to Castle Hill Dance Hall we went. She said she didn't want us drinking that white liquor and didn't want us doing the jitterbug with those nasty men that went there. But that was mine and Hazel's favorite thing to do. Get a little liquored up and do the jitterbug, the two just went together. We called it giggle water; Bootsie called it hooch. Why, even the name came from the jitters that alcoholics get," Lucy volunteered. "That jitterbug was a wild dance, and you almost had to be an acrobat to dance it. And we did steal a kiss or two—or three. We stopped counting," Lucy stopped. My guess is Mama wanted to shelter them from the gambling, moonshine consumption, and carousing that went on at that dance hall. I fancy their innocence was lost even before this.

"It was two in the morning before we called it a night. It was black as pitch. Bootsie was driving us home, and he was a little tipsy himself, but we didn't care, Hazel and me, because we were fuddled and foolish too," Lucy told me with a laugh. She told me they were rounding a curve much too fast when Bootsie ran off the dirt road, jerked the wheel hard, and went back across the road, hit the ditch bank, and that is when he lost control. Lucy's voice fell to an almost whisper as she continued the story, "I don't know how many times the car rolled over and over. I remember hitting the roof then the door then the seat then the roof. I thought it would never end. The funny thing is, there was very little noise with it all. It was almost like *bump…bump bump…bump.*" She said she must have passed out or was knocked out because she remembered waking up puzzled, not immediately remembering where she was, then suddenly knew. She called out to Hazel but did not get an answer. Then she called out to Bootsie: no answer.

"I was quivering in a panic." Her voice was a little stronger now. "It was so dark, not a star in the sky. I fished around in my skirt pocket and found my cigarettes then the matches. I pulled the matches out and struck one against the side of the little box. The stem broke before flaming. I struck another and the fire appeared. I held it high to provide more light. I figured out the car was resting on the driver's side with the roof crushed in so much I couldn't even see the driver's seat, let alone the steering wheel."

Lucy stopped and sat without speaking for some time. I peeled potatoes and waited. Then she continued, "I lit another match, but I still could not see Hazel, so I put them back in my pocket. I climbed up through the shattered window, dropped to the ground, twisting my ankle, getting all tangled up in that mess of a running board. *Thank God I am so small,* I thought as I nearly got hung up in the window frame." She said she must have walked five miles before she came to a house, knocked on the door, and pleaded with them for help. "It was an older couple," Lucy said, "and I did not even ask their names. They got dressed, grabbed an oil lantern off the front porch, and we drove back up the road. The headlights revealed it all," she murmured.

What could be seen from that vantage point was the under-carriage of the car resting against the trunk of a huge live oak tree. The man got out of the car and lit the lantern. Lucy said she and the woman stayed behind. The man disappeared behind the overturned car, but the light reflecting toward the sky from the lantern could be seen as he moved about.

"There's a girl in here, but she is slumped all against the door and I can't reach her," he yelled out to us.

"There is a man in there too," I yelled back, but the man didn't respond.

"I have to go back home and get the oxen to upright the car so I can get to the girl," he said as he drove away. Lucy said she feared the worst, that Hazel was dead. Lucy said it seemed forever before the man returned walking behind two massive yoked oxen.

Dawn turned to twilight as they watched the man uncoil the logging chains from the harness and attached them to the sus-pended wheels of the car.

"*Giddyup. Gee. Gee. Whoa. Giddyup. Haw. Haw. Whoa,*" he commanded the oxen, then the car came crashing down. He unhitched the chains and threw the oxen's lead rope over a sapling.

"It was a bloodcurdling scream it was, but I have never been so happy to hear such a sound. Hazel was alive. I ran to the car and watched as the man pulled her through the broken window. Her hair, face, and chest were matted with blood.

"She was wild-eyed," Lucy explained. "Hazel started half cry-ing, half screaming again and repeated over and over, 'Where's my teeth! Where's my teeth! My front teeth are gone!' and it took a minute to understand her because she had no teeth to place her tongue against to make the T sound," Lucy recounted with a little smile.

"What happened to Bootsie?" I asked.

Lucy continued, "The sun was just coming up. The man walked up the road a ways in the direction of the dance hall and I followed, leaving Hazel in the care of the woman. About fifty yards out, he held his hand up, palm out, motioning me to stop. He squatted down briefly then stood and walked back toward me. Somehow his body blocked my view as he walked there and back."

He put his hand on my shoulder and said in a husky voice, "He's back there. He didn't make it. His body is pretty broken up. He must have been thrown from the car then it rolled over him."

That is the night the 1946 burgundy Buick Roadmaster was totaled, Hazel lost her front teeth, and Bootsie lost his life. Lucy survived by the skin of her teeth. Who's to say it was the alcohol he consumed that caused Bootsie to lose control on their way back to Crossroads. Perhaps it was purely and simply an act of God!

REMINISCING

In the summer of 1998, I was hosting a cookout for friends and family. Aaron, my only son and the youngest of my three children inquired of me, "Is Uncle Harvey still alive?"

The question came out of nowhere, and I was caught off guard. I was suddenly consumed by the memories that flooded in. I was overcome by them. Lucy's was a life of hardship even unto death. Harvey was her husband, second one, to whom she was married for twenty-five years. They divorced yet remained friends until the end…her end.

Lucy, my dear Lucy, was a vision in her prime. I do not have personal memories of her beauty in her youth, but I have in my possession snapshots and one photograph she had someone hand paint of her with those steely gray bedroom eyes and that come-hither look. If only I had been so blessed, or was it cursed?

"He is still living, Aaron. At least I have not been told otherwise. The last time I saw him and talked with him was at your Aunt Lucy's memorial service, and that was three to four years ago." Aaron began reminiscing, telling those present tales of his uncle.

"Now, talk about fishbowl glasses! That's the way I remember him. Why did he wear such thick glasses anyway, Mama?"

"I don't really know for sure, but it had something to do with his medical discharge from the army. He didn't like to talk about it, but he was sent home from the Korean War. It was shrapnel. Lucy told me his body was the store-house for multiple war wounds left behind of shrapnel from explosions he was able to survive. The only physical limitations he sustained were the severance of tendons in his right ring and little finger and injury to his optic nerve," I said to Aaron.

"Now I remember," Aaron continued, "Uncle Harvey was awarded the Purple Heart, the Victory Medal, the American Campaign Medal, and others that I can't remember the name of for his valor in fighting for our country. Aunt Lucy did tell me about that a few years ago."

I closed my eyes and said a prayer for my dear sister; old enough to be my mother, but I ended up being hers. That was toward the end of her journey, her stay here on earth.

I'll bet she is sitting up there with the Angel Gabriel, St. Peter and St. John, and all the others, looking down at me, and… and…I can just see her, with her head thrown back, giving a powerfully deep belly laugh, steely gray eyes twinkling and saying to her court… "That's my sister. She's a nurse, you know. And she knows everything." And with her right-on-time sense of humor, she probably added, "And if you don't believe *me*, why, just ask *her*!" And laughter in the heavens would be so loud I would have mistook it for thunder.

Chapter Fifteen

Farewell

I SAW HER ONE last time. It was a busy day, packing, cleaning, and preparing for the big move. Items were removed from the shelves in the mudroom, wrapped securely in newspapers, and packed neatly into boxes. I was positioned with my back to the screened door that led from the mudroom into the garage. Suddenly, I felt the climate change. Goose bumps sprang up all over my body and my skin felt taut. The air felt icy cold, and there was a faint odor of what I can only describe as gunpowder about the air. I could hear my heart rapidly pulsating and sounding like thunder at my temples.

There she stood, blocking my exit from the door. She was very still, but her long skirt shimmered ever so slightly even though there was no breeze. Her image was more visible today, and I could see that she had very prominent, high cheekbones. Her eyes were the color of slate and held pools of knowledge and experiences.

Before she disappeared, I made brief eye contact with her, and my soul flooded with overwhelming emotion, for her eyes held such sadness. It is for certain she does not want me to leave. She is deliberately trying to prevent me from going out the door! The last glimpse reveals to me that she shall miss me here, and as she faded from sight, my tears began to flow. Was she sad because she knew I would no longer have the turmoil in my life that always willed her visits? Would she miss me in that way? My heart tells me that I have known this figure in other times and that we are kindred spirits of sorts. Will she follow me where I go? Can I manage to pack her into my belongings somehow and transport her with me? In time I will know. I will miss her…

Reflections of Angela and Aaron

I continued packing, cushioning porcelain and crystal glassware with newspaper, filling box after box, allowing my thoughts to wander. I reflected on earlier days when my children *were* children…

From the age of five, Aaron owned a motorcycle of some form or fashion. Santa gave him his first, then as he outgrew one, Douglas and I would replace it with another—and another and another. When he was about nine, he and Angela were playing chicken on their respective motorcycles. This would be incredibly dangerous because both of them were so headstrong and relentlessly stubborn.

I heard the whine of the engines, throttles wide open. I could see the two billowing plumes of dust rising high above the full-grown green stalks of corn in the field just a few feet away. The dust plumes got closer and closer in proximity, so I instinctively knew what they were up to well before they came into view. Right before my very eyes it happened; he didn't swerve and neither did she. Bikes and bodies flew up in the air then landed in a heap.

In the beginning, as I sprinted to them, neither Angela nor Aaron stirred. Then as I came closer, I could see Angela rise up on one elbow and then shakily stood. Not so with Aaron. As I kneeled down over his limp body, I could see that his right leg was bent at an unnatural angle. The bridge of his nose was flat with blood trickling across his cheek and pooling in his right ear. He was unconscious but mouth-breathing. My inventory of his injuries from a visual assessment: broken nose, fractures of the tibia and fibula, and a concussion to what extent I did not know.

He was rushed to the hospital, the same hospital where I was employed, the same one Sandra Jones was director of nursing, the same one where Mr. Albright was the CEO. In the emergency department, the emergency response team took over. Procedures were performed, IV started, then he was transferred to the critical care unit. For five long days, he remained unconscious. Reassurances were offered by the entire staff. "I am confident he will return to consciousness when the edema that is causing pressure to his brain subsides," one surgeon from the team said to me. He was right on the money because Aaron aroused late on the fifth day, and by day six, he was back to his normal level of consciousness.

He laughed out loud the first time he was handed a mirror to survey his facial injuries. "I have raccoon eyes, but where is my nose," he giggled.

My fervent prayer was "Thank you, Lord Jesus."

In time, the broken nose and the fractured leg healed. Aaron resumed his lifestyle of racing his dirt bike through the trails and logging roads around the farm. Early on, Angela was stricken with remorse, but we were not accusatory toward her. I remember saying to her, "Well, nobody can call either of you chicken now, can they?" She lost interest in bikes after that. I always thought she was just smart that way.

His love affair with dirt bikes and racing bikes lingered over many years. In his adult years, Aaron became a professional motorcycle driver and won many first place plaques and ribbons. He drove like a bat out of hell, fearless and ferociously competitive. His pit crew was his two sisters and his mama and what a fine crew we made. The following words I wrote to Aaron after his very first blue ribbon win.

My son, in the early morning hours, while you lay sleeping, I stand watch. My thoughts are like wisps of smoke escaping the chimney from the smoldering fire to the left of my chair.

Images and flash-backs of your early childhood flood my senses. The challenges and frustrations you dealt with; the accomplishments you mastered are so vivid as to embrace my very soul. This is the surrealism of deja vu one encounters only rarely.

Your attainment of manhood has, quite honestly, caught me with my guard down. I feel so exposed.

Do you see, in my eyes, the fear and sometime terror I have for you? Do you hear my heart pounding and racing away? Do you feel the tightness in my chest and know how hard it is for me to breathe again? Do you feel the overwhelming love, the insurmountable pride and admiration this mother holds for her only son?

There is no doubt. You do! This I know!!!

To Aaron from Mama after your first place win at Roebling Road Raceway, Georgia

YOU WILL COME BACK

"You will come back?" He said pretty offhandedly and shrugged his shoulders, looking far away into the distance…far, far away from me. I took a step backward and to the side just to be able to look at this kind, gentle, considerate young man who had become so very dear to me. The visual was so overpowering! His long, jet-black hair was pulled neatly into a ponytail just at the nape of his neck. His eyes were ever so black and flashed with energy and excitement only he and she could fathom. *More alive than I will ever encounter again, no doubt,* I thought to myself. His name was Jude; hers was Jasmine. Only a few hundred feet separated my house from theirs.

Our bond of friendship grew even stronger as the threats from Phillip became known to them. Jude, with his high-powered rifle at his fingertips at all times, swore to protect me and my property. Jasmine was forever on the lookout for any suspicious behavior or any sightings of Phillip. They knew I was making a getaway from the sleepless nights, the fear instilled in me by that demented ex-husband of mine.

With the patience of Job, Jasmine taught me the initial steps of how to use a computer then gave me the courage and confidence to move forward as the self-taught student evolved. She would sit on a short-legged wooden milk stool at my right elbow resolutely and respectfully giving me pointers. Then she would laugh and say to me, "Mama, can I make you another cocktail?" Oh, the memories…

"No. No. I will never come back. You must understand that," I said to him in a broken, melancholy voice. She understood. I could see it in her body language, in her lack of eye contact, impossible for this fleeting moment in time.

"Life goes on," I said. There has never been a "come back" era in my life because I am continually pushing forward, leaving ghosts and baggage of the past behind. And in this wake, I also end up leaving dear, precious friends behind. I am continually humbled by the people I have encountered, the friends I have made along the way, and the enrichment they have added to my being.

How remarkable this young couple. They are young in years but so fearfully old in the scheme of things and the experiences of love and life… I have learned from them—and learned well, I might add. They have taught me so much about charity and winning and sharing, and…I could go on. It is not necessary. They have given with shameless abandon, and that is exactly how I have taken… My dear friends, I thank you! Oh, how you will be missed… God, you love them so. As do I.

SINCAI

Jude and Jasmine were such a delight. They were proud owners of a Chow dog whose name was Sincai. They pronounced his name Sin-Say. What a splendid name for such a Grand Chow! Just hearing the sound of his name conjured up thoughts of exotic and far-away places. Looking into his eyes one would wonder how Sincai became so gentle, so acquiescent, for you just knew he had stories of grander days he could tell. His thick soft red coat was shot with blacks and grays now from his long years of existence. He was mighty in size and weighed nearly ninety pounds.

Rescued from an animal shelter many years ago, Sincai became their companion, their "third eye," and their guardsman. He stood watch over their domain and doted on the couple that made their hearts and home his. He had free run of the place they called Havenwood. Sincai was a fierce hunter and loyal friend, but time took its toll, and in his September years, he became blind and frail. Role reversal took place with his masters, with their ardent love, as they protected him.

Now, he is gone, and there is a void in the hearts of the couple who loved and cared for him so deeply. Good-bye, Sincai. Oh, how he will be missed. In time, the pain will become more tolerable, but today, they must mourn. And I shall mourn with them.

For today, Sincai quietly went to sleep with his masters, these dear friends of mine, by his side. He was aged and broken and had such little quality of life. Glaucoma had taken his vision, and he could just scarcely walk. He was buried under the magnificent two hundred-year-old oak tree that stands just outside their kitchen window.

IN MY LIFETIME

It is February 1999, and my mind wanders. What would I want to see happen in my lifetime? Oh, I don't know. Let me render this some thought...

I would like to see…

- rainbows on a more regular basis
- snow in winter
- my children, more often
- a grandchild on my knee
- spontaneous laughter, yes!
- less care for what people might think.
- ducks and geese on the pond
- Sheika Bear live forever
- my children, without difficulty or distress
- people kneeling in prayer
- more random acts of kindness
- understanding of those who are different
- acceptance of a Higher Power
- all men equal
- dancing as if no one was watching
- people taking time to think
- Jerusalem, the Holy Land
- Africa
- my mother, just one more time
- my oldest daughter free
- the pyramids of Egypt
- hands raised in thanksgiving
- no more hunger
- The end to all war
- no more cancer or AIDS or other incurable disease

- myself, in love
- the end to violence
- peace on Earth!

Some of these, I will probably see, for I have quite a few years left, I hope. If the whole world feels as I do, I truly believe most of these things possible. In the masses are the answers. If only I may be an influence to one.

Chapter Sixteen

Rebound

EARLY IN THE year in 1999, there was one match mate contact that piqued my interest much more than the others; his e-mails were eloquent, his voice was masculine, and his adventures excited me. His name was Randy Welch. He lived on the northern coast of North Carolina, and I lived in the sand hills region of the state. Interestingly enough, this small town was named Gibsonville. Eventually, we agreed to meet face to face. We began sharing weekend encounters and developed a bond of friendship, which left me thinking this relationship could grow into something positive.

I thought about signs and premonitions. Was I merely born under a bad sign? I was born on a Saturday in May. It is said that Saturday's child works hard for a living, and I most assuredly was a living testament to that. Taurus is the zodiac sign I was born under. According to astrology, Taurus loves peace and order in their lives. They desire the beauty of a happy home life; they yearn for a partner and a stable relationship. But last night, I don't know whether it was intuition or premonition that I felt.

Last night in a phone conversation with Randy, and again this morning, I felt coolness, an aloofness coming from him that I had not sensed before, and this made my blood run cold. Suddenly, Randy felt like a stranger. Six days from now, I plan to change my life forever! To do things differently…to be ready for the new challenges of a new day!

Today I have spent hours upon hours packing perishables for my new home and my new life with Randy in Gibsonville! What an opportunity this is, requiring courage and resilience! I will be starting my life over for the third time. So! What is wrong with me? Why do I have such a sense of uneasiness? I should not be so apprehensive about the future, about life, about my new beau—or should I?

I cannot be prepared for this if I have no information. How much do I know about this man I met on the airwaves, and how much do I actually want to know? We shall see when the final vote is taken!

On moving day, Aaron and Heather, Angela and Ricky helped me pack the 26-foot U-Haul truck and the 14 foot one as well. In addition to these two trucks we loaded an SUV plus the single-axle trailer hitched to the back. Luckily I had dispersed a large number of pieces of antique furniture. In all probability I would have no need for all the formal pieces I had acquired during the years.

Randy and I were married in a private ceremony, and we settled into a lovely old farmhouse there in Gibsonville that we rented; I started over yet again. Heartbreakingly, Megan's health continued to decline; she was in and out of the hospital, receiving more treatments that were followed by more surgeries. By this time, I had changed jobs again. I was employed by a government-funded health care agency, supervising private duty nursing in surrounding counties for those that qualified.

I fell in love with all of the coastal counties Shawano, Waupaca, and Dare, with the sleepy little towns nestled there. I especially loved the County of Dare, named after Virginia Dare, the first child born to English settlers. This is also near the site of the Wright brother's first struggling flight!

I began my search for a permanent home. Undoubtedly, I must have been shown fifty or more houses before I found the perfect location—on the Bradley Bay in Waupaca County! In April of the year 2000, the purchase was made, and we settled into our new home.

The Nor'easters were troubling, damaging but always compelling. The sunrises and sunsets portrayed God in all His magnificence. The difficulties of being with my dying daughter and her siblings became greater and greater, consequently leading me in search of yet another job, one that would allow me more freedom to be available when needed. Shawano Correctional Institute, a two-thousand bed all-male facility came to be my new employer and would remain so for the next fifteen years.

On the heels of our union, a cloud found the way into our relationship. It came in the form of betrayal: the pornographic sites I discovered Randy surfed long after I was in bed, his midnight e-mails to fantasy lovers, his seeking out young women, obtaining their phone numbers, placing secret phone calls to them. Just a year and a day after we were married, I filed for and was granted a divorce on the grounds of incompatibility. He begged me to try again; I refused. That ship had already sailed. He moved on. I was alone once more.

The Winn Dixie

The air is cool and crisp with the early fall days. It is 6:38 pm, a Friday, and it has been a long week at work. I rush through the food store, picking up items to survive the weekend. I am on a mission…rushing up and down the aisles, putting this and that in the basket and on to the check-out lanes. I chose one…aisle number 4…no one in line except this elderly couple who have placed most of their items on the conveyer belt. This is good, I thought, as I angled in and placed my items behind theirs. In the background, I could hear the PA system blaring, "Aisle number 7 is open with no waiting!" I am satisfied with my choice, feeling good that I have chosen an aisle that will move quickly, and I am next in line…and I continue to burden the belt with my choices. I glance at the cashier and identify stress in her body language and in the lines of her face…and I tune in…

"We need some Schick double-edged razor blades and I have looked all over the store, but I can't find them," the customer was saying to the clerk. Her voice falling on my ears sounded soft, like the texture of velvet—smooth, like Tennessee whiskey going down.

As I looked at the customer, I thought, "It's okay. It will only take a minute for the clerk to help her with this. But then, I took a closer look. In line, in front of me was this very fragile elderly woman, likely in her early nineties, back stooped with osteoporosis. Her silver, thinning hair yellowed, in need of a shampoo. To her right was her most significant other, her husband, with his four-legged walking stick clasped tightly in his left hand with his edematous right hand dangling uselessly at his side. *Left-sided stroke*, I thought to myself. A CVA occurring in the left hemisphere of the brain results in aphasia and right-sided hemiparesis.

The clerk returned to her register. "Here are the razor blades you were looking for," she said triumphantly. The line grows longer behind me. The old woman turned to me and said, "I can't find the chewing gum he likes, you know he has sugar diabetes, and he can't chew the regular kind…it's the Dentyne, sugar-free kind he needs. She is fumbling in the candy and gum section and knocking items to the floor as her significant other stands patiently, waiting for her. His right eye droops, and he is drooling a bit. I stoop to retrieve items strewn around our feet.

The line grows longer behind me, and I can see the impatient, exasperated looks, the mounting annoyance of those waiting to be checked out by this cashier. After all, it is Friday night, nearly seven in the evening and everyone has much to do to get their weekend underway. The clerk is not focused on them; she is intent on helping the customer at hand, making very concentrated efforts not to make eye contact with those lining up behind me.

I reach into the little cubicles that checkout lanes are famous for...stocked with all the impulse items we buy when we are bored with standing in line... "Is this what you are looking for?" I asked.

"Darlin', that's exactly what I have been looking for," she said as she retrieved a three-pack of Dentyne Sugar-Free Gum from my hand. They complete their transaction and with their purchases, they shuffle away; she pushing the cart, he dragging his right foot slightly, following a step behind.

I make eye contact with the cashier and see that she is very appreciative of my patience, and I think, "There, but for the grace of God, go I." As I weave my way to my vehicle, with my shopping cart full of the "necessaries," I have a heavy feeling in my heart, and I am saddened by the presence of this elderly couple. Time will place me in their footprints.

AND THERE WERE TEN

On Friday afternoon, the fourteenth of January 2000, I left Waupaca County to drive to Raleigh to visit with my children for the weekend. My financial situation was still decidedly bleak as final payments were being made on my deceased mother-in-law's funeral expenses. Additionally, my customary income was now reduced from $75,000 annually to $39,000. Starting over has more than one disadvantage.

The purpose of this visit was to be with Megan while she was going through yet another torturous event in her life. She was convalescing from a hip replacement, necessary for the reason of too much radiation. It was also to take some burden of care from

Aaron, Angela, and Ricky as they made all effort to never leave Megan alone. They took turns, leaving work early or arriving late, even missing work altogether for that very purpose. Collectively and individually we prayed for strength in our faith, courage to face the unknown. We prayed for comfort to be restored to Megan.

The days were memorable, and they flew by. Megan's body was ravaged with metastasis of the primary cancer. Her appetite was nil. She was prescribed Ensure, a dietary supplement; however, she had developed an aversion to that. To the eye, she appeared emaciated, and it was obvious the disease had now taken control of her ninety-pound body.

I cooked all the dishes that had been her favorite when she was healthy before the cancer. Try as she might, she was unable to tolerate most, resorting to a few nibbles of watermelon. Moreover, we all suffered from loss of appetite.

The Lord gave Aaron, Angela, and Ricky a quality of spirit, a natural virtue, which enabled them to endure the adversities they faced each day. With calculated temperance, they provided for all Megan's needs. Their compassionate care was unfathomable.

How difficult it was to leave the driveway and say good-bye to them today. Needless to say, I talked to the each of them at least once during the four-hour drive back to Gibsonville. Any one of us could win an Oscar for our performance at some time or other, and today was no exception.

I was able to hold back the tears—well, almost as I talked with Angela and listened to her give me advice and then with Aaron as he reminded me to read my e-mail as soon as I arrived home. Ricky talked about plans for my next visit. However, I was not so polished that I could prevent the steady stream of tears from flowing down my cheeks as I spoke with Megan. Listening to the breaking of her voice was heart-rending; my absolute soul was infused with anguish and grief.

At one point, just past Atkinsonville, I turned my vehicle around and headed back West, searching for highway US 301 and the journey back to Raleigh. Megan convinced me to correct this emotional, whimsical decision and continue toward my home. The drive back seemed endless.

With the usual anticipation for mail from any of my children, I grabbed my purse and an article or two and rushed into the empty house and hastened up the stairway to the study. Two clicks later, I was reading the e-mail from Aaron, which merely said, "Make sure you look under the floor mat in your vehicle. There is something there from your chilrin'!"

Out the door and down the stairs I ran. My heart was singing; I had this humongous smile on my face. How unique they always make me feel. The door on the driver's side swung open under my left hand; as I leaned against the door frame and peered under the mat, a white envelope caught my eye.

How thoughtful, that they would go to the effort to leave a love note only a mama could appreciate and make me have to work for it too! I chuckled out loud as I plucked the envelope from under the mat and eased the flap open. My breath caught in my throat, and I was motionless for a long, long time. My face was awash with overflowing tears, for there, in my hands, were ten crisp, new twenty dollar bills.

SUBSTANCE OF A MAMA'S SOUL

It seems that as I grow older; I realize that I love this son of mine with more intensity than I ever thought possible. When I look at his square jaw and crow's feet that are just beginning to emerge at the outer corners of his eyes, I realize that he, too, has now come of age; and it saddens me that his youth is past. He retains the ability to laugh and play and be foolish, and I pray he never loses this, even unto the end of his days, when he is old and bent and moving slowly…

Ah, I think he shall still have today's twinkle in his eye and air in his stride even when he is one hundred… And he will still be able to provide that little combination nod-wink to his sister, and her heart, too, shall melt. This narrative I wrote about Aaron, and it goes like this:

> Once upon a time long, ago, there lived a young woman in a house all made of brick. One day, as she was puttering about, doing mindless little tasks she realized there was an extremely vast space in her heart that had yet to be filled. And it felt like a tiny little ache that was not quite pain but a nuisance, still.
>
> So she thought and thought and planned and planned and wished and wished and prayed and prayed and low and behold a tiny baby boy was delivered to her on a warm June night. Oh, he was so warm and cuddled so softly and smelled so sweet.
>
> As time went by, she didn't think about the little space in her heart and the little boy? Well, he grew, and he grew, and he grew.
>
> The young woman grew older and wiser but still, she thought and thought and planned and planned and wished and wished and prayed and prayed...
>
> And a phenomenal thing happened. That great big space in her heart? Well, it just got bigger and bigger as the boy grew older and somehow the pain was different now...
>
> For this woman just knew her heart would burst because of all the love it tried to contain for the little boy who is now a man and will always be the substance of his Mama's soul.

I love you Aaron,
Mama

PRESSED BETWEEN THE PAGES OF MY MIND

The year is 2000! The world didn't come to an end at midnight on December 31, 1999, as predicted by the naysayers. I read somewhere that in the twentieth century nearly four hundred million lives were lost to wars, genocide, and mass murders. We also in that century saw development of the greatest technologies the world had known. Science, physics, biology turned quite evolutionary. What a blessing just to be alive!

"On the first day of Christmas, my true love gave to me..." tune was running through my head as I maneuvered the dense traffic on US Highway 13, heading home after a taxing work day. It was January 5 and old Christmas Eve. My mind drifts backward to 1949 when I was six years old:

I am sitting at my mother's knee while she patiently removes the brown paper sack wrappers that cause my brunette curls to bounce softly on my shoulders. I am picking-teasing-playing with my baby sister, Pam, who is four years old and is sitting on Mama's lap. She is as usual in a pout, with her bottom lip thrust outward. She pulls and tugs at each curl my mama unwinds, but I don't mind because I love my baby sister passionately.

Mama is recounting the story of old Christmas...how, way back in the days of Julius Caesar, the Roman year was organized around the phases of the moon...and how, before the calendar was reformed, England celebrated Christmas on the sixth of January and that is why in some parts of Great Britain, people still call the day old Christmas. It makes no sense at all to my sister or me as we are enchanted solely with our Mama's voice and what a good storyteller she is.

We feel a particular excitement this night because we expect Santa will be back to leave a small token gift in recognition of just what good little girls we assuredly are. All at once, Mama became quiet, placing her pointing finger softly over her lips signaling us to be quiet. She gently picked up the glass kerosene oil lamp and held it near the window, turning the wick up a bit to increase the intensity of the flame for better visibility. The heat from the lamp left a kind of halo-rainbow effect on the frosty window pane. Suddenly, there he was! We were able only to catch a glimpse, but without a doubt we knew, we just knew this was Santa Claus!

January 6, twelve days after Christmas Day, is the Day of Epiphany; "epiphany" is Greek for "appearance." January 5 is the Eve of Epiphany. Most Christian faiths believe it was this precise night over two thousand years ago that the three wise men found the infant Jesus in Bethlehem. The twelfth day of Christmas then is in commemoration of the day in which Jesus appeared to the Gentiles as our Savior.

I never thought to wonder how my mother obtained the many books she owned with topics ranging from history to art to religion to geography and faraway places. It never occurred to me that we were poor because Mama could create magic out of scraps of yarn or cloth or paper. And she could spin a tale...

She would tell us stories of hobgoblins and brownies that lurked around our house. We always knew they were only mischievous little buggers and had lots of duties. She would tell us the hobgoblins were tiny, furry little creatures primarily responsible for cleanup of the spilt milk, the scattered firewood by the pot-bellied stove or biscuit crumbs dotting the floor around the kitchen table. She said the brownies were much more agreeable and helpful and went about cleaning up behind the hobgoblins and helping her with household chores. Mama would tuck us in bed, telling us to go to sleep so the brownies could do their jobs because "they only come out while we are asleep," she said. As hard as we searched and as long as we tried to stay awake, there never was a sighting of a single one of these creatures. Well, maybe just once we imagined we caught a glimpse of one.

Mama cautioned us not to confuse hobgoblins with goblins, and that we should watch out a goblin didn't get us because they could be mean and spiteful. She said that was where all the commotion in the night came from. It was the goblins banging on pots and pans, knocking and thumping on the floors and doors, making the screeching sounds we heard that we thought was someone screaming. We certainly never did try to seek out a goblin. Propaganda or not, it sure put a sizable scare into the two of us! I have since wondered if Mama told us these things to conceal real and true events that occurred at our home after the sun went down.

Getting back to old Christmas, Santa did leave a small toy for each of us that old Christmas Eve. I don't know when this tradition came to an end. Probably about the time, someone tried to convince me there was no Santa Claus. Oh, for the age of innocence again…

CHAPTER SEVENTEEN

TIME GONE...

MEGAN WAS CONVALESCING in my home after recent surgery, radiation, and chemotherapy, in efforts to contain the spreading cancer. We shared so much in those two weeks. She especially spoke frequently about her brother Aaron who she worshiped with all her heart and soul. She was the inspiration for this writing about Aaron. I assembled the story in booklet form, and this I presented him as a gift.

> The air was calm and crisp that particular morning. She gazed through the tiny glass panes that looked out over the back lawn. For such a long time, she remained there, watching the little blond haired toddler as he moved about, entertaining his puppy, entertaining himself. And she thought out loud, "My heart will surely burst from all this love I have for my son".
>
> Days were busy with love and life and laughter. One morning she found herself standing just inside the foyer. She peered through the tiny glass panes across the front lawn and watched him board the big yellow bus for his

first day at school. And she thought out loud "My heart will surely burst from all this love I have for my son."

The weeks flew, and months and years had gone by. As she watched through the tiny glass panes of the back door, she knew he was happy. He greeted his friends as they drove away together to play their final Homecoming football game. What an upstanding young man this now dark haired boy had turned out to be. And she thought out loud. "My heart will surely burst from all this love I have for my son."

Time marched on and called itself "Time Gone". That spring, she sat on the bleachers of the huge football stadium. She squinted through the warm rays of the sun, and the tiny glass lenses of her binoculars to get a glimpse of him. She heard his name called over the public address system as a graduate of that lofty state university. And she thought out loud, "My heart will surely burst from all this love I have for my son."

Now, many years had passed. Times and circumstances had made their mark. The nor'easterly breeze across Bradley Bay lifted and swirled the water into foamy white-caps. She stood on the upper floor and peered through the tiny glass panes of the French door that led onto the veranda. The telephone rang, and she knew it was her son, calling just to chat, just to say hello, just to say "Mama, I love you" one more time. And she thought out loud, "My heart will surely burst from all this love I have for my son".

TERMINAL

"Terminal"… the word means "causing, ending in, or approaching death; fatal." This is the definition offered by The American Heritage Stedman's Medical Dictionary and was the verdict handed down to my daughter near the end. Hospice was arranged complete with hospital bed and IV morphine to relieve the constant excruciating pain she suffered…

"Megan! Stop! Stop screaming! I can't understand a word you are saying!" I said to her on the phone in October of 1999. "It's the cancer, Marmie, the doctor says I have cancer again— it's everywhere. Mama, it has spread all over my body…I know I am going to die!" She wept uncontrollably. That cold grip of fear seized me again, the perspiration began as I steeled myself against the nausea, the panic welling up inside.

Knowing her future was nil; I felt I needed something *tangible* just to touch, hold on to, and identify with…and so the search for the crucifix began. We went from store to store, Megan with me when she was able…searching, searching. From the most uptown jewelry store to the lowliest pawnshop we went…hoping to discover the perfect crucifix, a symbol that would represent our unwavering walk in faith and would solidify our bond even more resolutely.

This day, we stopped in at Welch's Fine Jewelry store. We perused the items locked behind the glass of the display case. There it was! It was attached to small silver embellished card. The clerk unlocked the case and removed the sterling silver crucifix, passing it over to me. Immediately, I knew this was the one. We stood quietly by as the clerk placed it on a fine silver chain. With soulful tenderness, Megan fastened the clasp at the nape of my neck. For eternity, this will represent our faith walk as we approach other battles that are sure to come.

Time creeps, crawls, inches. Time, you can't see it, touch it, smell it, or drink it; but it is there. It is a member of the measuring system, like a teaspoon, to help us sequence events, a framework for measuring the intervals of existence. Everything about my life was all at once obscure. Time held no real meaning. Looking back over those agonizing years that Megan fought for her life, I felt like I was moving through a dark, thick, heavy cloud. Everything seemed so surreal. The days were dull, lackluster, and quiet. Just one summer past she had convalesced on my second floor veranda, the one that overlooks that vast expanse of water, the Bradley Bay, that reflects such magnificent sunrises and sunsets. This is the same veranda that weathers all the Nor'easters that surge through these parts. Early mornings and late afternoons she would sit there watching sunrise, sunset, listening to nature, looking outward...looking inward. She was covered with a lightweight lap-blanket this day even though the sun beat down with penetratingly thermal energies. I knelt just maybe a foot away, pulling weeds from the flowerboxes that were overflowing with fresh basil, petunias, mint, lavender, and thyme. The air was filled with their delightfully diverse fragrances. The riot of colors was intense.

Neighbors walked by, bicyclists wearing helmet's made their way along the graveled road. Some passing folks remarked about the ambiance of this place, how inviting. These sounds were warm and familiar. The neighbors called it The House Swinging in the Trees. My house sits on the corner of Cypress and Seashore Lane; the total acreage elevated more than six feet higher than that surrounding me. It is not unlike a villa in Spain with the beautiful gardens and the large windows overlooking the broad expanse of water. Nestled under a forest of grand old oaks and soaring, stately Carolina Pines, the building rambles back and forth, this way and that. It is wrapped with decks, verandas and porticoes. Williamsburg Blue with navy trim, this home blends in quite naturally with the stunning backdrop nature provides. It is easy to see why one would call this place a house swinging in the trees.

I said to Megan, "I sometimes feel as though I am in a fishbowl looking out while others look in."

She laughed at that statement and then became pensive. "You know? This may be the most enchanted place I have ever been." At that precise moment, my home on Bradley Bay took on a name of its own, "The Enchanted Fishbowl."

I could write volumes about how Megan suffered: the pain and sorrow of those long days and nights. I could tell you about her questions of what heaven would be like when she got there.

She wouldn't like you to remember her for that brief time in her short life here on earth. What she should be remembered for is the native abandon in which she enjoyed her life, her joy, her laughter, and her delightful sense of humor, her strength of character. Each member of the family was profoundly affected by her suffering, her lengthy illness, and finally her death. Megan's faith was strong to the very end; she took her last breath holding her daddy's hand with her right and her brother Aaron's hand with her left. She must have been looking at the very face of Jesus too because she had the most tranquil, radiant smile on her face I had ever seen. I knew she had gone home to heaven, but I have said that already.

In sorting out her personal things after her death, I stumbled across an old wrinkled scrap of paper in her wallet. I pulled it out and unfolded it, taking exceptional care for the creases not to tear. This paper had clearly been unfolded and refolded numerous times. There in Megan's own handwriting was a plea to God. It was dated July 7, 1987, when Aaron must have been in his sophomore year at the state university. It said:

> GOD, YOU know there are a lot of things in this world that I don't understand or believe in. I do believe YOU hold the greatest power in the world. Because of this I have a lifetime wish to ask for. Please keep Aaron safe. He is the most precious thing in this world to me. He is one of the good guys, not perfect but close; but YOU know that I believe he could never do anything wrong. He has so much life and so much to offer. So try and forgive him, always. He is strong in a lot of ways, but not as strong as many think he is. Protect him and if YOU ever have to take one of us, take me; for if you take him, you will take us both. Amen

How prophetic her words, how foretelling—be careful what you wish for, my darling daughter, for it may be yours. She did adore her brother and was particularly helpful in his successes at professional motorcycle racing. I have a photograph that hangs on my wall of Aaron standing in the winner's circle at Road Atlanta Raceway, holding his first place trophy, his gaze cast downward, his head bowed in the direction of Megan, standing nearby. That evening, after his win, I wrote to Megan, and this is what I said:

> In Gratitude
> So, here you are, at yet another Crossroads of his life.
> All time has been dedicated to making it happen;
> Making it painless; making it perfect.
> He looks in your direction. You understand the cue,
> "I want... I need...." He projects and you,
> Well, you being You, Deliver.
> His wounds healed fast in your care. They still do.
> All wants, needs, dreams are fulfilled just by projections to you.
> There have been so many pitfalls.
> The years you were mother, sister, and confidant have now
> Culminated into a true and sweet success.
> Now he is a man
> And you are a woman with the gift of love, hope, and understanding;
> A view for new horizons. Who best to know?
> And understand and share.
> You run the interference. You are his protector.
> You are his Special Force. You see and share his dream.
> Celebration time is here!
> To Megan from Marmie for making it all happen, I love you!
> August, 1995

How contrary to nature it is for a mother to bury her own child. There are no words to describe the shock, the peculiarity of it. In late March 2001, Megan phoned me, asking in a faint, fragile voice, "Marmie, will you come stay with me until it's over?" Words just won't say it, how I felt hearing that—*until it's over.* And I did stay with her until it was over. Her exact words are embedded in my memory as though placed there by a red-hot branding iron, "Mama, will you come stay with me until I die? I know it won't be long now...and...tomorrow is my birthday..."

Because she was unable to care for herself these last weeks, Angela and Aaron insisted she live with them in the small house they had purchased on Church Street in the bustling town of Raleigh. The banker just two years prior, had unhesitatingly approved their mortgage with a handshake and verbal affirmation. "Thank you, Mr. and Mrs. Robertson, for your business," believing them to be husband and wife. After all, they shared identical stats—last name, address, and phone number.

I arrived early the next morning and held my daughter in my arms for a very long time. How thin...frail she was. She was not without her beautiful smile, but the smile did not extend to her eyes and my heart began to crumble. "Such little time is left," I thought. This day marked her thirty-eighth birthday, and I could not let it pass without the celebration we always had for birthdays. As I walked around the party supply store, I looked the fool as I chose balloons in pretty bright colors and paper mache decorations to hang from the ceiling. Surely everyone in the store must have wondered why I was shedding so many tears while planning a party. I still have those decorations wrapped in pastel-colored tissue paper and stored in a pretty box at Teach's Island.

Two weeks later, she passed away. Much transpired in those two weeks...the coming to terms with the finality of death... Megan planning her own wake, her funeral, choosing the music... the photographs that would be displayed...even the suit I would wear the day of...God, and time has softened my loss ever so minutely. I pray the same is true for Angela and Aaron.

I still cannot speak Megan's name without a floodgate of tears spilling over. But you know, I don't want to forget. I want to remember the slight herbal scent of her freshly shampooed hair, her cologne, sweet and strong as was she. I don't want to forget the first time I saw her face; I touched her tiny fingers, my heart swelled into dimensions that were unspeakable. I looked into her eyes and marveled at the revelations they held. In calling to mind, I think we both knew the fate that awaited her. She grew, we laughed and played. She looked at me with those enormous onyx eyes; I was paying attention, and it created in me a kind of uneasiness.

I don't want to forget how she loved to embrace and hold her family, how soft her arms felt as they encircled my neck. I want to remember the incomparably strong bond she had with her siblings. If only I could push back time. We could say more about forgiveness, unconditional love, understanding the uniqueness of our relationship. I wish I had been stronger, braver even. I wish I had told her even more often how much I treasured her, how extraordinary she was to me and how much I would miss her. How hard it is to realize I will never look into her face again.

She knew so little time in her short life. She gave so much—brought an abundance of happiness and in the end agonized with unbearable pain. I remember watching her, watch life…knowing all too soon it would be ending. And end it did in such an excruciating, horrible death. But with her was her family, her friends, those she so deeply and compassionately loved.

She was so afraid…didn't want to leave…to go alone *there*…although she had said in a prayer for her brother some years before, "Take me first, Lord, for if you take him you will have taken my life, my very breath away and my reason for being."

She was our driving force, a lamp to our path every day. She brought so much joy to our lives and made us laugh uncontrollably sometimes even in our darkest moments. Megan was so special in every way. She ran interference for her brother and her sister and many times received the brunt of her mama's punishment that should have been dealt to the two of them. She didn't mind. Somehow, she felt that was her reason for being.

"Mama, the pain is so severe I cannot bear it any longer. Mama, tell me again what heaven is like…" Her eyes were closed, and she lay very still upon the linens of the cold, hard hospital bed, a bed placed by hospice in the home of Aaron and Angela.

We would spend long hours as I told her of the joy and laughter and lack of pain found in the kingdom, a place where there would be no more death or mourning or crying or pain. I talked about beautiful sun-filled days and streams of clear, pure water surrounded by such beauty never seen by the human eye. She stroked my hand from time to time. She would tell me how comforting it was to listen to my words and hear my voice, that it took so much of the pain and fear away. Her breathing would become easier and the lines in her face, etched there by the long-suffering, would soften a bit.

I miss my daughter…the fragrance of her freshly shampooed hair, the lightly perfumed powder she would brush across her nose, the profound love one could feel expressed by those black, ebony eyes, her light, happy step of years gone by. I miss the little wisps of hair that fell softly around her face. I remember, in my distracted way, pushing those locks back and she would hold my hand and gently place her bangs right where she had them and we would look at each other and giggle.

Tonight, as I revisit those mournful places in my mind, I see photographs and memorabilia of this daughter of mine, and I weep. I long for her touch and her gentle embrace. I long to hold her in my arms just one more time and gently rock away her suffering.

The shutter of the camera opened on time…and as it closed… time was gone. My daughter, my "all-knowing" free spirit daughter is gone. But she left so much behind in ways no one can imagine except those closest to her. Her spirit will live on forever, in the hearts of those she touched so deeply. The day will come when we reunite. God is merciful—the joy is unimaginable!

CHAPTER EIGHTEEN

TWENTY-FOUR DAYS

THE ASSIGNMENT WAS larger than life, and Angela knew the future stability of the company would be heavily weighted with the outcome. Twenty-four days was the time frame allotted to prepare for this monumental task. New programs with supporting software must be developed. Bugs previously uncovered would have to be worked out, the whole nine yards rested on her shoulders. There could be no glitches and no surprises.

Her *all* was devoted to this assignment. She slept fitfully, having night sweats and cold sweats—nightmares, somewhat terrifying. She would awaken through the nights with yet another issue making its way to the surface of her consciousness. She would rise, jot down notes, make entries in the database she was preparing, and then return to bed and pray for sleep. Brief respites would find her still entrenched in thought and planning. She was consumed by this undertaking. The hot seat was hers.

Four days and nights preceding "The Day" found her with loss of appetite, insomnia, stomach cramps, and jitters. The gnawing pain of fear was always only a heartbeat away. Everyone cut a wide berth, giving her the space to create…to do what she must do. Then, "The Day" arrived!

Angela rose in the predawn hours and applied final touches to her presentation. "If ten o'clock will just get here…it can't come soon enough," she thought as she carefully placed the laptop in its bag, along with other important paraphernalia.

Angela chose her wardrobe for the occasion with deliberateness. She remembered pointers from Megan when applying her makeup, in styling her long blond hair. She donned a deep burgundy suit of soft wool-blended fabric over a cream colored silk blouse. The smoke colored hosiery complimented the outfit well. She added small diamond earrings and a thin white gold chain encircled her neck. On the chain was a tastefully turned cross, embellished with a diamond that matched the earrings.

As she stepped into her matching burgundy suede pumps, she ran through her presentation in her head. "Once I arrive and get set up, this case of nerves will disappear." She gave a nervous laugh and said out loud, "I don't know why I am so nervous. This is not my first rodeo, you know!" She paused for a moment, "Megan would have been entertained by that remark." A brief moment of melancholy washed over her as she remembered a remark Megan made to her on countless occasions, "You are so beautiful, Angela, perfectly beautiful, in every way."

Angela is six feet tall and weighs 132 pounds. She is very fit as her diet is healthy, and she works out at the gym daily. She can cut an intimidating path when she chooses. I do not believe she is aware of how sensational her appearance is.

The proposal was quite technical, requiring apt knowledge and skill. She said she heard words like *brilliant, outstanding, magnificent, polished, remarkable* in the buzzing conversation at the reception that followed. Obviously, the executives of the company were mesmerized and impressed with her relaxed style and professionalism.

"I cannot believe I was so overprepared. But it certainly paid off because they purchased the entire program and signed a five-year commitment! That will boost our sales a pretty penny!" Angela exclaimed in her excitement.

I could hear the satisfaction in her voice. She articulated how, when the presentation was complete, she received accolades, warm and friendly double-handed handclasps, and great big bear hugs from her audience. I, too, could feel her success!

"Mama, I could not wait to call you. And...not to make you sad...but...I so wanted to call Nana and tell her...and...I... I wish I could have told Megan too." She held her composure because she knew that I could not...not just yet! Not enough time has passed...

Angela, my only daughter now, is a strong, self-taught individual, one to be reckoned with. She sure knows her stuff, and she proceeds with such boldness. Her grandmother, Nana, passed away more than ten years ago, but she is still embedded in my daughter's most immediate recall. And Megan, gone now just a year ago, is no longer a constant companion to Angela every moment of every day.

Angela still searches for the little scrap of paper on which Megan scribbled some words then handed over to her during another crisis... And on the little paper were the words "Kazi Wazi was a Bear...Kazi Wazi had no hair...Kazi Wazi wasn't very ...was he?"

Last year, when Megan was near the end, Angela spent most of her days working from home, just to be with her dying sister. Angela would include Megan in everything she was doing. Megan would sit and listen to Angela attempting to troubleshoot problems with her employer's company. Angela would preserve her composure until she got off the phone then would either explode in frustration or burst into tears.

Megan kept her good humor, so she would do and say dumb funny stuff just to lighten Angela's mood. One day, she wrote another note and passed it to Angela while she was on the phone with her employer. Angela started laughing so hard she had to terminate the phone call and regain her composure.

The day will come when Angela finds that little scrap of paper…and she will shed many tears as the memories explode around her.

Chapter Nineteen

Times of Change

THE OLD-TIMERS, THE ones incarcerated for many years still refer to themselves as convicts. That word lost favor over the past several years as the word prisoner became more politically correct. As a health care professional, I came to understand convicts were the more trustworthy and respectful group while the new generation of prisoners reflected the changing times.

For fifteen years, I worked inside a penitentiary moving about safely and securely. The rule that every nonofficer in the facility must be escorted by an officer was rarely adhered to in practice. I would find myself going from zone to zone unescorted but with a feeling of total fearlessness. In short order, I learned the ropes and became a game player just like the prisoners. My duties were varied and left no time to become disinterested in the day-to-day routine.

Days were filled with incidents that kept me on my toes and caused the twelve-hour shifts to scurry by. To the prisoners, the environment was their community, their own town. After all, they could go to the barbershop, the laundry, shop for food at the canteen. They could read their favorite books in the library, continue their formal education or learn a trade. Dental issues were referred to the dentist who was in house Monday through Friday. Mental issues? There was a psychiatrist on the fourth floor. An in-house chaplain was available, and worship services were there for all denominations and religions. Most illnesses were treated by the resident doctors and staff, but in case of emergency, the local EMS was available for transportation to the nearest hospital.

Such an occasion arose one Saturday around noon. A medical emergency in Zone 14 was paged overhead. Upon arriving at the scene, I received a staccato run-down from the officer on duty. "He said he swallowed a handful of razor blades, but he doesn't act like it to me."

The fellow in question was alert and talkative, showing no signs of trauma or injury; however, this was still a medical emergency and would be handled as such. Just like in the civilian community, the doctor's office was closed for the weekend, which left the charge nurse as the medical decision maker. The warden was notified, the captain informed, EMS contacted, and the inmate was transported to the local hospital.

This episode sounds simple and straightforward enough, but one needs to understand the amount of time these simple steps consume. Each doorway and barrier between me and the patient had to be opened at my request by an officer stationed nearby or at a remote location. A physical assessment of the prisoner had to be made before movement. The route then retraced to the medical department, the prisoner secured in the infirmary behind a locked door with an officer stationed there. The captain then assigned two armed officers to ride in the ambulance with the victim. These officers would stay with the prisoner until he was returned to the prison. If the hospital stay was extended other officers would rotate the assignment. There was never a moment the prisoner was without a multiple officer escort. Arrangements were made by the captain for two additional armed officers as back up to follow the ambulance in a chase car.

No shortcuts are taken. The prisoner must be packaged for the transfer. Handcuffs, leg chains, and chains connecting the hands to the feet are secured. The EMS technicians also make their own physical assessment, and when satisfied, the prisoner is loaded and transported.

At the hospital, the CT scan revealed four razor blades, three inside the prisoner's stomach and one wedged in his esophagus. The doctor in the emergency department that received the prisoner to her care called me, saying, "I have called Lifeflight, and we are airlifting the patient to a hospital in Norfolk!"

"You can't do that. You can't transport prisoners across the state line!" I yelled at her then depressed the switch and placed a call to the warden. "Even the warden can't authorize that," I thought.

The impatient doctor called back, confrontational and outraged, saying, "I don't know who you think you are! You are *just a nurse*, but I am a *doctor*. You have created the biggest FUBAR I have ever seen."

So another call was made to the warden. "I guess the doctor thought because I am *just a nurse*, that I would not know what the term FUBAR means," I said to him. "I'll take care of it" was all the warden had to say, and I believed he would. And, he did—in a matter of just two days; her name was no longer on the hospital staff roster.

With ridged conformity to the rules and regulations of the Department of Corrections, the patient was transported to a trauma center in the state of North Carolina. He was returned to the prison three days later. The medical report stated something to the effect they manipulated the blade in his esophagus, allowing it to pass into his stomach and make its way through the digestive tract along with the other blades. Nature at work...

Prisoners like these were disciplined for their bad behavior. He could be placed in solitary confinement and/or placed on a behavior modification diet called the Nutraloaf. Prisoners simply called it the loaf. It could be prepared as vegan or carnivorous. These are the ingredients: spinach, beans, cabbage, carrots, apple-sauce, instant potato flakes, and dry milk powder; throw in some tomato paste and bread crumbs then grind it all up together. Add in a little ground beef for the carnivores. This concoction was measured and weighed then baked in loaf pans. Prisoners were fed this diet until they exhibited positive behavior changes. The taste and texture of the final product was disgusting! I know because I sampled it.

I think the intent of the Loaf was to avoid the use of uten-sils to prevent the prisoner from hoarding items that could be used for self-inflicted injuries or as weapons against another. Or it could just as well have been under the guise as more punish-ment. But where there is a will, there is a way, as Mama used to say. And the prisoners were crafty and cunning. They had their ways of obtaining smuggled goods. Batteries, razor blades, plastic sporks were common contraband they hoarded.

Prisoners are allowed to have money that it is kept in a trust fund account at the prison where they are incarcerated. There is no limit to the amount of money that can be deposited to this account. Inmates with large bank accounts were capable of pur-chasing illegal drugs, cell phones and weapons from corrupt offic-ers. Friends and family, too, would smuggle them in on visitation day. There was no end to the weapons they could fashion from just ordinary items.

Sayyid Mourad Muammar

The first time I laid eyes on him and his eyes met mine was defi-nitely the beginning. The expression on his face was as though he was startled. I am sure my face held the same disconcerted appearance. But let me begin at the beginning…

As the nurse in charge, it was my responsibility to escort our newly assigned physician from the gatehouse through the main lobby and up the four flights of stairs to the medical suite. There, in the gatehouse, I watched him as they scanned his body with a metal detector, commonly called the wand.

He stood six feet tall, and if I offered a guess, he weighed about 195 pounds. I watched as his large biceps and quadriceps strained against the tasteful black scrubs he was wearing. With body search over, we made our way to medical, as it was referred to by those inside, exchanging small talk along the way. His skin tone was olive; his thick, neatly trimmed hair was black, and his eyes were dark brown. His movements were fluid; he walked on the ball of his feet, which immediately brought to mind an image of the endangered cat, the black panther.

I took him on a full tour of the facility, introducing him to upper management folks, that first day. He began familiarizing himself with the floor plan of the sprawling structure. "I can smell the odor of the concrete and steel, but it is hard to describe," he remarked as we made our way to the human resources department to have his photo taken for security and identification purposes.

"It brings to mind the odor of coins when they are held too long in your hand. Or the same smell as a ring full of keys," I replied. But the truth of the matter of my thought processes were menacing. My first impression of the scent was likened to the odor of the blood Phillip rubbed from his face the afternoon I broke his skin with the egg bucket. Repulsive…

On his second day, he was presented with an identification badge that gave him access to medical without an escort. The third day, he arrived with a tattered gift-wrapped package. "In the guard shack, when I came through, they said they had to open it for inspection," he said contemptuously through tightly clinched teeth. Instinctively he knew the officers did not appreciate being called guards. They felt the term was outdated and offensive. I gave him a puzzled look then laughed out loud at his little pout. His face softened a bit as he handed me the package.

"It's for you, now open it," he said in a much more unperturbed manner. We walked down the corridor to the lounge and sat facing each other; our knees touched. Like a lightning strike, yearning washed over me. I looked into those dark electrifying flashing eyes and knew he felt it too. I opened the package, turned back the tissue wrap, and there was a pair of scrubs identical to the ones he wore, black pants, and tunic, V-neck, short sleeve. "Now go change into these. Can you swagger? We'll be quite the couple as we make our rounds throughout this prison." We both broke out in laughter.

We took on the appearance of the Bobbsey Twins but only in our attire: black scrubs, black sneakers, and black socks. Out of unashamed curiosity, I wondered whether he wore black undergarments just as I chose to. The similarity to the twins stopped there. Now the staff and prisoners whispered, "Here they come, Sheik and Sheba." Obviously, there was a more familiar, sensual bond in the making.

As Dr. Muammar's assistant, we became inseparable for the twelve hours we were on duty. I learned a considerable amount about his background, how his parents fled Iran when he was a very young boy. He told me about the many trials he experienced because of his heritage.

We held long conversations by phone almost every night and most days on the weekends. Such a bond developed between us that we became what I can only describe as one soul in two bodies. It was magical, this emotional connection. "You remind me of that free bird Maya Angelou wrote about," he whispered in my ear one day, and it went straight to my heart. He insisted I call him Mourad, saying, "The name means desirable one." "That is an understatement," I thought. The desire I felt for him was pretty overwhelming; however, I continued to call him doctor. Didn't being single again give me license to live out the yearnings of my heart?

We dined by candlelight at the old flagstone restaurant a short driving distance away. We danced with much abandonment. His karma was mesmerizing as he recited Hafez poetry to me into the wee hours. "You know I have two wives, and for each of them, I built a magnificent house. Of course number one wife and number two wife are aware of each other, as this is our custom," he shared with me over dinner one evening. "This brings me to this question," he continued. Whether by serendipity or design I did not want this interlude to end.

"Don't ruin this," I thought to myself.

But ask he did, "Will you marry me?" I contemplated his query as I sipped my wine. The tremble in my hands was obvious. He reached across the small round banquet table and took my left hand in his right. Clumsily, I placed the stemmed crystal goblet on the table, spilling a few drops of the burgundy liquid on the white linen cloth.

"I can't be your wife number three! My values and principles won't allow that," I eventually replied to him.

"But listen! I will make you my first wife, the one most important... I will build you the grandest house of all and put you first in every way," he replied intensely without hesitation.

Maybe I wanted this to merely be a limbic brain experience and nothing more. I was saddened by this turn of events as I slowly and deliberately stepped back and away from the relationship. I felt so discombobulated; we had never embraced except for a dance, we had never kissed, we had never touched in an inappropriate way, yet our souls were so interconnected.

"Will you be my wife? Please reconsider. Will you please marry me," he asked so forlornly on many occasions following.

My response was always "Even though you promise I will be number one, there will still be number two and number three, biding their time...and I am a fierce competitor."

Father Time, dressed in his heavy ornate, robe carrying that hour glass, which represented times constant movement, stepped in. Doctor's tenure ended, and he returned to whence he came. The phone conversations continued for a while then dwindled and finally stopped altogether. Another chapter of my life... closed.

Chapter Twenty

Mark

IN LATE AUGUST of 2001, I received an e-mail from Mark Byrne. His e-mail opened with "I don't know if you will remember me or not…" How could I not remember? He was my first childhood sweetheart, my first crush. The earliest recollection I have of Mark was when we were seven or eight years old. His mother Sudie was sister to Cousin Frankie's wife Tillie. Mark and his parents lived in the District of Columbia and would vacation in the summers in Crossroads, visiting with family.

I couldn't wait to walk or drive the Allis Chalmers tractor to the general store to play with my cousins during these visits as I knew it would be an opportunity to see Mark. Well, the feeling was not reciprocated because each time I would appear the cousins would start teasing Mark about Kat, and he would run away in tears. He was such a cutie with his timid smile, pretty blue eyes, and eyelashes to die for. Time passed as it has a way of doing, and Mark's visits ended when we were about fourteen. I thought about him often in my high school years, but as time passed, my interest waned. I married my high school sweetheart and started a family of my own. Mark did the same; our paths diverged for yet awhile.

As the years passed, Mark, his wife and two sons, along with his mother, would visit Crossroads. I came to look forward to these visits and would find myself in his path, whether attending church services and functions or just visiting with my cousins during these occasions. Our eyes would meet, my heart would skip a beat, and he, being the gentleman he was, would stand, extend his hand, and nod his head slightly, a minuscule smile would emerge at the corners of his mouth.

Although we never acted upon it, there was always a little spark between the two of us. He has since admitted to having thoughts of me over the years as well and was still teased by his cousin Wallace about Kathleen even as an adult.

The arrival of his e-mail was no significant surprise. The message was thoughtful and straightforward, to offer condolences for the loss of my daughter Megan who had passed away in April earlier in the year. He was not aware that I was alone nor was I aware the same was true for him. He referred to me as country girl, and I referred to him as city boy. Here is an excerpt from one of the initial e-mails I sent to Mark:

> To the City Boy, I was just wondering if you knew that I had such a "crush" on you when we were like 7-8 years old. I remember looking forward to summers because you would be coming to visit "our cousins." On my, what, a turn life takes…

And here is Mark's response:

> Hey Country Girl. I remember waking up in the mornings with my cousins. I was extremely bashful of course. My beloved Cousin Bertha just teased me to death about "Katieeeee." I remember you coming to the store in the mornings, walking or driving a tractor and Bertha would

say "Oh, Markeeeee…Here comes Katieeeee." My cousin Wallace just directed one of his silly snickers at me. I wouldn't know what to do or say in response. I think that I just ran off. They never teased me about Sarah, another girl our age who lived in Crossroads. Years passed. I remember coming down there with my mother in the winter of 1967. I was a state trooper then. There was snow on the ground. There was a gathering at the community building on highway 305 for a cake sale, and we all went. You were there with your husband and two small children. I didn't recognize you. It had been years, and we were grown. I believe you were wearing a red skirt that night. I remember asking Wallace, "Who is that beautiful woman." When he told me who you were, I remembered those times years ago, and being no longer bashful, I thought how neat it would be to roll those years back and to have the opportunity for Bertha to have a repeat. I certainly would have had a different response. The few times that I have seen you after that, I have always enjoyed your outgoing and friendly personality as it matched up well with your natural beauty. Such an occasion was in the summer of 1976. We went to the Baptist church, and you were there with your family. You and your family came to Aunt Tilly's later in the day. You were always a pleasure and easy to be around. Certain particular things and people just seem to remain with you through life. Yes, life does take turns. One thing that I have learned is you don't take it for granted and there are no guarantees. Also, the things that you least expect to happen, do happen. Have a lovely day tomorrow and stay out of trouble. Mark

This is how our romance began… Our e-mails turned into phone calls, our phone calls turned into visits.

After one holiday weekend with Mark, after he told me good-bye for the thousandth time, after he drove the long distance back to Washington, DC, I recorded these words:

In a little while
I will be turning back the covers on the aged antique bed.
I will be remembering last evening, when he was here...
when he held me gently and held me
Fervently and held me possessively.
I will be remembering the waves of passion that washed
over me throughout the night as we
Turned in unison...touching softly and gently.
In a little while
My telephone will ring, because he promised...
And he always keeps his word. He will comfort and console me as in many nights past.
The sound of his voice will lull me to sleep.
I will be at peace and feel comfort because he has identified that as his job.
In a little while
My life will take on more meaning because of the good man he is.
I will rise to new heights and reach goals I have, until now, thought to be unattainable.
I will persevere for patience, knowing I will be the loser if I do not.
My feelings are fierce and intense!
In a little while
My life will be complete. I will no longer look wistfully to my future,
In search of that one good man.
He is here; he is present and I so want to honor him in all ways.
I have known Mark for sixty plus years. It seems like I have known him for centuries.
It is as though I have known him since the beginning of time.
The cells remember...

The foundation for our relationship took shape and form, and in June of 2002, we were married in that little country Baptist church, in Crossroads, North Carolina. The following story that I had penned was inserted into our wedding program.

He Walked Into My Life

I was seven maybe eight years old. It was the early 1950's and I fell in love for the first time in my life. It was summer time in Crossroads and life was modest then.

For many summers to follow I eagerly waited for the annual July vacation that would bring him near to me once more. Abruptly, for reasons I did not understand, the visits ended. Time moved forward and life's events occurred.

Some ten years later I saw him again. I was both astounded and taken aback by his presence. How handsome he was...so tall, so trim, so quietly sensual and my heart skipped a beat. He was married as was I. And in my eye a teardrop formed.

Life moved forward, not waiting for anyone and once again he appeared. More distinguished, more masculine and even more handsome than I remembered. The same truth was evident...we were both still married. The teardrop, now so prominent, was poised and waiting to fall. My heart was more than a little saddened by it all.

He presented himself to me again, not so very long ago. Circumstances were a little different now. I again married and still in search of "real love" as described by Margery Williams in The Velveteen Rabbit. The turn of events had left him with no strings attached. And the teardrop slipped quietly down my cheek.

Trials and tribulations occurred in my life. All at once, I was no longer married. I toyed with the idea of making contact with him but did not. He, being the person he is... walked into my life once again. The teardrop is no longer evident. Today, we pledge our vows each to the other and our lives become one...the new beginning of a relationship that began as an embryo those many decades ago.

STUMBLING BLOCKS OF A NEW JOB

For the first year of our marriage, we lived in his home in DC. I took a job at the Oberlyn County Adult Detention Center, and Mark continued working with the Oberlyn County Police Department. My securing that job was no easy task. My first interview was with the medical administrator; the second interview was with the medical administrator and the high sheriff. "We just can't be too cautious," the sheriff said then continued, "You will be scheduled an appointment with our psychologist, and a full psychological profile will be developed. You will then be required to take a lie detector test. Naturally you will undergo a full medical exam."

I was beginning to feel somewhat overwhelmed, downright flabbergasted at such stringent requirements. I wasn't applying for a spot with the FBI or the CIA for goodness sake. The administrator took over the conversation, saying, "The results from these tests will be meticulously analyzed by the sheriff and me. We will reach a decision at which time you will be notified."

So I went to the office of the psychologist. He interviewed me briefly then handed me what felt like a five-pound packet of papers in several folders. "Fill these out completely before you leave. I will see you again next week, and we will discuss the findings," he said as he curtly dismissed me to a tiny cubicle. There were four hundred multiple-choice, cross-referenced questions. There were neuropsychological assessments, intelligence assessments, and cognitive assessments. Then there was the big one, the Minnesota Multiphasic Personality Inventory with hundreds of yes-and-no questions.

At my initial follow-up visit with the shrink, I was given what he called an inkblot test, which consisted of a stack of cards that were spotted with inkblots. The theory was to look at the inkblots, describe the image my mind's eye depicted, then describe how it made me feel. As I offered a description of the image on each card, he always tried to make a sexual connection to them. I envisioned one card to represent two children playing pat-a-cake; he asked whether I likened it to a vagina. Another image I described was a bird in flight; he queried whether it brought to mind a penis. This occurred with every card. It was revolting, and I felt distinct unease in his presence.

He reported to me at the final visit that the tests revealed I was aggressive, authoritative, and forceful with men and with women. You don't like children and your sex drive is… By this time I had tuned him out and was whistling Dixie in my head. I stopped in at the lab and had blood drawn for the medical exam I was scheduled to have the next day. "Yes, I ate breakfast and lunch today without even thinking," I replied to the technician when asked. Truth of the matter, I was too disconcerted by my conference with the psychologist to remember I should be fasting for accurate blood test results.

"You have a 45 percent loss of hearing in your right ear and a 49 percent in your left, and I see that you wear contact lenses for corrective vision," the physician's assistant said to me. "You might want to exercise more and eat less because you are flirting with disaster as indicated by your cholesterol levels." He turned a deaf ear on my explanation about the nonfasting thing.

The kicker was the lie detector test. I had been married less than a month, moved to a different part of the world, had a new address and a new telephone number. When the officer was satisfied I was sufficiently strapped and buckled in the hard, straight-back wooden arm chair, the procedure began.

"State your complete name and address" was the very first question.

My breathing quickened, my heart rate increased, and I gripped the arms of the chair. I tried to explain to him my relatively new living arrangements but he barked at me, "Let's just start over. State your complete name and address!"

At least I was able to give my name, but I still stumbled over the address. The questions went on and on, but when he asked me, "When was the last time you had sex with an animal?" I almost jumped out of the chair. I was doomed from that moment forward.

The following week, I met with the administrator and the high sheriff for the final interview. By this time, I was feeling pretty intimidated and had told Mark that morning that I most likely would not get the job.

The administrator opened the conversation, "The written report that was submitted from the psychologist in essence indicates you not qualified to work with inmates. Your hearing tests results are alarming in that you may not hear if an inmate is walking up behind you so this would create a potential threat to you physically. The stress of a job in this facility may be too great because the report from the physician's office indicates you may be at risk for a heart attack or stroke."

The sheriff spoke for the first time, "And frankly, we are rather puzzled with the results of the lie detector test. To be honest, we have never had anyone fail so miserably. Can you, would you enlighten us?"

By the time I finished explaining, they were both reduced to tears from all the laughter. We chatted a little more amiably for the next thirty minutes or so. I excused myself and went into the lobby, waiting for them to confer. Not even ten minutes later, I was summoned to return to the office.

"If you will accept it...," the administrator began.

The high sheriff interrupted her, "The job is yours!"

I was grinning like a Cheshire cat as we shook hands on the deal.

THE FIRM

I came to know an inmate at the Oberlyn Adult Detention Center... The first time I saw Mr. Bittenhauser was in July of 2002. He was on his side of the slider, the slider being the cell door, and I was on mine. "Mr. Bittenhauser!" I yelled through the secured door as I unlocked the food slot for the trap door to open so I could pass his medications through. The noise made by the ninety prisoners and the deputies who watched over them was deafening. There was nothing to absorb the noise, just thin, lumpy mattresses and understuffed pillows.

As he approached the door, I thought he must be in his early sixties about my age, in fact. His once black hair was gray, and he moved with confidence and poise. "Very impressive, an attractive man," I reflected as I pulled the little blister packs of pills from the drawer of the medication cart. I carefully sponged off the circle of water that was forming under the gallon-sized iced water pitcher atop the cart.

I do not know for what purpose this person is an inmate. I have no need to know. It makes no difference to me. I am neither his judge nor jury. I am his health care provider. He is an inmate here *as* punishment, not *for* punishment. He told me he was "guilty as charged" and is awaiting placement at a prison. There the term will change from inmate to prisoner.

"Good Morning, Mr. Bittenhauser. And how are you today?" I asked as he came closer.

"Very well, and what is your name, nurse?" He wanted to know.

"Byrne…Nurse Byrne," I responded as I poured the pills of many colors into his hand. I watched as he placed the handful of pills in his mouth and washed them down with the cup of icy water. He knew the routine. He opened his mouth wide and stuck out his tongue to assure me he had indeed swallowed the pills. Inmates and prisoners hoard pills to sell on the underground black market that thrives in prisons across the country. Mr. Bittenhauser was not one of those.

"Well, have a good day, Nurse Byrne," he said, and we both smiled as I locked the food slot and slowly pushed my medicine cart away, toward another door—another inmate.

"Mr. Bittenhauser!" I yelled on another medication run. He appeared at the door and held his hand out the opened slot for his medications. "You know, wouldn't we be impressive as a team of attorneys with names like 'Byrne' and 'Bittenhauser.'" I laughed and said, "Only if I can have my name first on the shingle." He conceded that would be possible.

Then this week, *just this week,* I watched as Mr. Bittenhauser approached the door. His shoulders were slumped, his head bowed, and as he came nearer, I could see tears slowly wending their way down his cheeks.

"You want to talk about it?" I asked as I poured the pills into his hand yet another time.

He looked me in the eye, swallowed back the tears, and simply said, "I have *cancer.* The doctor told me today."

I pushed the medication cart to the side and signaled to the watch-tower for his slider to be opened. We stood outside his cell door and talked for a long time. We talked about the power of positive thinking, about fear, pain, and suffering. We talked about how one can "arrange" his mind to think healthy. We talked about God and the power of prayer. We ended the conversation. He reentered his cell and the door slammed shut, such a final sound. We will talk again, maybe more about "The Firm" next time.

Prisons are overflowing with the Bittenhausers of the world. I have seen on too many occasions that the punishment didn't fit the crime. The structured sentencing system leaves much to be desired. As the prison population ages, chronic medical conditions occur. The older *convicts* fall prey to the younger *prisoners.* All too often an officer will be on the take and turn a blind eye to the atrocities that take place.

In October of that year, the metropolitan area of Washington was besieged with the tragic rampage of snipers, murdering victims at random. I recall how nerve-shattering it was just to drive into a service station to top off the gas tank. I remember Mark and I standing in each other's arms and saying if the sniper took one of us, he must surely take us both.

Eventually, the juvenile Lee Boyd Malvo, along with his partner John Allen Muhammad, was arrested. At the time, I had no way of knowing I would be the nurse assigned to provide for the care of this murderer, Malvo, the younger of the two Beltway Snipers.

I am so humbled by working in such a place. I think this is where God wants me to be at this point in this life.

Rare Indeed

His name is Lugo. Luis Lugo. "I am Mr. Luis Lugo," he said as he introduced himself to me. His skin is the color of toasted almonds. His hair is uniform and cropped close to his scalp. When he turns his smile on, it automatically elicits the same from you. He is one of those folks who just make you feel good to be in their company. Mr. Lugo has not always had such occasions to smile. Who knows the real history behind his incarceration?

According to his medical records, from a hospital in DC, Mr. Lugo was diagnosed with lung cancer in 1992…ten years ago. Just last week, Mr. Lugo was admitted to our infirmary with diminishing breath sounds, decline in sensory level, severe abdominal pain, possible bowel obstruction, and high fever. I offered him comforting words, words of hope and faith. We whispered a prayer together as he was packaged for transport. He was rushed to the nearby medical center where he was admitted and housed for four days.

I was on the telephone today, behind the thick glass walls, when I looked up and saw Mr. Lugo walking by, escorted by a transport deputy. Mr. Lugo is six feet two inches tall and weighs 240 pounds and appears to be in perfect health. His eyes met mine briefly, and he sent me a wink across the way, and that great big smile erupted. Naturally, I grinned back just as boldly, and I felt a sense of knowing and such a sense of peace for him.

Later, over lunch with colleagues, I listened to all the banter about…

"But his reports say there is no evidence of lung cancer, all the tests were negative."

"The man does not have lung cancer, how can that be possible?"

Susan looked at me and said, "So what is that smile on your face all about? Do you know something we don't?"

I hesitated, all eyes turned to me and I responded, "You know about *miracles*. You may not believe, but I certainly do…miracles happen every day".

Who knows why God removed the cancer from this individual? Who knows what Mr. Luis Lugo will do with his new freedom from this dreaded disease? Who knows the direction his life will now take? God knows…

THE JONATHAN AFFAIR

And then there was Jonathan. Jonathan's story left me mortified, depressed, sad, questioning…and a little rattled. I allowed myself to become too attached to him emotionally. He was the same age as Aaron—and good-looking with an intense reckless façade that he presented to the world. I say I was too attached because I held too many emotions for him; I held a herculean desire to fix what was broken, to soothe his fears and tears. He left me angry, outraged, and irate. The embodiment of my very soul poured out to him…

So, what did you think would happen when you pulled that gun on the cashier at the Quick Stop in the wee rainy hours that early Thursday morning? When you pointed that steely gray .38 at his chest and pulled the trigger; watched his chest implode; watched the shards of bone and droplets of blood as they were propelled rapidly in the direction of your own clothing and skin?

What did you expect as your nostrils filled with the hot sweet scent of his blood mixed with the pungent odor of burned gunpowder; as you looked on, watching the pool of blood creating a rivulet that surrounded the patent-leather shoes protecting your feet and listened to the wheezing and gurgling of your victim as the life drained from him so senselessly. In return for his life, you gained only pocket change. Not nearly enough to buy your next fix.

Oh, Jonathan, I followed your case, you know, like a blood-sucking worm attached to your ankle, mesmerized by you, wanting to get inside your head, to examine with you all the why's that confounded me so. I remember you well, Jonathan, with your glib tongue, your exotic good looks, your dissing everything!

What did you think as the sun came up on your fragile, lax body as you lay in your drug-induced stupor, spittle and vomit trickling from your lips, filling your ears, spilling over to your jet-black coiffed hair? You lay there in the street, beneath the Washington Post as your shield, sprinkled with morning dew giving a surreal camouflage to your wasted appearance. Could you hear the sirens wailing as the emergency team rescued you one more time?

What did you think would happen to you, after we patched you up and gave you sustenance, food for your body and soul and sent you packing into the wild blue yonder, out on bail by some bondsman? And, you went your way, your way.

Tell me, what did you think would happen when the authorities pulled you kicking and screaming from your mother's home? Old withered men shuddered, and shrunken aged women peeked at the spectacle from behind rag-covered windows. Young children stood quivering and saturated in the cold sweat of fear. What, exactly, did you think?

I was there, watching you. What were your thoughts as you stood in that rank-smelling basement of the jail before the Magistrate, with yourself all puffed up and arrogant, sending fleeting dagger-looks all about? And as you were placed in B-Cell our eyes met… why did that have such a startling effect on you? Were you afraid I could see into the windows of your soul and all your vile, nasty secrets would be found out?

Now, you have returned to the place the high judges say you will forever know as home. I see you have added a third tattooed teardrop at the corner of your left eye. Your body language portrayed definite self-importance, but your eyes are vacant and I know it is only a matter of time…

In the subculture of convicts, a teardrop tattoo means you have killed someone. Each teardrop signifies another person murdered.

Jonathan was found, in his cell, hanging from the bracket that held the television mounted to the wall in the corner of the concrete walls. He had fashioned a noose from a flimsy, cotton rag called bed linen at the jail. He was alive, but his brain had suffered irreversible damage due to lack of oxygen. Jonathan was sent up-state to live with all the other dead souls still walking around in the state mental institution. God have mercy on him.

Chapter Twenty-One

February in the North

$\mathcal{I}$ NEVER TRULY BELIEVED "Southern Hospitality" was a fact. That was before I was exposed to *The North*... There is so little sunshine and the weather is so frigidly cold. The people of *The North* are even colder. People won't glance in your direction for fear of making eye contact, and I have yet to see a smile on one's face. They walk swiftly past you, their heads twisted away, even their pace quickens. The high crime rate in this part of the world may be responsible for this bad-mannered behavior, resulting in the people just being downright scared or intimidated.

Could it be blamed on the destruction of the Twin Towers and the attack on the Pentagon by terrorists in September of 2001? Could the reason be the snipers' bloody rampage, in and around Northern Virginia, DC, and the Beltway resulting in the senseless killing of so many, and the shattered lives left behind? We too, crouched by our vehicles at the gas tanks, embracing our own bodies, trying to make ourselves lesser targets for the unseen shooter's bullets. These incidents may contribute to the unfriendliness of The North. Mostly though, I think the aloofness was already in place.

Neighbors turn away with their body language blaring, "Don't speak to me!" There are no children on our street, so there is no laughter or chatter seeping through the closed, bolted doors. Youngsters walking by, giggling, arms linked, and whispering secrets to one another are as foreign to this place as *South* is to *North*. The postal service worker, with her canvas bag slung over her shoulder, looks away as she passes over the day's mail and mumbles to my smile and cheerful greeting.

A Southern transplant does not do well here. My heart aches for the gesture of friendship from a stranger in the car I just met on the street; it aches for dear, cherished friends and their warmth and laughter. It longs to be held close by a colleague. But there is an unwritten rule of *"Do not touch."* How I wish to be back home, in northeastern North Carolina by Bradley Bay.

If only I were there, I could take a walk in the rain or watch a beautiful light show in the sky and across the water, courtesy of our Father, during one of our remarkable electrical storms. I could watch the rapidly descending, graceful swoop of golden hawks, with the sun on their wings, brilliant in color. The geese would probably be awakening just about now. Slowly, one honk would turn into ten, twenty, then thirty or so. They would raise their fat, plump bodies from the water and circle the sky until their formation was complete. The afternoon would find them back on the bay, nestling among the old cypress knees.

I could watch the squirrels scampering up and down the tree trunks and branches and across the lawn. Neighbors walking past for their morning exercise might stop to chat as I sat on the veranda. Later, I could hold onto the young boy's dog that had broken away from his master, leash all tangled in the Pampas Grass and English Ivy. The child would linger for a while with the perfunctory twenty questions that only a child could emulate.

Eventually, I will be back on the Island in our home over-looking the bay, with friends sharing camaraderie and solidarity, merriment, and laughter. They'll not shun from touch or holding me close as is the habit and spirit of Southerners. I will be in closer proximity to my children so the trips to visit can be more frequent. How many visits do I owe them now? How sorrow-ful I feel that I see them so rarely. There was a time when that was not so. Today, my heart is heavy. Tomorrow, perhaps the sun will shine.

How mournful this all sounds. February is a dreaded month for me. If I can just make it past February…my spirits will be lifted and my heart less heavy. Was it not for the wonderful man to whom I am married and share my life, my spirit surely would die.

A Conversation with Mark

His expansive, powerful shoulders shook as tears streamed down his gentle, line-creased face. His forehead rested in his hands, and he was audibly weeping. "Oh, Lord," I prayed. "Please take this agony from this dear man, the man to whom I will spend the rest of my life." I moved over to the love seat and situated myself beside him, hugging him close for a while then sitting quietly by, with my hand on his shoulder; his sobbing subsided a little, and he began to speak.

"She saved it all. She saved everything. My little pocket knife, my daddy's knife, and even the small ring and bracelet I wore in the hospital when I was…" his voice broke, and he was unable to take the sentence to completion.

The heart-wrenching task this man had chosen for this day was finally to explore the boxes that contained his mother's prized possessions and to sort through the items stored there. The boxes were filled with bits and pieces of his mother's belongings when she passed away over ten years ago. He expected it to be painful, but I think he was surprised to find the chore to be this heartbreaking.

He was an only child, cherished so reverently by his mother. She wore her pride in him like bejeweled armor or stately medals earned. She had reason to be proud. As a child growing up, he spent many, many hours in the company of his mother where he learned to be a good man, to respect others, and to believe in the power of faith and prayer. She taught him the laws of Christianity as he humbly sat by her side every Sunday when they attended church services.

What a good mother she was and such a good example for her son, teaching him the right and wrong and how to treat his fellow man. She could be a clown as well, with such a good sense of humor. She wrote poetry and prose; Mark has those writings to this day. His goal is to have those pieces published to share with the world.

Toward the end, when his mother was in such poor health and not expected to live, the burdens he carried about in his own personal life were seemingly insurmountable. His wife of so many years (and the mother of their sons) was positioned to start life anew…with someone she had already developed a relationship… a relationship that did not include Mark.

Just out of the blue one day, his mother had said to him, "I'll bet if you and Kathleen found yourselves in the same area you would find a way to see each other." But he, being one devoted to family and responsibility, took this as a whim of his mother's fancy, not dwelling on the impact this possibility could have on his later life.

Sudie died an agonizing death in the throes of chronic lung disease, so common in our older generation, who knew little of the evils of tobacco. Her death has left a tremendous cavity in the heart of this great man. He cherished and adored her so.

FOUND COUSINS

I find myself reminiscing about childhood days spent with my cousins. How long has it been? So many years from when we used to play in the sun and giggle and whisper secrets one to the other...

Time sped onward, and in the interim, we grew up and grew away from our roots. Oh, but such a lasting impression of joy was stamped indelibly upon my heart. Aged, crinkled, and yellowed Kodak prints embellished with dates of 1951, 1953, 19... are proof of that. There we were, drinking Kool-Aid and eating sugar cookies from Mama's oven.

How happy we were just to hold hands, walk arm in arm, be together. I can close my eyes and hear the laughter, see the dimples and the shining faces. I see us in our homemade shorts and halter-tops and lustrous dark hair. Is that red, red lipstick I see? There was a well-trodden path from our house to theirs and times when the dust particles rarely settled.

Now it is 2003...virtually a half century later. I hear the same laughter and feel the warm smiles. Again, we are playing together, holding hands and whispering secrets, giggling late into the night. But now, we drink espressos and gingerbread lattes and eat baklava and fine Belgium chocolates... We wear diamonds and gold and drive expensive sleek vehicles.

The path is longer now, but the trips are as easy as when we walked that winding dirt mile just to be together. There is a knowing in our eyes that this is *the forever*. The bond has been renewed and will stay with us until the end.

At night, after the lights are dimmed and the house is quiet, my mind travels to the days of sun and sand days filled with affection and camaraderie, and I send up prayers of thanksgiving for yet another miracle sent to me by God. And I am humbled yet again. How blessed I am to have found my cousins again and forever!

Not unlike the feelings expressed by the unknown author of *Found Pennies* who said, "Found Pennies are from Heaven, at least that's what my grandpa told me…" And these are my feelings for these dear cousins of mine. They feel more like sisters, and I think, in a way, they are, for we share the same childhood packed with secrets only we can understand.

WINTER 2003

This winter has been bitter with snowfall after snowfall after snowfall. Lucky for us, the north is remarkable in keeping the roadways cleared for safe travel. Even northeastern North Carolina has been blanketed with snow with the outer banks receiving the greatest snowfall in over ten years. I am told every county of North Carolina was covered with the beauty of bright white snow! It may be some years before this phenomenon is repeated.

Soon, winter will be gone, the budding and blooming of spring will begin. We will feel renewed, refreshed, excited about The Enchanted Fishbowl and the reuniting of old friends and the opportunity of making new ones. This weekend, we made our grand escape from the north to spend some quiet time at Teach's Island, laying plans for the future.

Our entourage this year will include "found cousins" and their families. How blessed we are in this good fortune. Already our calendar is filled with scheduled events, just to be together, birthdays, anniversary celebrations, Fourth of July celebration in Raleigh, Thanksgiving at the Enchanted Fishbowl on Teach's Island, Christmas in the north. As time passes, dates and events will be added, and our excitement of being together will build.

This morning, as I look across Bradley Bay, I see thin ice covering the still waters. Mallards and Canadian geese are flying low, searching for an area of water that is free from the slush, to set down for a rest. Yesterday, my dear friend Albert reported counting twelve beautiful white swans floating on the bay. It is not unusual for us to see snow geese here. This also begins a new year for The Enchanted Fishbowl. Our inventory of garden art is growing, and the pieces are more beautiful than ever. How blessed we are, in love and in good health.

WILL YOU SPONSOR US?

It is April 2003, and it has been a wonderful weekend…a wonderful Monday with my baby, Mark. Sunday, we visited my children. And on Sunday night, we reminisced about family and friends and past lives. Monday, during our good-byes, we stopped at Gloria's Kutz and Kurlz to drop off Happy Stones that Gloria had ordered. Gloria's Kutz and Kurlz is where I get my hair cut, purchase hair products, but mostly visit with my friends.

Gloria was so excited asking, "Will you sponsor us for the walk-a-thon for cancer this year? It's in June, and I thought, well…you know, because of…I mean, with Megan dying…oh, my God! I didn't mean for it to sound like that!" And it was so hard to concentrate on her request. Memories and thoughts of Megan flooded my brain waves, and I screamed at my inner self to push them away so as not to make such spectacle of myself. I stumbled through a response, letting her know that I would do as she asked.

Megan's death was still so new to me… Somehow, I know this is how it will always be. I remember her begging Angela and Aaron to "please take care of Mama after I am gone. My death will be hard for the two of you but for Mama…"

My life has been filled with such crooks and turns and screeching halts. Sometimes, if I hold my breath for a long, long time and close my eyes, I can see a light that intercepts my journey… and, should I name the light, it would definitely be Mark. So in June, I will sponsor Gloria's Kutz and Kurlz in honor of my oldest daughter, Megan, who succumbed to cancer the prior spring. I miss her with every beat of my heart.

In just two months' time, we will be returning to Teach's Island and the beautiful waters of Bradley Bay forever. The thought of this lifts my spirit and warms my soul.

Chapter Twenty-Two

Catharsis

ONE'S BRAIN CAN be likened to an egg, the brain being contained in the skull as the egg within the shell. Yet there is no containing one's mind. This being said to help you understand the power a mother can exert over a child such as in the case of my brother Nick. It was late July 2003 and Nick was visiting Mark and me for a few days. We talked about old times, good and bad; Nick sipped his whiskey sour, Mark enjoyed his brandy, and I delighted in Grand Marnier over ice. Acknowledging it was late, we turned down the lights and went to bed. I could hear Nick cough occasionally in the guest room, tossing, turning. Mark's soft gentle snoring soon lulled me to sleep.

It was Nick's screaming that awakened me. Shrill, incessant, and nerve-shattering... So agonizing was the sound my blood ran cold and the hairs on my neck stood up. I lay frozen, waiting for the screaming to stop. And I began to sweat, just like in the old days. His screams turned into sobs, such an empty, hollow sound. Then there was silence...a deafening silence. The grandfather clock chimed twice for two o'clock in the morning. I watched the minute hand of the meticulously painted surface of the porcelain clock on the table by my bed sweep slowly, slowly as if suspended in time. I knew that sleep for this night was over for me and over for Nick.

As I lay there, my breathing shallow so as not to miss a sound from the guest room, such sadness came over me, and I began to weep, for me, for Nick, and for Mama. Our mother, who could, yet to this precise day continue to plague Nick, through dreams and nightmares, even in the eighth decade of his life. It is amazing what the dormant mind, in a deep sleep, can extract from suppressed childhood horrors. I tossed and turned fitfully, unable to obtain more than a tease of a nap.

It was now four o'clock in the morning. Sluggishly I got out of bed and made my way into the bathroom. The face looking back at me from the mirror showed signs of aging. "How much I resemble my mother," I thought as I leaned forward over the porcelain lavatory with the gold embellished fixtures. I splashed water across my cheeks, patted my face dry, taking a deep deliberate inhalation.

Walking down the long dark hallway, I could see faint light from the dining room casting shadows on the rich plum-colored carpeting of the conversation room. A thick layer of smoke from too many cigarettes hung motionless in the air. Smoking inside my home was not allowed, well, except for Nick. He knew the answer to his question even before he asked. "Well, of course, it's okay for you to smoke inside Nick. I know how badly those old, tired bones ache from moving about," I said to him.

The aroma of rich, dark-roasted coffee enveloped me, momentarily distracting me from the smoke. Nick was there, sitting at the breakfast table, steaming cup of coffee in one hand and a brown tapered cigarillo in the other. I leaned over, gave him a kiss on top of his thinning hair, and sat down opposite him.

"Mornin' to ya. Coffee's ready. I'll pour you a cup," he said. He rose slowly, positioning his four-legged walking cane squarely on the tiled floor, painfully moving toward the coffee station in one corner of the kitchen.

"Restless night, huh?" I asked offhandedly. He shuffled back to the table where I was sitting and put my coffee mug down, his trembling hand splashing a few drops of the dark liquid onto the aged, handmade tablecloth that topped the timeworn oak table. The ash from the cigarillo he held between his lips fell unnoticed onto the floor. Nick did not respond until after he had repositioned his chair with his walking stick and settled in, comfortable again. The chair moaned in opposition as he shifted his tired, frail body, reaching for the ashtray. "Yeah," he said, rolling the word off his tongue until it came out in three syllables.

"Want to talk about it?" I asked, wondering if I should have asked and even if I wanted to hear his response.

There we sat in silence for a long time before he spoke again. Absentmindedly, I rearranged the perfectly arranged wildflower bouquet in the crystal vase that sat in the center of the table, and I waited.

"It's Mama," he said in a quiet, choked voice. "It's Mama. I'm better than I used to be. Time was I would have these nightmares about her two, three times a week. Now it is only two, three times a month. I'm grateful for that." I sipped my coffee. Nick sipped his. I brushed imaginary crumbs from the table. I gazed into the darkness surrounding us, Nick and me, inside and out.

"Do you remember how she used to beat me? How she always took my things away from me? Tried to take my very spirit away from me?" He asked in a broken, grieving whisper of a voice.

I remembered better than anyone. Even to this very day, my heart and spirit acknowledge the pain for him that it did all those many years ago. And in my mind's eye, I could see him, my brother, at fourteen years old, with little trickles of blood, finding their way down his slim, tan torso and legs as she switched him incessantly with the thin flexible bough she had him retrieve from the shrubbery growing nearby...such was the result of my mother's unbridled rage toward him. Neither of us could ever understand why.

I remembered, as a child, standing barefoot beside my mama in the hot sand, waiting by the mailbox on our rural route, for the mail delivery, waiting for the allotment check that would arrive without fail near the first of every month...a check for forty dollars...a gift of love through hard-earned military dollars from a son to his mother. This money would provide food for the table and pay for fabric for new clothing for my baby sister and me. He kept for himself twenty-two dollars. This check arrived, uninterrupted, from 1953 until 1956 as a love offering from Nick to his family...and then he married Lynette, and the checks arrived no more.

"She is still chasing me, you know...beating me, finding me, no matter where I hide, to this very day. The counseling I've had has helped some... But I don't think I will ever be completely rid of the nightmares." I waited through the silence again. His cigarillo, left lying in the ashtray had smoldered to dry ashes and our coffee was cold. The grandfather clock chimed six times, the air was still.

What a powerful influence Mama still had on Nick...a true man's man. Even after his distinguished twenty-five-year military career as a paratrooper, retiring as a sergeant first class. Even after all the horrors and dangers of the Vietnam War. The Vietnam War lingering over twenty-five years, when in the 1950s, the US began sending our troops there. Nearly three million young men and women were sent to fight for what some would say was such a controversial cause. Nick, now in his waning years, reduced to tears because of the tyranny vented by his mother.

Without speaking more, Nick slowly rose from his chair and walked out on to the veranda and into the beautiful brilliant sunlight that filtered through the Carolina Pines. He stood and watched the foaming whitecaps on Bradley Bay break against the bulkhead. Catharsis of the soul...

God only knows the poisons lying repressed, trapped in Nick's mind, waiting, lurking in the shadow of his thoughts, to be unleashed unexpectedly.

THE AROMA OF BACON

It is unnerving sometimes just how or when flashbacks and memories are triggered. It is February 2004. This morning, I have the kitchen window open about six inches. The brisk, frigid northeastern wind is strongly forcing its way in, and I am frying bacon for breakfast. Suddenly, I feel exhilaration, and in my mind, I hear the first rumbling sound of the big engines of racing bikes. My nose and fingers are raw as I see myself standing by the barbeque grill, frying bacon, cooking pancakes, and scrambled eggs.

I hear the muffled voices of early risers at Road Atlanta and see the guys as they go about, stretching, rubbing sleep from their eyes. One by one, they make their way to our canopy, a dozen or so good-looking young men, following their noses so to speak. Their coffee cups are steaming as I pour them yet another. They stand around, making idle conversation with Aaron, Angela, and Megan as plans are laid for the day of sprint racing. The day will be filled with labor and friendship and sharing. Some will experience heartbreak and disappointment, physical and emotional pain. Someone will take home the gold. Who will take the honor of winning first place today?

In my mind's eye, I see their racing leathers being readied; the visors on the helmets polished to being virtually undetectable. The bikes, sitting on their stands with tire warmers in place assuring optimal traction into the first turn. Fuel levels are topped off, and the suspension settings checked one last time. The bikes are meticulously cleaned before each sprint race to make certain the sponsors stickers are glowing.

It was impressive to me that the folks that managed the racetracks arranged for a church service each Sunday morning at nine o'clock. It was pretty informal but always intensely spiritual lasting about thirty minutes. What a striking mood elevator this was for everyone.

When the bikes fired, the odor of racing fuel filled the air; the rumble of the powerful engines was near deafening. Slowly, each biker made his way to the start-finish line and took his place. The excitement built; underneath my feet the earth trembled as the uniform roar from twenty-thirty bikes rose to a thunderous crescendo.

I watched as the one designated to perform the task held up a two-minute warning board giving everyone time to locate their grid position. With only thirty seconds to go, he turned the board sideways. As the grid marshall was assuring everyone was in place and ready, the thirty seconds elapsed. The green flag was waved, triggering the release of the clutch as the bikes rocketed forward.

I recalled the dreaded red flags to indicate the race must come to a halt because somewhere on the track a driver was down… The white flag was the most anticipated as it signaled only one lap to go. How addicting this professional motorcycle racing!

Big strong arms encircle my waist as kisses are planted on my cheek. I am brought back to the present by my mate Mark. I am not at Road Atlanta at all but in my galley kitchen on Bradley Bay. The bacon is still frying as I turn to smile at Mark. I am fulfilled; I am loved and respected. He doesn't know where I have been in my wandering thoughts. No need to share. Some things are just too personal. I will leave my memory bank for now… God knows I will be back.

HAPPY MOTHER'S DAY TO THE QUEEN OF MOTHERS

This is a poem my dearest Mark wrote to me on this special day on May 9, 2004.

My wonderful wife and wonderful mother, the best that
can be
How lucky we are to have her, those wonderful children
and me
Having her as my wife, God's blessing alone by far
And her attention to motherhood, Oh, how lucky we are
Her children now grown, traveling the paths of life
Still seek and adore her, Kathleen, my wife
She has been by their side, since they were born
Sharing life's experiences whether joy or to mourn
Their love for each other, no others can compare
Side by side, life's adventures they will always share
So Happy Mother's Day, my Kathleen and wife
To your children and me, you are our life

Your husband, Mark

Chapter Twenty-Three

What I Believe

I BELIEVE THE BIBLE was divinely inspired and written by men who wanted so fervently for us to accept their teachings. It may be skewed a little, but I don't believe it is propaganda. I think that throughout the centuries, in interpretation some of the meaning may have been lost or altered. I do believe in the "core teaching" that is there though.

I believe "even the hairs on your head are numbered" even before the embryo is fertilized. I believe God has a plan for each of us, and that we have lessons to learn, lessons to teach. I know how we all agonized in prayer to God from the precise moment we knew Megan had cancer, and that what we begged for, Megan to be cured and live a long happy life was not granted. But God answered needs in all of us with Megan's passing. I know that I yelled and screamed at God to heal my daughter, and I am confident he did. Maybe I didn't understand what needed healing in Megan, but God knew the future, and he knew it was time for Megan to go home. I have never been angry at God for taking her. I do believe Megan's illness and death helped put my life in order and lead me to Mark. I believe it helped place my son

Aaron on safer ground, no more motorcycle racing or driving all night to arrive at the track on time, no more burning the candle at both ends. I believe her illness and death brought my children's dad back into their lives or perhaps for the first time. I believe it gave my sister Pam and her family the opportunity to do the right thing, which they did for the short run, but they faltered and are now lost in their own selfish world again.

I believe Megan's illness and death gave Angela and Ricky a stronger bond than they ever could have had. I think Megan lives on through Angela and Amber to this very day. I have faith that God will always prevail and answer my prayers even though many times I do not know what to pray for. But He knows my every need.I believe this gave Hazel and her children an occasion to right a wrong. They chose not. I think it gave my children's paternal family the opportunity to ask forgiveness and to right the wrongs they had done to us as a family unit. Only one of Douglas's sisters stepped up to the plate. She carefully whispered in my ear with her hand cupped close to my face to be sure her words were not overheard, "I am so sorry for the way I have treated you all these years, but don't tell anyone I said that." I doubt that did much to alleviate the guilt she harbored in her heart.

I do believe God is in control, yet with free will, He allows us to move forward with inferior ideas, unfavorable decisions, and contrite temperaments. This is when I think we are on our own…I believe in divine forgiveness, and I believe in heaven and hell. My heart's desire is to go to heaven, and I want all my family and friends to go there with me. It is so hard for us to talk about Megan and her death. Maybe, if we could…

BLESSINGS ARE LIKE SHOWERS

Blessings appear in such diverse shapes and forms; they can be imperceptible or concrete. They may present to any one or all of our senses. We may be conscious of a blessing, or it may appear in the form of an unconscious nature. In the duration of one split second, blessings abound, we may recognize it immediately or as an afterthought. This brings me to these thoughts.

I know that God has a host of angels surrounding me and mine at all times. It is like being surrounded by an iridescent shield and the protection this affords is of extraordinary magnitude. When sleeping, the shield settles over and around my home, protecting me from any outside forces. When moving about, during the day in the workplace, the shield moves with me, the invisible bubble that allows me to be safe in an unsafe environment.

As I travel the highways, the shield protects me from harm by others. I am given the added strength and endurance, with help from the angels so that I may complete tasks that others only dream about. Lately, it seems, the blessings are coming in storms! God has placed us on the chessboard of life and directs our every move. My daughter is to have a child that her heart and soul has so longed for. My son has found a true sole mate to share his life with. I have a companion, a wonderful man that one could only perceive in fairy tales. Finally, with my children as with me, our homes are safe havens.

Even now, I shed many tears for the loss of my firstborn, and I suppose that will always be a reality for me. God, in his wisdom, shielded her as well and took her home. My arms feel so empty with the knowing I can never hold her near me again… My heart aches with such fierceness that I cannot hear her laughter. But God has a plan…

In a little while, I will be able to hold a tiny baby in my arms to fill some of the void there… Soon, I will hear the ringing of wedding bells as my son and his mate join in matrimony. I just have to be careful as I walk about… Seems I keep bumping into angels at every move I make.

CHAPTER TWENTY-FOUR

MY SISTER PAM

LIFE DOES TAKE some quirky turns. Maybe the psychologist was right when he said I was too authoritative, too aggressive. Without getting mired down in all the muck of the specifics, Pam and I had a falling out over Nick. I have asked for her forgiveness. So far, I have not been forgiven by her. I have placed phone calls to her, and if I can catch her with her guard down, she will answer. On most occasions, she does not.

"I beg for your forgiveness, Pam. If we can't proceed as sisters can we at least be friends," I asked of her in the last conversation. Her reply was, "I am not the person you used to know. No, I don't think we can be friends—certainly not in this lifetime." That cut to the very core of my being. I send her a birthday card every year, and a Christmas does not pass without her receiving a Christmas card from me. I send her notes I have written about her. Looks like we will go to our grave with her heart as cold as a stone.

I Thought About You...

I sat there, filling out my medical history, detailing the events when I had spinal meningitis, and I thought about you ... I thought about the days you spent with my family and me, nursing me back to health.

I took a walk through the woods, and I could feel the damp cushion of moss beneath my feet, and I thought about you. I was reminded of similar walks we took with Mama when we were little girls.

I thought about you when I heard familiar laughter in the corridor. My head turned abruptly, but it wasn't you.

In my bathroom, I discovered, tucked away in a drawer, an old pack of stale cigarettes and I thought about you.

A question popped into my mind about an event I couldn't quite remember, and I thought about you. I knew you would know the answer.

I watched my son patiently re-comb his 4-year-old niece's hair after her "messing it up" over and over, and I thought about you. It was déjà vu with Larry combing your hair when you were 4.

Turning the pages of the November issue of a magazine, there was an advertisement for pork and a picture of a beautiful crown pork roast, and I thought about you.

To refresh the air inside, I picked up a container of "Claire Burke Original Fragrance" and I thought about you.

Today, I will make a chocolate pound cake from the recipe you shared with me those many years ago, and without a doubt, I will think about you.

DUSK AT TEACH'S ISLAND

Tonight, as I was driving home, I decided to stop by and see an old friend. He is known as mountain man, a name he so rightfully earned because he loves God's creation and is a recluse of sorts, spending too many hours alone deep in the forests. Actually, his given name is Amos, and for him, I hold a lot of respect.

I turned down the seldom traveled driveway, which leads to his ramshackle house. It was dusk, the beginning of the evening as I wound my way to his dwelling. I was creeping carefully maybe a half-mile an hour, and in the semi-darkness, I could see flashes of red, gray, and white motion. Gently, I applied the brakes and came to a stop.

There, almost within my reach were three white-tailed deer. The doe, gray in color, tossed her nose in the air and snorted quite loud. Her two baby fawns, hind quarters sprinkled with tiny white spots, so red and fat and sleek, froze in place.

The doe stood there with her right front leg bent in absolute stillness. She stomped her right foot solidly on the ground and snorted loudly. The two fawns mimicked her exactly. She tossed her head and lifted her left front leg only to stomp the ground even more firmly. And she snorted again.

The air was chilly, and this snort from her exuded a frosty mist from her nostrils that wafted upward. How magnificent she was…

This I watched for at least fifteen minutes as the show continued. Occasionally, they would cast a glance toward me but did not seem to be alarmed. Their ears would point to the direction in which they were gazing and their tails would pop up and fan out, then would be tucked down quite low again as they surveyed their surroundings.

I did not want this experience to end. How graceful they were, so in charge of their own being. What glorious specimens they were. But as the dimness closed in, they were lost in the shadows, disappearing into the night before my very eyes.

I slowly removed my foot from the brake; the car moved forward, the spell was broken. What an opportune moment I had just experienced, viewing nature in all its rawness and splendor. This is Amos's world, I thought as I progressed onward to knock on his door…

A Walk by Bradley Bay

It was an unseasonably warm early November day here on Teach's Island. Such a perfect day it is for raking leaves and tidying the yard for the winter that is sure to follow. My granddaughter, Amber, is nearby, pretending to be a water princess, secluded under the soft billowy fronds of the weeping willow tree. Her tiny hands part the boughs and she peers out at me. I talk with her in make-believe fashion for a few minutes then return to the task at hand. My indiscriminate thoughts were starkly interrupted by the sound of an agitated fowl of some sort. "Grandmother, what is making that sound?" Amber asked. Searching for an image, my thoughts rushed backward in time, probing my memory to identify a bird that matched the tone.

Even before it came into my field of vision, *I knew*, I just knew it had to be a guinea! *Nothing* sounds quite like an agitated guinea! There she was, walking hurriedly toward us with her head bobbing to and fro, but she was white, not speckled as the ones I remembered from my childhood back in the 1940s. Nevertheless, she was a guinea—a white guinea.

She just walked out of the woods to greet us, unafraid of me or Amber. She followed us to the clothesline where Amber passed me clothespins to hang the laundry. She followed us to the dog run, flew up, perching herself on the gate. It was obvious she wanted to be a part of this family.

We know she is a *she* because of the various sounds she makes and because her helmet and waddle are relatively small. We don't know from where she came or how long she will be here, but for the present, she has been dubbed Aunt Minnie the guinea.

Should you be wandering around by Bradley Bay, keep your eyes keened down the little roadways and streets of Teach's Island. At any moment, you may stumble upon Amber, Aunt Minnie, the guinea, Sir Lancelot, the Great Pyrenees, Marco Polo, the Tibetan Mastiff, Ms. Katherine Hepburn, the Persian cat and their auspicious friend, Mark taking a late afternoon stroll.

She brought the entire neighborhood pleasure and entertainment. Then, on January 15, 2009, she disappeared just as mysteriously as she had arrived some fourteen months earlier. Good-bye Aunt Minnie. You will be missed by all!

NEXT IS...

Tonight, sleep evades me for one reason or another. Just cannot settle down to that restful feeling that normally is upon me by 8:00 pm. So many issues are on my plate right now they are almost overwhelming. I pace the floor.

Issues: the season of my oldest daughter's birth then death; my home in disarray from projects unfinished. Frustrations at the workplace, the shabby spirit of my baby sister and her family that is directed toward me and mine. Ageing…growing older. I could identify more, but they may be even too intimate for me to share.

I turn the TV on then off. I turn the computer back on and surf the Internet. Abruptly, without warning, I am brought into sharp focus. I receive an e-mail from my son. Aaron, without a doubt, would give me the world if he could. He truly believes I hung the moon. The e-mail says, "*And next is your trip to Africa.*"

Africa, a place of dreams…warm humid winds, tropical rains, mosquitoes, sleek fat animals in the wild…cocktails, soft, sweet music…a place to lose-find one's self. In all probability, Africa I will never physically see, but in my heart and in my head, I can retreat to this place and find peacefulness there.

His dreams, wants, and desires for me are parallel to mine, illusive, and spectral. But the desire is so powerful. So remarkable is the fact that we can look upward and forward to *"And next is…"* even in the face of the greatest of losses and insurmountable disappointments. What a measure of character that is.

The witching hour is near, but I remain captivated by the feeling of affection my son projected to me in what he thought was an unassuming e-mail to dispel yet another of my disappointments. Such ordinary words that were written with so much enthusiasm and admiration, intended for the purpose of lifting up his mother. *"And next is your trip to Africa."*

I Danced
On rapier tip and cross sword's periphery, I danced,
to music heard solitarily by my own ears.
I Laughed
With a robustness rarely heard in womankind, I laughed.
And Gabriel and Peter and John laughed with me.
I Sang
With the heart of ten thousand angels, I sang,
Lamenting and wailing at the injustices abounding.
I Played
With white-hot, immortal yearning, I played,
Like a destined pilot flying into the heat of the last battle.
I Lived
With a shameless desire to make a difference, I lived.
I searched for means to heal the emptiness within and the
suffering without.
I Loved
With unabashed fierceness and never-ending devotion, I
loved,
knowing I would not come this way again.

Chapter Twenty-Five

Outpatient Surgery

T IS 5:45 AM, and we are sitting in the designated parking area for the outpatient surgery center in Chesapeake, Virginia. I'm nervous and quiet and hungry. Mark is nervous and talkative and hungry. My back hurts, and I'm cold.

"Ouch! Another back spasm," I grunted forcibly.

"What? We can go back home. I don't have to have this surgery, you know!" Mark responded between half-clenched teeth.

"Just take me to a bathroom. I have to pee," I pouted.

As he started the car and shifted into reverse, he remarked in softer voice, "Well, they have not unlocked the doors anyway—all these vehicles have people waiting in them," and he waved his left arm in an arc that encircled the half dozen or so cars that had preceded us here.

Mark pulled back out onto Battlefield Boulevard and easily found a fast food restaurant just opening their doors for the early 6:00 am crowd. I hastily beat a path to and fro. At 6:05 am, we were back in the outpatient parking area and found the others who had been waiting had entered the complex through the heavy glass automatic doors.

We entered the elevator, and the door closed behind us. At our destination floor, we stepped into a lobby with several people already seated, with others lined up at the reception desk. Mark took his place in line, and soon, it lengthened behind him.

The lone receptionist efficiently processed each person individually, maintaining her fixed smile and a minimum amount of confidentiality. It was now 6:40 am. Folks were in their own little cliques, speaking quietly, reading the newspaper or nervously flipping magazine pages.

For lack of a better term, a "tour guide" appeared. "Good morning to everyone," she said. "Please follow me." The group of about 16 folks stood in unison and filed in line behind her. "This is where…" and her soft voice was lost to most of us. "And here…"—she motioned to her left—"is the…" She spoke too soft; I didn't understand. "Now, this is the…" she said animatedly, and she pointed to her right. I don't believe anyone completely understood, but as I looked around at the group, heads were bobbing in the affirmative and lips were turned upward in smiles.

What good little puppets we are, I thought cynically.

It was obvious we had now reached the pre-op area. There, against the west wall was a tall, long desk with assorted medical paraphernalia scattered about. Along the east wall were about sixteen cubicles. The group huddled.

From a folded piece of paper, she extracted from her pocket, she began, "Let me see…Mr. ah… Jenkins. Your stop is here at K3…Ms. Adams…yes…there you are [chuckle, chuckle] you are K 4. Yes, just go right in, and Mr. Bar… Mr. Bla… [chuckle, chuckle]"

"Byrne!" I interrupted her.

"Right. Right. Mr. Byrne, you are assigned to K5. Yes, that's right, just step inside…"

So we stepped inside. How can a room so full be so bare and cold? First of all, the two straight backed chairs were extremely lean and would have defied anyone over 160 pounds trusting their luck with them. Then there was the small square table, wedged in one corner. It boasted deep scars on top, desperately trying to find their way out from under the weight of the Holy Bible, compliments of the Gideon Society. The most pitiful piece of furniture, however, was the thing they called a chair-recliner-gurney sitting a little askew and jutting out into the center of the room. Surely, they didn't expect my six feet tall, 260-pound spouse to utilize *that*!

There we stood, looking at nothing, looking at each other, lost in our own private thoughts. "I have to pee," I said as I opened the inner door, only to find a younger man and woman standing in the middle of the bathroom floor…staring back at me.

"Oh. I see you all have discovered the shared bathroom," this "tour guide" said. "Let me demonstrate the door lock—it is on the wall here, see? Just press this pad and both doors will lock." And she did a little curtsy and stepped back with such a satisfied expression you would have thought she had just explained Einstein's Theory of Relativity.

I just kept advancing into the bathroom and reached out to "press the pad." The other couple exited, and I had the bathroom to myself. "Whew, just in time!"

At 7:10 am, a female, dressed in faded cartoon scrubs, entered the room. She is wearing a name tag that says "Jeanie, Registered Nurse. She exchanged pleasantries with my husband. I just stare at the back of her head. "What are you having done today?" she asks of Mark.

"Well, I am having the same thing done here…"—and Mark weeble-wobbled his right hand upward, then down—"as I had done here," and he repeated the process with his left hand. The nurse rolled her eyes as she took the purple permanent marker and wrote "yes" in giant bold letters on the web between the thumb and forefinger of his right hand.

She then explained to him that she now would start an IV and proceeded to tell him why the IV had to be situated in the left *hand,* not the arm or ante cubital area. She remarked, after gently tapping the back of his left hand, "I'm glad to see you brought your good veins with you today."

Nurse Jeanie chatted away as she began preparation for the IV insertion. Another knock at the door and there entered a man in green scrubs with a cap to match. "Good morning. I'm Dr. Getties, your anesthesiologist," he announced in his sing-song voice as he made his way to the chair at Mark's right side and planted himself there.

Jeanie was now struggling with the intracatheter, to which she wished she would be able to attach the IV tubing. "What happened there?" Mark asked as she piled gauze pad after gauze pad on top of the railroad-tie vein, trying to control the bleeding. "No one has ever had trouble hitting *my* veins."

Nurse Jeanie laughed nervously and said lightly, "Oh, there was a valve in the way. That happens sometimes."

Dr. Getties made a lame joke that I could not hear and Jeanie followed with "And I stayed at the Holiday Inn Express last night." They both broke up in laughter at their own senseless conversation as Jeanie reapplied a tourniquet to Mark's upper left arm to attempt another IV site.

"And what surgeries have you had?" the anesthesiologist asked as he referred to the documents he pulled from his hip pocket.

"Well, I had a release of ulnar nerve entrapment of both elbows, and I had the same job done to this hand that I am having done to this…" Mark began but was interrupted.

"Have you ever had any problems being put to sleep?"

"No!" Mark said to Mr. Green Jeans on his right and to Jeanie on his left he said, "I thought you said you needed to put the IV in my *hand* because you needed my *upper arm* for blood pressures?"

"It will be okay," Jeannie mumbled distractedly as she probed and retracted and probed and retracted that stout pink-hubbed angiocath deeper and deeper into the left ante cubital space on my husband's arm.

On Mark's right, Green Jeans was asking, liltingly, "So you don't have any teeth you can take out and show to your friends?"

"*No!*" Mark replied.

"Open your mouth and let me see," chimed in Mr. Green Jeans. After opening, then snapping his mouth shut Mark said

"What? Did you think my teeth would fall out in my lap or something?"

Jeanie was taping the now functional IV securely to Mark's arm then connected the tubing to the no. 18 Gauge needle.

Dr. Getties continued, "I'll put you to sleep and Dr. Williams will…"

"What agents will you be using for anesthesia?" I asked of him.

He turned slowly and deliberately in his chair, looked at me in disdain, then turned back to Mark and said, "I will be using various agents. Versed, Propofol, Ketorolac…"

I interrupted him again, saying, "That is what I wanted to know. You've answered my question."

The room became unusually quiet. Jeanie drew to attention turning first to look at Mr. Green Jeans then at me. Green Jeans turned slowly in my direction, making eye contact. I could see the anxiety on Mark's face, and I thought, "Mercy me, why do I have to pick a fight with his anesthesiologist just before he is going into surgery?" And in my mind, I began to shy away a little.

"So what are you, a drug person?" he asked, referring to a drug representative, with even more contempt creeping into his voice.

"Why do you ask that? Do you think one has to be a drug person to be a knowledgeable person?" I responded.

He ignored me and my question and turned back to Mark, glancing in my direction from time to time. "Oh, Kathleen, keep your mouth shut!" I kept saying over and over to myself.

Green Jeans took a deep breath and started over, this time, appropriately. "And you will be under *general anesthesia* [stolen glance at me], and then we will…"

It was 8:55 am, and the anesthesiologist was interrupted again when the OR nurse entered, introduced herself, and escorted Mark out of his cubicle, into the common area of the pre-op suite.

"Ah-ha!" Dr. Williams shouted as he turned away from the west wall desk toward the chair/recliner/gurney my husband was being transported on. "The man of the hour! Allow me to shake hands with the man of the hour!" He said laughingly as he shook Mark's hand. Then turning and holding my right hand between his hands. "Everything will be beautiful!" he said to me, and I waited for the rose petals to fall, and the orchestra to start playing. The consent for anesthesia was never signed by Mark.

I kissed my husband gently and watched as the gurney disappeared down the corridor and the steel, fire retardant doors closed between us. It is nine fifteen, and I have to pee again, but this time, I am alone. As is typical for me, I have about thirty pounds of papers, journals, day timer, and notepads weighting me down, but they are a welcome distraction from this horrid wait. I leave the paraphernalia behind in the chair as I head for the ladies' room. Walking there and back to the chair was painful enough. It was more of a shuffle than a walk. I must make an appointment with my chiropractor, and soon! My lower back is in dire need of adjustment.

The hands of my watch were stuck. Was it only nine forty-five? Did they say it would take two hours for the surgery? What? That can't be right. It must be later than ten forty-five! "Excuse me," I said to another person-in-waiting. "What time do you have?"

"Eleven o'clock," he said without looking up from his magazine.

Goodness, wouldn't you think someone would at least come and say, "All is well…" It is eleven fifteen, and my cell phone rings. "Hello?"

"Yes, this is JoAnna's florist, and we have a delivery for Mr. Mark Byrne," the voice said.

"Never mind the delivery. I will pick it up on our way back into town this evening." And I clicked off the phone.

At 11:20 am, there he is, Dr. Williams, perching himself in the empty seat beside me. "Everything went well, really well, just beautiful. He will be in a little splint...his joint was totally worn out...he needed that...they will call you back in a few minutes... any questions?" Then he was off and running. And the waiting, for that part, was over.

At 11:45 am, I was finally summoned back to the cubicle K5 only to find my husband not there. Instead there is another nurse named Mickey!

"Where is he?" I asked anxiously.

"Oh, in the bathroom...Mr. Byrne, are you okay? Do you need any help?" she queried through the closed door. There was no response. I walked over, tapped on the door, then opened it an inch or two.

There he stood, with a most puzzled, exasperated look on his face. "I peed on my foot! How could I have peed on my foot? Baby, I need some help, I was thinking...but I never heard the water..., and my right foot got warm...and then I looked down and...oh, baby, I peed on my foot."

"Here, let me help you," I said as I grabbed his left arm and guided him back to his chair/recliner/gurney to help him sit, and I was thinking that the chair defied Mark's height-weight any-way! "Let's get off those wet hospital socks and put on your own. And let's just get dressed as your gown is wet too." We both burst out laughing. What a perfect ending to a perfect surgery and in reality a pretty good day all around.

"COSTA DEL MAR: SEE WHAT'S OUT THERE"

His voice, steeped in anxiety, caused me to stop abruptly in the pet supplies aisle of the local Wally-World. I looked backward in his direction. "*Baby!*" he said, clutching at the V-opening of his

Henley T-shirt. His face was pale, and his lips were dry. "They're gone! My sunglasses are gone!"

Just nine days earlier, I had given Mark a pair of expensive-designer-polarized-lens sunglasses as a "hurry and get well" gift after his right thumb joint arthroplasty. He was so funny at the vision center, agonizing and choosing just the most appropriate frames. He preened, and he posed and he discussed this pair and that pair with the sales associate. Finally, Mark decided on the "Costa Del Mar: See What's Out There" design.

He whirled around and began retracing his steps throughout the store. I followed suit, moving in the opposite direction. Up and down the aisles we went, independently of each other, our paths crossing now and again. We both just looked at each other and wagged our heads in the negative upon passing as we continued our search.

"Have you seen a pair of sunglasses? My husband has lost his here in the store. He leaned over, I guess, and they just fell out of his shirt collar, and he didn't notice at the time and…" I said to every associate I could find.

Their response unanimously was "No. No, I haven't."

And I thought sarcastically to myself, "Of course not. Why, that is like dropping a $100 bill on the floor and expecting someone to turn it in at the lost and found."

My back was hurting, and I simply could not take another step. I found a bench and sat down to relieve the pain. I still had not made that appointment with the chiropractor. We had been in Wally World for more than an hour now. My heart was sinking as were my hopes of ever finding his glasses. Mark has such an appreciation for everything, and the glasses were terribly meaningful to him. I just couldn't bear the thought of them being lost in such a way.

"So they are lost" I thought. "It is just a thing. No big thing. We will just go back to the vision center and get an identical pair on our way home this afternoon." I was fighting back the tears for him, doing my positive self-talk thing when I felt a hand on my shoulder.

I looked up and there he stood—with his Costa Del Mar: See What's Out There sunglasses plastered firmly on his face. "Baby! You will never believe this!" he said, and the story unraveled.

"After I walked all over the store and retraced our steps several times and having gone to customer service twice, I decided to go to the car in hopes I had left them there. Well, they were neither in the car nor in the parking lot. As I was entering the store, I asked the greeter who was doling out carts if anyone had turned in a pair of sunglasses."

Mark continued, "At that point, I was feeling somewhat skeptical of any chance of ever seeing the glasses again but still not wanting to give up hope. He was just one last person to ask. As I was speaking to the gentleman, a woman and her granddaughter were leaving the store and overheard my question."

She stopped and said to me, "My granddaughter found a pair of sunglasses on the floor back there, and we gave them to the salesclerk in the jewelry section."

Mark took off his glasses and continued the story. "I hurried to the jewelry section, looking at the glass counter tops, hoping to see my glasses there, and when I didn't, I asked the clerk 'Did someone turn in a pair of sunglasses?' and she said, 'They sure did. I have them locked up right here.' And sure enough, she opened the locked box, removed a pair of sunglasses and presented them to me, and they were *mine!*"

I couldn't help it. I started to cry. Over a pair of lost-found sunglasses, over the one-in-a-million chances this could have ever happened. See how delightful things happen to a wonderful person like Mark?

Chapter Twenty-Six

Nathaniel Morgan, MD

ODAY IS WEDNESDAY, January 10, 2007, and I have an appointment with my primary physician. I loathe doctor appointments. I know my blood pressure will be up, and my heart rate will be rapid as it always is when I visit a doctor's office. My doctor always laughs at me saying, "I can't believe you. You have been a nurse all these years, but when you are the patient *you have the White Coat Syndrome.*" If he only knew...

Doctor visits bring forth memories I try to repress, memories of Dr. Morgan, Nathaniel Morgan. Back in the 1940s, there were no "specialists" in the rural counties of North Carolina. In fact, there are very few in existence in that small town even today! Nathaniel Morgan was our family doctor, he was *my* doctor.

I remember the steel band he kept clamped tightly around his head. Suspended from this was a lighted bulb, bright white and glaring. I can see him reaching up to direct the bright beam like a beacon from hell, glaring into my eyes, temporarily blinding me. I remember the foul odor of his pungent breath as his head came closer and closer to mine. I do remember the Bright's disease that I had when I was two, and that should have been enough memories for a child, but there was more—much more to come.

His medical practice was on the second floor of the cluster of buildings on Main Street. The stairs were dark, steep, and narrow and smelled of mold and mildew. Directly at the top of the stairs was a door, the upper half being translucent granite glass. Gold lettering on the glass read, "Nathaniel Morgan, MD." Upon entering, a receptionist would greet you then you would sit and wait and wait and wait… The floors were made of tongue-and-grooved linseed oil-soaked boards that felt spongy under your feet and made squeaking sounds with each step. The sweet sickening odor of diethyl ether and alcohol permeated the walls.

Then there was the examination room…a chamber of horrors for me!

In retrospect, I think Nathaniel Morgan was an emotionally twisted individual who probably lived on the edge for the most part. I remember him pinching and twisting my nipples when I was only five or six years old, telling my mother I would never have nipples at all unless she "pinched and twisted them like this." His skin was pale, nearly the color of cornstarch; his boney hands and fingers were icy cold. I never quite understood why it was necessary for me to have nipples in the first place. I never understood why my mother did not intervene.

My most intimate parts he pinched and probed, squeezed and twisted, and pinched some more until I wanted to scream, swallowing back the urge to throw up, but I knew I could not for I would embarrass my mother. She had such admiration for this doctor who had saved my life. I often wondered whether my mother was that naive or if she just turned a blind eye. She simply may have never known or noticed what was occurring. I remember having kidney infections until I was about ten years old. I remember his nurse, Ms. Dulles, with gray, wispy hair that crept out from her scalp like tendrils, coiling around and attaching to her starched white nurses cap. She reeked of strange odors that were repellant to a child. I prayed and sweated and prayed some more that I would never have to visit this repulsive place again.

Along about the time I was ten or twelve years old, still being subjected to visits with Dr. Morgan, an event occurred that saved me from the evil sickness of this doctor. I wonder how many other innocent children were exposed to his vile behavior. Surely I was not alone, although that is exactly how I felt.

⁜

The night was cold, with snow and sleet being driven sideways by the constantly strong north wind. The roadways became practically impassable. The culverts and side ditches were littered with cars and trucks that had lost their traction spinning uncontrollably off the highway.

The situation turned to blizzard conditions, a virtual whiteout with fierce winds and blinding driven snow. However, the driver of one particular car was oblivious; he was heady with desire and intoxicated with Hennessy cognac. His companion snuggled closer as they travelled onward. Suddenly as they rounded a sharp turn in the road, they were struck head on by an eighteen wheeler! They were both killed instantly, tangled in that heap of twisted steel, half-empty cognac bottle a few feet away. The driver of the big rig escaped with only minor injuries. No fault was found except to blame it on the weather...

The law enforcement officers tried to keep it hush-hush, but nonetheless, the gossip mill cranked up. The story was out. Estella Morgan, wife of Dr. Nathaniel Morgan, was identified by her husband as the passenger in the car. Matthew Murphy, the only African American attorney in this sleepy little town was identified by his own wife as the driver of the car.

Nathaniel Morgan never recovered from losing his wife and was unable to pull himself up to face the public after all the nasty gossip. He became reclusive and paranoid but maintained a semblance of medical practice, haphazard as it was. His client base declined; his medical practice was in permanent jeopardy.

It was early one morning that Nurse Dulles placed the key in the lock and opened the door to enter the reception room of the practice. She hung her blue wool cloak on the coat tree. A dim light was visible under the door of the office where they kept patient records and such.

"How strange," she thought as she walked quickly and quietly across the floor toward the study door. "Doctor has never arrived before me."

Nurse Dulles tapped lightly then pushed the door open, and she began to scream. He was slumped half-in, half-out of his chair. Shards of bone and brain matter covered the maple wooden filing cabinet to his left. Blood was everywhere. She fainted, collapsing onto the floor.

It was just three months after the tragic death of his wife that Nathaniel Morgan took his own life. He committed suicide in his office by placing a hand gun to his temple and pulling the trigger. Beside an empty vodka bottle, a note was found, a note cursing and blaspheming the person responsible for his wife's death, penning as many racial epithets as he could bring forth.

Chapter Twenty-Seven

The Blessings Continue

THE YEAR 2007 brought many blessings to us, some of them in disguise, we often say. Over the winter months, I battled uncontrolled hypertension with stressors of working as a registered nurse in the prison system. Compounding these issues, Mark was recovering from reconstructive surgery to his right thumb. In the spring, I left my position with Department of Corrections. For the first time in my adult life, I was unemployed! Mark insisted I take "time-out" to revive and restore myself.

Well, I took his advice (sort of) and threw myself into refurbishing the exterior of our property and buildings, gardening, cooking… And what a good sport he was. Never did he complain about all those long to-do lists. He could see the magic it was working as my blood pressure gradually came under control and returned to normal!

Our grandchildren took turns spending long intervals with us over the summer. We had picnics at the park, water fights on the decks, pool parties, and cookouts, but mostly, we shared lots of fun and affection. The highlight of their days, though, was Mark relaxing in the hot tub with them.

We both continued to work with the Gibsonville Community Theater backstage, costume design, producing and acting as stage manager. We held auditions with lots of fantastic talent to choose from, so casting parts were a breeze. I made reconnection with an old friend, Della, that fall. This relationship promises to be fruitful and revealing. I think it will come fast and furious.

On October 6, Aaron and Heather were married after a seven-year courtship. That was a celebration to behold! Without a doubt, it was the most beautiful and dramatic wedding I have ever attended. They were so meant for each other!

That same month Mark and I made the decision to become Guardian AD Litem for our judicial district and are both now sworn officers of the court to defend and protect the rights of children. This is a truly humbling position in which to be, and we think we were led here by a power greater than us. Mark continues to work full time as a private investigator for a national company.

He has evolved into an exceptionally professional photographer, and I have further polished my computer skills. We have utilized our abilities to create a new business of producing VCDs, professional brochures, and weddings, special events, personalized special occasion cards, business cards, etc. We receive instant gratification and experience the joy in just being together!

We got a year older and, hopefully, wiser. We certainly have become more thankful for all the blessings God has bestowed upon us. Some of our blessings, as I said earlier, just came crashing down on us, like an anvil. Others were more subtle; nonetheless, they were all recognized as blessings from above. For our family, we pray for smooth sailing and roads that are not too rocky and that God's blessings will continue their deliverance.

Chapter Twenty-Eight

Presume

I T IS WINTER again. Cold, blustery, rainy days give me pause to reminisce and wish I had more control over the black hole in my heart that causes me to drive people away. Such is the case with my sister, Pam, whom I miss so painfully. This is my mournful message to her:

> Presume my days turned dark and turbulent, and I became unable to decode the woman that once stood before me.

> Presume my eyes could no longer distinguish the smile that lighted your face, and it's radiance I could not see.

> Presume all sound fell on the deafness of my ears, and I could not hear your laughter or hear you call my name.

> Presume my being, as I knew it, ended today, and all my tomorrows would never be could never be the same.

> Presume my ability to miss you so terribly and to care for you so deeply vanished quite suddenly and I had remained hushed.

Presume I reached my hand out to you today and your
fingers touched mine releasing love. Oh what a rush

Of joy that would be for me, for us to be together, once
more, sharing secrets and fun and family.

Presume my plea fell on ears that have turned deaf, and
cold toward me? What if, my sister, again I will never see?

Presume I could just roll back time...

FAMILY REUNION 2008

No matter how hard I tried, I could not prevent it this time. The
tears began to flow uncontrollably, and that was weeks ago. In the
deepest corner of my heart, there lurked a fear and a deep, deep
sadness that I could not quite identify. Did I honestly want to?
Somehow, I felt a tremendous letdown even as I began to make
plans for this event.

I moved forward... The gardens must be cleaned. A winter's
worth of leaves, limbs, and debris brought down by near fifty-
knot winds across the bay. All must be dealt with and removed.
New cushions for the wicker furniture on the upper deck would
convey cheerful refreshment to our arriving guests. Menus must
be planned. Spring cleaning must be completed. Then, last-min-
ute food shopping and preparation must be finalized; fresh flowers must be picked and placed.

Not one task evoked any sense of weariness. I felt quite ener-
gized by it all and made long, detailed to-do lists to fill my days.
A couple of months ago, Mark and I had what we thought was a
marvelous plan to bring our children together with us for the first
time ever, a family reunion of sorts. We talked about how delightful it would be to have our children and grandchildren together
to celebrate the spirit of family. We both feel quite strongly that
the spouses of our children are our children as well and acknowledge them as such.

Then it began…

"Mama, I thought you knew we won't be there because Ricky and Amber will just be coming home from Seattle that Saturday night, and I will have to be at the airport to pick them up. You remember, Ricky always travels at this same time of year to be with his mother, to celebrate her birthday, and to be with his parents to celebrate their anniversary." I felt Angela spoke quite nonchalantly as she relayed this information to me.

"How's my favorite Mom?" Kevin, Mark's youngest son queried, some weeks ago as an opening to the phone call he placed to me. "We are looking forward to Easter weekend with you guys. I know you said you were going to ask each family to bring a dish, but Sabrina wants to do the all the cooking. And I have already decided how we will do the egg hunt. I will buy about fifty plastic eggs or more and Dad, and I can hide them. We will give Stevie a head start because you know Horace is much older and can find eggs much quicker than Stevie and…" I sighed inwardly. It would not be reasonable to ask the entire family to eat the type of food Sabrina prepares nor for their food to be portioned as she does for her family.

I suggested to Kevin all the children in our family join the children of the community at the lodge for an egg hunt. This idea was inspired by the many delightful Easter egg hunts I enjoyed as a child at the Baptist church, with all the children of the neighborhood. I further interjected my feelings about real eggs and the symbol of new life they bring to the Easter season. He totally disagreed with me and abruptly ended the conversation. I did not hear from him again regarding the invitation.

Suddenly, the momentous weekend was only two weeks away…

"Hey, Mama, no, we won't be there for the reunion…we will probably be visiting with Heather's aunt…her parents want us to go with them to Virginia…"

"But, Aaron, we have had this planned for over two months. You both knew we were planning the reunion and genuinely expect you to be here…" I stammered into the phone.

"Well, we won't be there…" he remarked as flatly and coldly as any stranger would say to another in stating a decision reached. I quickly changed the subject, not allowing myself to crumble emotionally…

I struggled with how to tell Mark of this latest turn of events. Mark, the one who championed Aaron on many, many occasions would say, "He always does the right thing. Aaron always does the right thing. I have never known anyone quite like him." There was no way to sugarcoat Aaron's decision. It was what it was.

Mark was as hurt as I. The two of us were shaken. Neither of my children or their families would be available for our family reunion. And neither would either of his! I cried; Mark cried. We talked about how ridiculous it was to proceed with the theme of a family reunion. I was simply too upset to respond. Mark agreed to send an e-mail:

> Hey All, we have been notified by some of you of developments that will prevent you from attending the family reunion that Kathleen and I had been planning for all of us over Easter Weekend. Regretfully, the family reunion focus of the weekend is cancelled. We wanted to advise you of this to enable you to make the best plans for yourselves over Easter weekend. We fully understand any decision you make. We still want those of you that can come over the weekend and can be with us to please do so. For those of you who have not given us a definite answer, please do so where we can plan accordingly.

On Tuesday morning, I received a phone call from Angela on her way to work in Lexington. "Mama, we got Mark's e-mail, and I am sorry. I am sorry we messed the weekend up, and I am sorry Aaron and Heather have made the decision not to come."

On Thursday, March 13, Aaron called mid-morning. "I am sorry I hurt your feelings, Mama." I told him how deeply I was wounded. I accepted his apology. A little bit of my heart died that day.

Adam (Mark's oldest son) responded that they would not be able to come and offered reasons why. He asked if he and his family could visit in April. It is now Monday, March 17, 2008, with the weekend just four days off. We have heard nothing from Kevin and Sabrina.

And the joy I felt at being with all our family, hearing laughter, watching children playing together, had disappeared. My heart still aches from the emotional pain. Maybe it was not a good idea for us to arrange a family reunion after all. Times have changed; the need for each other has vanished from our culture, not just in our family alone.

OUR NATION

The very fabric of our nation appears to be unraveling. Murder and mayhem, terrorist attacks, mass murders on grade school and college campuses. All this at the hands of maniacal individuals inflicted with an insanity that is incomprehensible. There are such a vast number of children who have no father figure in their lives, more people are living at the poverty level, and the illegal drug market is growing in leaps and bounds.

Our nation is divided. The scriptures are being lived out. When we take an indirect course of action, circumventing God, what can we expect?! Our hearts become deceitful. Sure we trust in God when we are at the bottom of the barrel, when we are brought humbly to our knees to call on Him because we have nowhere else to turn. Yet when the strife of that particular issue has subsided and we are distracted by untoward motives, we are apt to spend less and less time in the Word and on our knees. That is, until another crisis erupts…

It is the unjust use of power that smothers the spirit of many. When I hear of the oppression of children of alcoholics, drug users, dealers, abusers, thieves, and murderers, I have an over-whelming feeling of heartsickness for them. They are victims of a lifestyle in which they too may repeat the cycle.

Today's economy finds us holding our breath more often than not, afraid of what is to follow. Rising gas prices at the pump has led to increase in costs for shipping and delivery of all goods and products. This leads to less cash flow for individuals and encumbers even more the abilities of the average person to provide for his/her family.

Answerability, responsibility, and liability are used synony-mously with accountability. Accountable simply put means being responsible for something or to somebody. Remember the story about Cousin Frankie and his wife Tilley? This is a prime exam-ple of the affluent taking advantage of those not on the same level. At their country store, you could purchase almost anything: nuts and bolts, hoop cheese, salt pork, candy, even chicken feed. Their sleight of hand at the weighing scales cheated many people, but this only happened to customers from the lower strata: the rich exploiting the poor.

My observations and signs of the times…

> Some Wednesdays and all Saturdays in the sultry South
> Our mothers hawked their pastries, called it Curb Market.
> My generation pedaled Amway and swore it was not a "pyramid".
> Today's children peddle porn and drugs; calling it enlightenment.

VALUES, BELIEFS, AND MORES

It is true; I think that one must determine his own values—the importance of anything, the relative worth that a thing holds. I read somewhere that loving things and using people only leads to despair, that using things and loving people is the way it should be. So it must be that somewhere along the way I chose to be uniquely me. But God had His hand in it more than I knew.

Why didn't my mother intervene with my daddy's atrocious behavior toward me? Was she plagued by guilt? We are told that guilt is the state of being responsible for the commission of an offense. Perhaps an emotional experience that occurs when a person realizes (or believes) that he or she has violated a moral standard and bears significant responsibility for that violation.

Why didn't my daddy intervene when my mother so ruthlessly beat her own son? Rumor has it that Nick may have been fathered by someone other than the man he called daddy. Further rumor has it that my daddy also "liked little boys." Could guilt be the premise of the Machiavellian-like behaviors by the two of them? How did I escape those evil genes I believe them both to have carried? Or did I?

I must say my mother was not racially prejudiced as was evident in her behavior and in her acceptance of the colored folks in our community. The term "colored folks" considered racial by some was not a disparaging term in the period in which I was reared. A dear friend of mine who is African American said to me once, "The term 'colored' they used in the old days was not meant to be derogatory. It's old-fashioned and outdated but not offensive."

Thomas Jefferson, the principal author of the Declaration of Independence, said it so eloquently and succinctly in the final wording of the best known sentence in the world; it cannot be improved upon:

> We hold these truths to be self-evident that all men are created equal that they are endowed by their Creator with certain unalienable Rights that among these are Life, Liberty and the pursuit of Happiness.

This is a self-imposed motto I try to live by. Truths, beliefs are interchangeable words. I hold a truth, a belief that we are all truly of God's creation, that we will share the same heaven or hell, whichever the case may be, regardless of our skin color. Mores? I look at that a little differently. Mores from a sociology standpoint are a specific society's virtues or values, rather what is "normal" for that particular group, the accepted traditional customs of a particular group. Would not the movement of the Ku Klux Klan fit that definition? So I am particularly mindful of mores, customs, and traditions.

I never thought to wonder the *why* of Ambrose Underwood's vile behavior. First of all, I was an extremely young child when these tragic events occurred; secondly, it was years before I could even bring myself to think about it. Now, more than seven decades later, I do wonder why, how people become pedophiles. Why didn't I tell my mother? Certainly I could not have told my daddy. That would have caused him to love me even less if such a thing were possible. The key, I think, is in Cousin Ambrose's parting words: "Your mother won't love you any longer."

Isn't that what predators do? They use a child's natural desire to be loved to keep them silent. That is exactly what Ambrose, the perpetrator, the vile predator, did to Pam and me. I would not tell, and I forbade Pam to tell, and he went to his grave scot-free.

I am still left with the why of one's ability and desire to corrupt the purity of a child. I have believed, all my adult life, the cells remember…that behaviors and personality traits are handed down, generation after generation, that some behaviors truly are genetic. Studies are now evolving supporting that theory.

Who knows what memories and experiences are clouded or hidden in the time warp of seventy-five years? I recognize one's personal awareness is held as the truth by the perceiver. It requires a particular mental attitude to overcome life's adversities. Somewhere along the way, I gained a harmony within myself; I learned the difference between knowing the truth versus being true. Assuredly, my relationship with God has brought me here. I do believe faith can move mountains.

THE PEBBLES

It was the Sunday before Memorial Day, May 31, 2010. Mark and I traveled to Crossroads, in lower Concord County, the community in which I was reared. Just to give you a little "back story," my brother Larry, who had lived there all his life, died last November. His daughter's husband also passed away just before Christmas last year.

So today was to be a reunion of sorts with my sister-in-law, Marie, and her family. Marie and I have always shared a mutual respect and deep-seated love for each other; I was eager to see her again. She invited one and all, to come together, in remembrance and fellowship. It was a wondrous day; family from all over gathered, just to bond and reminisce, to share common beliefs and values.

On into the day, I said to my niece Julie, "I would like to go to the cemetery to see my brother's grave site." The cemetery was located behind the little Baptist church of my childhood and the church that still shepherds my family and friends in the Crossroads community.

So it was not surprising that Donna, another niece and daughter of my brother, came to me and said, "Let's go to the church. I want to show you the grave marker Ma got for Pa."

How funny they were those two nieces of mine, saying they did not know how to use the key to my car and Donna pawning the key off to Julie. "You don't need a key, just press the button on the dash," I instructed her. Well, we finally got out of the driveway and drove the one mile north to the church. Julie turned into the driveway and pulled up close to the cemetery behind the church.

Donna got out of the car and quickly walked toward the back of the building. I said to Julie, "Where is she going?"

"Oh, to gather some pebbles," she said as if I would understand what that meant. Julie and I walked together, moving closer and closer to the grave sites of our loved ones. Donna was already there, standing by the tombstones, adding a few pebbles to the base of her grandmother's headstone, moving over to her dads and depositing a few more there.

As she turned back toward my own daughter's grave, I could see tears just streaming down her face. I looked at Julie, and her face, too, was flooded with tears. Donna bent and gently placed one, two, and then a third pebble on the base of Megan's headstone, increasing the number already there and...

Suddenly, it was revealed to me like a bolt of lightning! And I began to cry. Each time, these two young women visited the gravesites, they would place a pebble or two on each monument to acknowledge these loved ones, to demonstrate someone had been there...that someone still cared.

Chapter Twenty-Nine

Deja Vu

IT WAS SUMMER 2011. My six-year-old granddaughter Amber sat all buckled in the back seat of the car I was driving, and I watched her in the rearview mirror as she sang made-up songs to me and to her doll. We were traveling east on a pretty difficult highway when suddenly I hit a washout in the pavement. "What was that?!" she cried out in an alarming little girl voice.

"Just a bump in the road, Amber," I responded calmly. "It's nothing to worry about." Suddenly, repressed events came roaring to the forefront...

It was as though it happened just yesterday. I was about eight years old, so it must have been around 1951. The faded black 1946 Chevrolet rolled along, following the winding country tar road. It was pitch-dark, so dark it felt heavy. Then it happened! I can still hear the thud as the vehicle struck the object in the roadway. I could feel the rise and fall of first the front end of the vehicle then the back...the back where my baby sister and I sat whispering and giggling to each other.

My brother Larry brought the car to an abrupt halt leaping out of the car. My dad, and then my mother, both exiting from the front passenger side, retraced the path we had just covered. Unexpectedly, we were not giggling anymore; I began to sweat. It was eerily quiet. An inordinate amount of time passed before they returned to the car; now their voices were low, nearly indiscernible, nearly voiceless. It was as though my mother read my thoughts, tossed back over the seat in a voice sounding not like hers at all, "It's nothing to worry about. It was a big tree limb, just a log in the road, so no need to talk about it to anyone!"

We did not complete our trip that thick black night. We returned home and were promptly told to get ready for bed. I could still hear their voices, even though they kept them subdued.

My mama's voice, "He... drunk... fell... highway... notify sheriff..."

My daddy's voice, somewhat louder than my mother's, "Accident... dead anyway... just a nigger... shut up... no law." Larry was silent.

In bed, I pulled the homemade quilt up to my chin, trying to stop the trembling, but I wasn't shivering from cold, it was from fear; the kind of fear that always causes me to sweat. Many years later, I came to realize what I feared happened that night actually did. My brother had struck and killed a pedestrian, a Negro man. No agent ever asked questions and no one ever told; however, I knew.

That car, the '46 Chevy certainly held no good memories for me. There was Ruth Johnson, a hardworking single Negro mother with a house full of hungry mouths to feed. Her husband had just up and left one day and never came back. She had four boys ranging from age four to age sixteen. Ruth lived about one hundred yards from our front door but on the opposite side of the sandy dirt road. It was early on Sunday morning, and we were getting dressed for church when we heard it, the explosion that rattled the dishes in the cupboard and shook the window panes in their frames! The sound wasn't deep enough to sound like the dynamite Daddy used to blow stumps out of the new ground. But it did sound like it came from the direction of Ruth's house… At that moment the ear-piercing screaming began.

Daddy bolted out of the front door, Mama and Larry out the back. Pam and I trailed behind. There was Ruth, running toward our house carrying in her arms…so much confusion, yelling. *Oh my God, I could see it was her baby, the four-year-old toddler but where was all that blood coming from?* Everything slowed to a snail's pace, and the voices were just a roar in my head. Ruth and my mother in the back seat of that '46 Chevy, the child wrapped tightly in quilts that could not prevent the blood from spilling through onto the dense nappy fabric of the car seat. They sped off with Larry's trembling hands at the wheel. The child was doomed from the precise moment of the explosion. He died in his mother's arms before the hospital more than twenty miles away could be reached.

I heard the grown-ups talking. They said they found little heaps of small cylinders left around the trunk of the pecan tree. There was a claw-tooth hammer nearby plus a small wicker basket with even more of the cylinders. They said he must have struck one cylinder, which set off the entire stack. They called the cylinders blasting caps, small tubes filled with detonating substances used to detonate high explosives. Their assumption was that possibly the toddler thought he was cracking nuts at the roots of the tree or simply trying to open them up to see what was inside.

You know, my mother scrubbed and scrubbed the moquette-covered back seat of that car, but she never could get rid of all the bloodstains. Or maybe that was my imagination, running wild. Now and then I indulge in memories of the past, of that Sunday morning. I remember the pain, the sorrow, the unnaturalness of a mother losing her baby boy, such an innocuous little one. Why Ruth didn't lose her mind over that I'll never know. My thoughts linger, and I wonder how she and her surviving sons were affected by this tragedy.

That October, God humbled us all with a devastating hurricane named Hazel, striking the United States near the border between North and South Carolina, as a category 4. This hurricane caused extensive destruction and ruin. It made landfall near Calabash, North Carolina. In Long Beach, only five of approximately 350 buildings were left standing. Nineteen people were killed in North Carolina, hundreds more injured. With vengeance, it roared through Crossroads on that Friday, the fifteenth day of the tenth month, 1954.

I recall lying face down on Daddy's cot in a cold sweat that afternoon, praying as only an eleven-year-old can pray. I felt the house shudder and shake from the heave and ho of the storm raging outside while I lay there on the cot my daddy called his, just steps away from my mother's bed where she, me, and my baby sister, Pam slept. In the aftermath of Hurricane Hazel, rebuilding and reconstruction of Crossroads began, and the memory of the death of the little toddler was pushed aside. I didn't forget.

MARGIE

The night is warm, the doors and windows are open. My fingers move over the black and white keys of the antique baby grand piano, playing the old familiar hymn "Rock of Ages." There is a warm, gentle Southeastern breeze making its way through the open windows. Suddenly, my mind wandered back in time, and I could smell the sweet, damp, freshly tilled earth; could feel the warmth of summer sun on my face. I was transported back in time to the farm where I was raised…

Her name was Margie. Her skin was dark and looked as though it had been polished to a fine satin patina; her hair was tightly braided with coarse strands finding their way out of the little compact heaps that fell softly on her shoulders. The sclera of Margie's eyes were as white as the cotton growing in the fields around us, and when she threw her head back in laughter, the contrast of white teeth against that ebony skin was mesmerizing. She was trim and busty and carried herself in a very self-assured manner.

My youngest brother, Nicky, was slight of build but muscular in a wiry sense of the word. His usually pale skin was now bronzed by the hot penetrating rays of the summer sun. He almost never wore a shirt and his cut-off britches were loosely fastened, falling just below his navel. His sun-bleached hair was cropped closely to his scalp, thanks to our mama.

Margie and Nicky were about the same age chronologically... at the age of innocence soon to be reckoned with...history in the making for the two of them. I could not fully comprehend all the frivolity and electricity taking place between the two. Nevertheless, it was obvious something changed between them as they became quite secretive in their jaunts together. Their friendship took on an air of familiarity only known to lovers.

Nicky went off to war, and Margie moved up north to live with her grandmother. Somewhat later in life, the two chanced to meet as adults. I was there. The moment was extraordinary and undeniable. The electric charge was still present! The encounter was tense and a little strained at first.

"Yes, I have more than twenty-five years with the US Army under my belt, a wife, two sons, and even a couple of grandkids," Nicky said in his deepest baritone voice. Margie replied, "And I have a daughter who is about to finish college...going to be a pharmacist, she is." Then, with complete abandonment, they were in each other's arms, this beautiful, beautiful lady and my staunch military brother. How simple yet complex our lives were then.

Chapter Thirty

Should I Grow Pensive

ARK, I WANT you to understand my pensive nature so that you will never consider it a personal affront to you. You are the breath of my life; the beating of my heart and our spirit is as one. As surely as it happened, I think God brought us together rightly so, in our later years. We have many years ahead of us to continue to nurture and grow our relationship into an even stronger bond. Whatever the case, these words are for the sole purpose of communicating to you that when I am meditative, it is not because of you or anything that you have done.

I will say this is so definitive of the way I feel at times, times when I have spent solitary moments visiting the past, pulling from my memory bank the events of my life. I pray you will remain the understanding, broad-shouldered, even-tempered, clear-headed, loving fellow you are today. I pray my love does not leave you disillusioned. You are my all. You know; God knows.

For all the times I am withdrawn into myself, I wish you could know it is not about you. For all the times I am contemplative and seem preoccupied, it is not because of you. As difficult as it is to stay in the present, in this magnificent world I now live in, sometimes I fail. And this is not fair to you.

So I strive to focus on the present and all the magnificent treasures it holds. Without question, you are the greatest human treasure I have ever known. It is unfortunate that I carry all this baggage, but the weight has gotten lighter over time. And this is because of you.

May God bless us with patience and understanding and may we learn to practice unconditional love. As with unconditional love, we must learn acceptance. I want you to know you are the most important person in the world to me, and I love you with my all. If how I love you is not what you expected, for that I am sorry. My love may not be what you want it to be, but it is all I have.

About Rainbows and Patience

When I was just a tiny child to Mama I would say
"Where is the pretty rainbow? It won't come out today."
And in my mama's wisdom she'd sit me at her knee
To tell me about patience…what it would mean to me
To learn to wait and watch. "Take heed!
For patience is the thing you'll need
In dealing with most everything
That fate, in life, to you will bring.
And summers eve would find me there
A child with not a single care
Except to watch for rainbows glow
And stand in awe of God's great show.
Her lesson taught, I learned it well
And to my children I did tell
Of rainbows' magic, lessons there
How Mama molded with such care.

Afterword

I OFTEN WONDERED WHY I was the only sibling with a professional photograph. Some years later, Mama explained this was to be a keepsake for her after I died. The hand-colored pastel shades of pink and blue have faded with the passage of time, and the paper stock is yellowed. Perhaps I will take it out of hiding, dust it off, and find a special place to display it. No. Not yet. Did I know how sick I actually was at the time? Maybe it could explain the defiant, intense gaze that looks back at you from that photo. It's the *fight* mode of the *fight* or *flight* hypothesis and still takes place with me when disconcerting events are at hand.

Pam and I wore clothes sewn by our mother from chicken feed and flour sacks, and for the longest time, I was not aware this was not the normal attire for children. As my awareness developed, I turned inward. Praise God for His grace and the scope of my mind since I was able to envision a better life and I did have my dreams!

Child abuse and neglect is as old as the ages. The same is true of child molestation. Children are ashamed and afraid and usually will not tell of these indecencies, so parents should be ferociously on guard. Were there other children in Crossroads experiencing the same adversities as I? Was there an *Ambrose* lurking in other little girls' lives, seeking sick satisfaction? Some years ago, when Pam was speaking to me she talked about Ambrose, she thanked me for protecting her from that revolting individual.

Watching Vinnie's mother suffer brought fear to both Pam and I. Mama never explained Ms. Mary's disorder to us, never tried to soften the audible and visual impressions of her screaming or her twisted, contorted body. I do not recall when she died. Nod's dying was my first exposure to death. His condition, Downs Syndrome, seemed like a natural occurrence to me. Death and dying was never discussed.

What to make of Daddy, on three separate occasions, trying to take his own life? Then there was my young cousin who succeeded. Earl was short and skinny and spoke with a heavy nasal twang; his voice emitting through his nose and from his mouth. He was born with a cleft lip, undergoing several surgeries for repair, but it still left his face very disfigured. His limp was attributed to polio, the virus that ran so rampant in the early 1950s...before the Salk and Sabin vaccine, before the March of Dimes. No doubt his psyche was damaged, leading to his psychosocial problems.

When Daddy experienced the stroke that took his life, there were no first responders to intubate victims, no front-line lifesaving measures in place, no EMTs or rescue squad. Doctors actually did make house calls, and the local funeral home transported critically ill patients to the nearest hospital—if the doctor so ordered. Even with the advances in science and the medical field today, it is doubtful he would have survived a CVA so massive.

I believe my baby sister, Pam, lives with demons of her own making. Being nouveau riche allowed her to have upward social mobility. She definitely owns the materialistic goods that signal membership in the upper echelon. Those with old money still look on her as vulgar and tasteless with her flashy diamonds and other jewels weighting her body down. Further, she is lacking in the social skills appropriate for this lofty position. Although

I love her deeply and miss her terribly, I wonder if she will ever look on me as her sister again.

Larry lived a relatively long and happy life, content never to leave the home place. He continued farming the land until his death. Nicky, more aspiring of the two, traveled the world extensively and lived in exotic, far-away places. Today he resides in Barcelona, Spain, at the edge of the Mediterranean Sea. I questioned if he was putting distance between him and his memories of childhood.

I pondered intently and at length Hazel's withdrawing from the family unit. Whether she did this intentionally or subconsciously matters not. What is important though is that she has been estranged from her entire family for more than twenty years, so there is little hope of reconciling any wrongdoings. The last time I was in her presence, she was exhibiting signs of Alzheimer's, and I prayed she had righted herself with the Lord.

Mama calculated Lucy was born at around seven month's gestation. Delivered at home with the help of Aunt Eudie, Lucy, beat all odds. In rural Crossroads, all babies were delivered at home with the assistance of midwives. NICUs had not even been dreamed of in the 1920s. Of course, God had his hand in all of it because as written in the gospel according to Matthew 10:30 KJV, Jesus said, "But the very hairs of your head are all numbered."

Sometimes I wish I had questioned Mama about the relationship between her and Daddy. I wish I had asked about my biological father. Maybe it is just as well I didn't. Let sleeping dogs lie.

Don't compare me with old "Camel Knees," James, the Lord's half-brother, but I have spent many hours in prayer about our broken family. Maybe the day will come when we can celebrate a family reunion with those of us left behind.

It took years for me to forgive my daddy for the way he scorned and abused me. I often wondered if Mama's behavior toward me was linked to resentment of having a love child. That wouldn't explain why she inflicted Nicky with such physical and psychological pain. Unless the rumor was true that he was not fathered by Barnabas either.

Time and the Lord have helped me I have come to grips with my fears and anger toward Phillip. I have often thought how interesting it would be to return to Gibson and interview the folks who knew him, who knew him long before I met him. That option has not been ruled out. Nevertheless, I am not one to dance on the graves of my enemies.

In reference to my sister-in-law, Sally, who suffered emotional and physical pain most of her adult life. Over the years, Steven built her a bigger, grander house; bought her grander cars; gave her unlimited access to the bank account to spend as liberally as she wished but he could never quite make her happy; there was always something amiss. Their relationship flickered like a candle in the wind. Steven grew stoic, tolerant, and distant. She became spiteful and mean to her firstborn and to my firstborn as well. Eventually, she disowned this son while fiercely attaching herself to the younger one. She and I would never be friendly, only polite.

Sally battled ovarian cancer for most of her adulthood. She slipped back into a deep depression about two years before she passed on, opted to stay heavily sedated with barbiturates and antidepressants waiting out her death sentence. She refused to die at home with dignity, choosing to die alone in a cold, sterile hospital bed. Maybe that was the key, maybe she preferred the loneliness.

The actions of Douglas's family never altered toward me. There was an occasion, at Megan's Wake, a brief truce was put in place. However, that passed with the moment. I learned about social rejection at an early age, all the while knowing the pain and suffering was wrapped around my brain like tentacles of a squid. Researchers have found in a recent study that emotional pain is felt just like physical pain. The heartbreaking events of my life didn't actually *break* my heart, although I felt the pain somewhere in there. There were no physical signs—my eyes didn't bleed, my nose didn't fall off. But the symptoms were there: loss of appetite, loss of desire to mingle, anxiety, and fear.

There is a despicable expression some nurses' use and it is "Nurses eat their young." This is reprehensible and casts negative connotations on the entire profession. There is a new catch word in the nursing field today, and it is termed incivility, which obviously is a more polite term for bullying. It has been said that some typical uncivil behaviors include spreading rumors, failing to support a co-worker, public reprimands, badgering or back-stabbing, or damaging someone's reputation. Incivility was Sandra's lifeblood.

For twenty-five years, I held on to a union that died within weeks of its conception; I walked away. The pain of it all so unbearable at times it took my breath. I learned much in those years. I learned that I had never been loved by anyone until I felt the strong positive emotion of regard and affection of my children. Their relationship was and remains undeniably complete.

When I allow myself to reminisce, the images are quite vivid. I can feel the crispness of the fall afternoons when Aaron literally leaped off the school bus and climbed into the old blue and white Chevrolet step-side pickup truck with me. We would wander through the swamps and river bottoms, digging up dogwoods and river birches that grew natural to the area. We would carry them home with us and replant them in our yard.

I remember Angela taking a two-week "vacation" from school one spring to help me paint the horse barn and stables. At the end of the days, we were exhausted and our arms trembled with fatigue. The important outcome though was the bonding of our spirits. Now, Megan was a different story. She was smart as a whip but was not keen on doing anything to cause her to break a sweat—too vain. There was nothing tomboyish about her. She would be doing dishes, folding laundry, or helping prepare supper. Then in a trancelike state gaze off into space.

I would ask her, "Penny for your thoughts, Megan." She would respond, "I don't want to grow old, ever. I don't want wrinkles or old age spots or any of that. I just don't ever want to grow old, Marmie." And she didn't. Megan had a cone biopsy of her cervix performed in July of 1996, had a radical hysterectomy in September, and received radiation treatments from Monday through Friday of each week until January of the following year. In August of 1997, she was pronounced cancer free and again in 1998. It was a black day indeed when the following year it was confirmed the cancer had metastasized to multiple areas of her body.

She was thirty-seven years old that spring. The following spring, she went home to heaven. From that day forward, this home—this domain in which I live is known as an enchanted place, a fishbowl of sorts: The Enchanted Fishbowl!

My mate Mark, daughter Angela, her husband Ricky, my son Aaron and his wife Heather have been my strength, my anchors, and my hope over these last years. They, independently, one or the other, have kept me alive, kept me sane. Their love for me runs smooth and deep. They have allowed me to grieve in my own way and have stood by me. Without them, life would have been pointless; without them, there would be no reason to face another day. What blessings I have received from God, allowing me family to share *my* life! I ask God daily to bless them just as He has blessed me.

Observing my surviving daughter and my son, I see they have internalized my same values. Their faith is exemplary; their work ethic is impeccable. Their honesty and integrity are unquestion-able; they are of a forgiving nature, and they love unconditionally. The icing on the cake is that they chose partners cut from the same cloth! What a legacy for a mother to leave behind! It was with the birth of my children that I began to understand the true meaning of love. This was the first time in my life that I felt I was actually loved by another...

That was before Mark. Never in my life time did I expect to find such perfect happiness in a soul mate. I am overjoyed and content; I am safe and secure. Mark is my every wish and dream come true. Our hearts beat as one. I believe with all my heart that God put us on the path to each other when we were children. The mountains and valleys were necessary so that I might appreciate the kindness, gentleness, and love of a good man. I have more than enough for my needs. "The Lord does not look at the things people look at. Man looks at the outward appearance, but the Lord looks at the heart'" (1 Samuel 16:7b, NIV).

The phrase I learned as a child, "Sticks and stones may break my bones, but words will never hurt me," has stayed with me throughout these seventy-five years. I have to admit, though, words do hurt. They have a powerful impact on a vulnerable child. Even in childhood, my prayers asked for soothing of my heart. When God gave me the strength and courage to forgive, my wounded persona began to heal. Praise God; He made me *uniquely me!* He molded in me a heart that is kind, generous, and forgiving. He has made it possible for me to share my life and my good fortune with friend and foe alike. The sticks and stones were necessary building material to get me to today. His blessings are bountiful. Going forward, I ask God to use me in the way He has planned for me.

> "For we are God's workmanship, created in Christ Jesus to do good works, which God prepared in advance for us to do." Ephesians 2:10 NIV

And When I Go

And when I go, I will be sad to leave you all behind. Sad, because I will not be able to participate in my grandchildren's lives…to see them grow up…to suffer with them the agonies and woes of childhood, adolescence, teenage years, and young adulthood. I will be absent to share in their joys as well. I won't be able to sit in the church pew as the "matriarch," all filled with pomp and circumstance as I participate in the weddings of those grandchildren and watch them have children of their own.

The saddest event will be leaving my dear Mark behind. What a man he is! He sure is a mind-boggler, with his extraordinary, exceedingly literal approach to all aspects of life. The *Encarta Dictionary* tells us that literal means "factual and unimaginative, simple in a clear unimaginative way that sticks to the facts and avoids embellishment." That is Mark.

Being an officer of the law for forty years is the very thing that molded this man in this fashion. Consequently, the only way he could serve as an honest enforcer of the law was to become and remain literal. A forty-year habit is hard to break. Why should he anyway? It is an endearing attribute to his incredible personality.

My heart will be sad to leave Angela, my surviving daughter, my clone. We have always had a kindred spirit, understanding each other, communicating on wave lengths of intuitiveness. How imperfect the two of us are in our perfect world. She lives her life with immense passion, just as I have, except that her head is on much straighter than mine ever was. If I ever could grow up, my desire would be that I could be just like my daughter, Angela. What an awesome woman she is!

Aaron. What can I say about Aaron? He is my every heartbeat, so thoughtful, so tender, and so full of caring for others. His mind is constantly in motion, wondering how he can make life better/easier/fuller for each and every member of his family. I have always feared for his financial security because of this very thing.

But go I will, in God's time, when He determines that time is here. There, I will go to meet my Heavenly Father and all my loved ones who have gone before me. The joy will be unimaginable… I parrot the plea of my mother, which was "I want to keep my right mind, be able to provide for my own needs and to die in my sleep."

MY WAY...

So here we are the end at last,
And as I face the final curtain
I said it all, I said before, how glad I am.
I know for certain
I loved and laughed and waxed and waned,
You know it's true; it's so be-fitting.
For all to know the final show,
I did it My Way.
Now all is quiet, the pastor prays,
The family does the necessary.
Kind words are said, verses are read
And now... The end of story?
Oh, please hold on. It is not true;
The story? It's still unfolding.
'Cause if you knew, if you only knew,
I did it my way.
I'm on my way, a brighter day;
A day of such rewarding.
I'm rich, you know it's true
Oh Wow! Such a fulfilling...
For in The Book, these things are said
And here I know that there'll be sharing.
Words are said, The Book is read,
And I go forth with such divining.
God saw me through as He shall you.
Let me say, with jubilation,
I shout with joy, my life was good.
I DID IT MY WAY!!!!!!!!!!!!